Gunfighters of the Dr

A Trilog

By Pete Chiarella

Edited by Lorina J. Faes

Cover Art by Gregory C. Giordano and Kelli Manhart

Book II Art by Colin Rogers

'Nydia' by James Nester

http://linktr.ee/gregorycgiordano_art

GUNFIGHTERS OF THE DRUNKEN MASTER: A TRILOGY

First edition. July 12, 2023.

Copyright © 2023 Pete Chiarella.

ISBN: 979-8223602897

Written by Pete Chiarella.

Table of Contents

DEDICATIONS

Gunfighters of the Drunken Master was originally published in 2014. The sequels came a couple of years later. The series biggest cheerleaders were actor & stuntman Gary Kent, star of Day of the Dead, Gary Klar, and author and friend Jack Ketchum. Both Garys saw a movie in these books. Before Gary Klar became ill with ALS, we had planned to rent a cabin and hammer out a screenplay.

Sadly this never came to pass and I had to sadly say goodbye to my friends as they have all left this mortal coil. So this new version of the series is respectfully dedicated to the real "gunfighters".

Gary Kent-1933-2023

Gary Klar-1947-2020

Jack Ketchum-1946-2018

John "Bud" Cardos-1929-2020

Special thanks to my editor Lorina J. Faes who made me believe in myself again and has inspired me to keep writing and creating.

Praise for Gunfighters of the Drunken Master:

"I wondered what would happen if you wrote some fiction. Impressive as you nailed it." -Jack Ketchum, author of The Lost, Off Season, and The Woman

"Peter, I see a movie in this, actually I see a couple of movies. Great storytelling." -Gary Klar, Steele from Day of the Dead

"A relentless story that, at times, makes you beg for mercy. Vivid, nightmarish, subversive and dripping with the vibes of the 42nd Street aura." -Cory Udler, writer/director of Incest Death Squad

"Gunfighters reads like cinema, like Mad Max only with balls. Where else can you hang with an army consisting of two men, six women and a dog called Dog? There is enough testosterone in these books to float an aircraft carrier. Just sayin." -Gary Kent, writer, actor and Stunt Man Hall of Famer

Gunfighters
of the
Drunken Master

by
Pete Chiarella
a.k.a. "42nd Street Pete"

The Death of the Earth

In the end, ignorance and greed killed the planet. During the gas shortage of the 70's, they told us that oil was running out. It wasn't, but we were given an offhanded choice, pay more at the pump or wait in the endless lines. We paid more, a lot more. And we continued to pay, but the oil never ran out as expected. The fossil fuel boys bought politicians at discount rates. They paid very little, if no taxes.

Any attempt at 'clean' energy was shot down. If there was a hurricane, prices doubled for months. These businesses did not ever lose money, we paid whatever they wanted. Other things changed, people became ignorant, as that was the plan. Things children needed to learn weren't taught anymore. These people wore their ignorance as a badge of honor. They were cleverly manipulated to violence by the politicians they blindly followed.

Then Mother Nature said 'fuck you'. Again, we ignored her. Summers were blisteringly hot, so hot that it became a health hazard to stay outdoors. Around 2016 forests started to burn. Some fires were caused by lightning strikes. Some were set by religious fanatics eager to bring The Rapture to earth. Some just started because it was too fuckin hot. Then we had a pandemic that our leaders ignored. Hundreds of thousands died as a result. By 2020 half the world was on fire, the other half under water. Then it stopped raining.

Crops died, animals died, rivers and lakes started drying up. Food riots broke out, a reality TV star was elected President. He ignored everything, disputed scientific facts, and had crackpot cures for the virus that ravaged the world. His hardcore followers murdered anyone who spoke out about the situation. Abortion clinics were bombed, everyone had a gun, the daily carnage was appalling. Then the solar flares started.

In some areas, the heat was a killer. With everything dry, fires started easily and there was nothing to put them out. The entire East and West coasts burned. Nothing was spared, nothing. At Riker's Island, a prison in New

York, prisoners were baking in their cells. One convict was determined to get out. He was a rough old bastard, age was around 60 or so. His name was Leroy Davis, but people called him The Blindman. He wasn't really blind, but was near sighted and had the start of cataracts. He was a career criminal and was doing time for two murders, one that he committed in prison.

Leroy smelled smoke and knew he had to find a way out. He kept hearing screams and gunfire. The guards were getting even, they were shooting the prisoners in their cells. Leroy made a decoy out of his blankets. He used his boots to make the figure on the bunk look real. Then he got into a rather difficult position close to the ceiling and waited. A guard named Taggart walked up to his cell with a shotgun. "Bye bye, you blind fuck," he said as he blasted the figure on the bunk. The figure was turned to rags. Taggart muttered "Where the fuck could he be?" Taggart unlocked the cell.

Leroy dropped on him and grabbed the gun. He blasted Taggart and ran. He kept running. A guard saw him and Leroy blew his ass away. Leroy got out of the place as the flames grew. He found a Ford station wagon with the keys in it. He started it and burned rubber. He headed west, avoiding people who tried to flag him down or stop him. He knew once the gas in this thing ran out, he'd be on foot. He had the shotgun and the orange jumpsuit. He needed to ditch the jumpsuit.

He was on the Pennsylvania turnpike, almost to Ohio, when the car sputtered and died. "Looks like I'll be strolling a bit," he said to himself. After a couple of miles, he spied a rest area ahead of him. It was deserted except for the dead. Seems a battle took place here. The buildings were pocked with bullet holes and a few baked bodies were lying on the ground.

A quick look around found no one waiting in ambush. Leroy found a place that had clothes. He found a pair of black jeans, a rust-colored thermal shirt, some work boots and a floppy hat, plus some socks and underwear. He ditched the jumpsuit. He needed ammunition for the shotgun. He prowled around in the service station and came up empty.

Then he decided to check the abandoned vehicles. A bullet ridden squad car had what he needed. The cop in it had been shot in the head. He had a 12-gauge Remington pump shotgun and a full box of shells. He also had a Sig Sauer 9mm pistol that was still in the holster. He took that and the cop's ammo for it. Then he noticed that the car had a full tank of gas. "Wonder if it will start," he said to himself.

Expecting nothing, he turned the key. It started right up. It seemed that the only vital thing hit was the cop. Leroy took the dead pig out of the car and drove it closer to the shop. He found some food, some bottled water and a lot of liquor. He loaded what he could fit in the car. Blindman stayed on the interstate, driving around dead and wrecked vehicles. Nothing was living, the dead littered the streets. He hit a roadblock when he crossed into Indiana.

It was a crude barricade built out of junk. Several men were sitting around drinking. Blindman took a swig out of a pint of Old Crow. He jacked a shell into the Sig Sauer. A fat, sloppy man with really bad teeth approached The Blindman. He was followed by a skinny guy wearing the colors of a biker gang. That guy carried an AK-47. Blindman counted four others behind the barricade.

"This be a toll road, stranger," the fat man said.

"Since when?" The Blindman asked

"Since me and the boys took it over, that's when."

"So what's the toll?"

"Everything you have in that car. But we'll let you sample some young pussy before we send you on your way."

"So you're raping little girls?"

"Yeah, like who's going to stop us?"

"Me, that's who." Blindman pulled up the Sig, fired at the fat guy and missed, though he did manage to clip the skinny guy in the chest. Five guns exploded in his direction. Blindman emptied the automatic without hitting anyone. He ducked behind the squad car as bullets ripped through it.

"Damn this nearsighted shit," he said to himself. He picked up the shotgun. Two of the group rushed him, firing AK-47's from the hip. Blindman waited, then blew them to rags.

"Throw down your guns or we'll kill a couple of these kids!" the fat guy yelled. Blindman didn't move. A few minutes went by.

"Didn't you hear me?" Blindman said nothing. He heard them discussing what to do.

"He must be dead."

"Yeah, I think one of the boys nailed him."

"Wait a few minutes, then we'll check."

Blindman laid on the ground next to the squad car. He saw the three walking slowly toward him. He let them close in, then opened up, firing under the car. Five loads of buckshot shattered their legs and dropped them. The fat man was the only one still breathing. A shot to the head cured that.

"Whoever is in there, ya might as well come out, these scumbags are all dead." Four men, six women and ten children from ages ten to fourteen fearfully came out.

Blindman looked at the group. They were battered and beat up, visible bruises and cuts on them. It was obvious the women had been raped. The squad car was leaking coolant and other fluids. His ride was ruined. One of the men thanked him.

Blindman gave him a hard stare. "I'm not judging you, but you people need to defend yourselves. I'm not hanging around. Take their guns and ammo," he said, pointing to what was left of the dead men. Anyone fucks with you, kill them."

"We appreciate what you did, we really do," a man said, "but we have no supplies, those bastards used them all."

Blindman pointed to his ride. "That car is loaded and now I'm on foot. I'm taking what I can carry, you people take the rest." Blindman filled a sack with liquor, a bottle of water and a lot of beef jerky. He started walking away as the group cleaned out the car. "I'm not taking anyone with me," he muttered to himself. "A caregiver I ain't and I need to figure out a better weapon 'cause I can't see for shit." Little did The Blindman know what the fates held in store for him.

The next day, he wandered into a residential neighborhood. The place was deserted, bodies lay around, mummified by the heat. Finding a downtown shopping area, he spied a gun store. The store hadn't been looted. He found a lot of 12-gauge shells, some with big slugs of lead in them. Pumpkin balls, they used to call them. He found a .38 revolver with a long barrel that he pocketed. He looked at the boxes of buckshot. He remembered reading Civil War history and how soldiers would put any kind of metal in shotgun shells.

"Might as well make some custom loads," he said to himself. He emptied a box of two dozen shells. He opened them up and dumped out the buckshot. He looked around for plunder. Sheet metal screws, a roll of dimes, snips of barbed wire, steel nuts, washers and broken safety glass filled the shells. Sealing them up with wax, he felt he was better armed now. Loading up, he saw no reason to linger.

Blindman was almost at the edge of town when he heard something, a mournful howl. "If I was smart, I'd keep on walking," he said to himself. Following the howls, he came to a brick building with a caged in small yard. Pacing around the yard was the biggest dog that he ever saw. It was brown, shaggy and had to weigh in the neighborhood of 150 pounds. Blindman and the dog locked eyes. The dog snarled, then whimpered. Not trusting the beast, Blindman ripped open a package of beef jerky and threw it into the yard.

The dog pounced on the bag and ate the contents. "You must be thirsty." Blindman opened a bottle of water and stuck the neck though the fence. The dog approached cautiously, then guzzled down the water. It then sat down and waited. "Want out, don't you?" he asked the dog. The beast's ears stood up and it wagged its tail. The cage was padlocked. Blindman smashed the lock with the butt of the shotgun. The door swung open, the dog took off down the street. The Blindman watched as the dog vanished from sight.

"I guess that's better than trying to eat me," Blindman chuckled. Blindman started walking, he was a couple of miles from the town when he was challenged. Two men with rifles stepped out of a wooded area by the road.

"Well looky here," one said. "Guess you wandered from some nursing home, old timer, we'll just take the pack." The guy had a filthy sleeveless denim vest and dirty jeans. His rotten teeth said he was a tweaker. The other guy had on a ragged flannel shirt and cutoff shorts. His hands shook as he held the rifle.

"Why don't you two assholes just suck my dick?" Blindman told them.

The tweaker raised the rifle, "That was rude, you old bastard. Now you can die." He never got off the shot. A brown blur crashed into his back, slamming him to the pavement. Before the other guy could move, the dog ripped his throat out. Blood spurted out of his ruined neck. The tweaker tried to get up and Blindman kicked him in the head, snapping his neck.

Blindman searched the bodies and came up with nothing except a pair of brass knuckles. He slipped them in his pocket. "Might come in handy," he said to the dog. The dog looked at him and wagged his tail. "So I guess we are even. Or we are pals," Blindman said. "I never had a pet and I suck at naming things, so I'll just call you Dog." Dog stared at him. "Well, let's get to moving, nothing for us here."

As they got deeper into Indiana, the terrain changed. Lots of fissures in the earth, crumpled buildings, burnt out wrecks, and sand. A lot of sand. "I guess we missed the Apocalypse," he said out loud. Dog just snorted. A free-standing bodega type store was riddled with bullet holes. Blindman looked inside, saw a few bodies. "These guys ain't been dead too long," he muttered to himself.

The store had been gutted, nothing much left. It looked like an organized clean out. "Now I wonder what I'm going to walk into," he thought. They walked a couple more miles and they came upon a bus. Dog's hackles started to rise. "Yeah, Dog, something is off here." He jacked a shell into the breech. As he got closer, he smelled the stench of death. Dead women and children were in the bus. They had been used badly and slaughtered. Three men in the bus had been bound and their throats had been cut.

"Fuckin scumbags, this was a massacre," he muttered. He punctured the gas tank and set the bus ablaze. "Best I can do for yas, no time to dig a grave." He and Dog watched as flames consumed the bus and its unfortunate occupants. "Let's go," he said to Dog. They kept on walking west. Blindman wondered what kind of scum would massacre a bus full of people. He would find that out shortly.

About a mile from the bus, there was a Ford F-10 pickup truck turned on its side. Three bodies by it, one still breathing. "Well if it isn't RT Tyler, pedo and rapist, guess you got out of Riker's a bit before I did," said Blindman.

RT was an emaciated piece of human garbage. Right now he was leaking blood from a bullet in his shoulder. "Hi Leroy," he said. "Good to see you. I could use some help."

Blindman nodded to the two corpses. "Had a little falling out with your pals, I see?"

"Yeah, they are part of The Drunken Master's bunch, thought I was too, but they felt different about it," RT explained.

"Now who the fuck is this Drunken Master?" Blindman inquired.

"Remember that big biker, 'Satan' he used to call himself? Well, he led a bunch of us off Rikers, then we got to that federal pen in Marion, Indiana and let those boys out. He set everything up in an old depot. It's a regular army we got and we take anything we want."

"Like that bus a few miles back?" Blindman asked.

"Yeah, that was fun, we made the men watch. Boy could those women holler, we had them for a couple of days. Too bad The Master got tired of it." RT finished.

"And you want me to patch you up so you can join up with that scumbag and rape and kill again?" Blindman snarled.

"Hey, not my problem if people can't protect themselves. You got anything for pain, or can you get this slug out?"

"Oh, I forget that you're hurtin, pain really that bad?" Blindman asked.

"It's fuckin killing me," RT replied.

"It's not going to kill you, RT. I am." Blindman blew off his head with the shotgun. "Never liked you anyway."

Blindman pondered while he worked on a fifth of Maker's Mark. If RT was telling the truth, this Drunken Master has gathered an army of thugs and is wiping out anyone in his path.

If I keep going, odds are we will tangle ass down the road. But then, what do I care? "Dog, let's go."

After two more days of walking, they came upon a small group walking toward him. Six men armed to the teeth. "You're going the wrong way," Blindman told them.

"So are you," a tall scarecrow of a man said. "That Drunken Master and his band of psychos is behind us. They are fighting everyone, including each other."

"Seriously?" Blindman asked.

"Yeah, they are having gunfights, like in the old western movies. The Drunken Master got his hand shot off and he's looking for the guy who did it. Too bad he was a bad shot."

"Where are you going?" Blindman asked.

"Away from here. I wish you luck if you keep going, but be warned, these idiots will try to take you out."

"Thanks for the advice," Blindman said, "but I know what's back there: nothing."

"Suit yourself. There may be nothing back there, but there is something really bad in front of you."

Blindman wished them luck and continued on. They came to some big sand dunes when they heard gunfire. Climbing to the top of the dune, he saw what looked like a store and a battle was taking place. Raiders were trying to take the store.

Blindman jacked a shell into the breech, looked at Dog and said, "Let's go."

Gunfighters of the Drunken Master

1

A group had been attacking the Quick Mart for days. At least 20 or so bodies were putrefying on the asphalt. So far these fuckers had the upper hand, but the thought of water, pure drinking water, was drawing every cut throat for miles around. Yeah, water, or any soft drink in a plastic container was worth killing for. Six months ago the world went bonkers as strange solar flares irradiated the earth. All fresh water was evaporated by a strange radiation. Any liquid stored in a metal container was also contaminated.

Drinking any of the tainted liquids would lead to a slow, painful death. The liquid would dissolve your insides like acid. Anything in a glass or plastic container was safe, and precious. Alcohol was in abundant supply. All of these raiders were drunk and had been drunk for weeks. Maybe if they weren't, there would be so many rotting in this parking lot. Ninety percent of the world's population was dead. The planet was a dried out, desolate hulk, as there was no more rain. Fires were common and burned out of control, fueled by the dried vegetation. One man controlled this part of the wasteland.

That man was a former special ops soldier, trained in dealing death. He was known as The Drunken Master. He held his territory in a death grip, killing any and all in his way. But on one fateful raid, he ran into something he couldn't handle, El Roacho Rio, the fasted gun in the wasteland. The Master caught three bullets during the face off with El Roacho, crippling his gun hand. Knowing that El Roacho was a threat to his little empire, The Master put a bounty on El Roacho's head: 100 cases of bottled water. Now, maybe he had the water, maybe he didn't, but just the thought of that much water brought in the baddest of the bad.

Nomadic killers, fueled by alcohol, roamed the wasteland blowing each other away. Gun fights were a daily occurrence, but due to the drinking, a gun fight could last for hours.

A barrage of gunfire interrupts the deathly quiet. The raiders have mounted a mass attack on the Quick Mart. The group numbers about a dozen. A guy with an AK-47 has made it to the entrance. He empties his weapon through the door, shredding the shooter behind it. As he kicks in the door there is a loud blast and his head explodes. Coming from the direction of the blast is a man wearing a rust-colored, ragged thermal shirt, drawing a bead on another raider. The guy's chest has a huge hole blown through it. A streak of brown runs past the guy, taking down another raider. It is a huge mountain cur that rips the raider's throat out in a fountain of crimson. The huge dog is followed by the shooter they call The Blindman.

The Blindman is one of the most dangerous killers in the Wasteland. Supposedly, he was from New York City, one of the few that blasted his way off the decimated East Coast. Rumor has it that he was on Riker's Island awaiting sentencing for murder when the world went nuts. He has a shotgun with a long barrel that he loads himself with nails, bits of barb wire, sparkplugs, and broken glass. He carries a sawed-off with a cut down stock as a back up.

Somewhere between NYC and this shithole, he picked up this huge dog. Weighing close to 150 pounds, the dog, for whatever reason, stays with The Blindman. While all of the other dogs have died off due to lack of water, this beast drinks the blood of whatever it or The Blindman kills.

Another raider has his arm blown off at the shoulder. Blood fountains high in the air as he eats the pavement. A couple of shots from the Quick Mart drop two more raiders. The rest give up the attack and run off. Blindman shoots one in the back. He now turns his attention to the Quick Mart.

"Ok, fuckers!" he yells to the occupants. "I just saved your asses so show some fuckin appreciation and toss me something to drink." No one answers. "Come on, you no-good bastards, don't make me come in there because if I do, I'll take it all and burn this fucker down." The door opens and a little girl pushes a shopping cart out. Her dirt-streaked face is full of fear.

As Blindman approaches the girl, a bullet buzzes past his head and pings off the cart. One of the raiders isn't quite dead. Blindman turns and kicks the gun out of his hand before he can fire again. Blindman drops knees first on the raider's chest.

"Fuck with me, will ya?" he screams as he pulls a pair of brass knuckles out of his jeans and turns the raider's head into jelly. Fresh blood joins the dried blood on Blindman's shirt. Turning to the frightened girl, what passes for a smile crosses Blindman's face. "Go back inside, honey. You don't need to be out here." Blindman looks to see what's in the cart. Two gallons of water, a couple of big bottles of soda, a few bags of beef jerky, a can of tuna and a couple of boxes of Pop Tarts.

"Not a bad haul," he mutters to himself. "Dog!" he yells. The cur trots over, blood still dripping from his jaws. Blindman rips open a bag of jerky and gives it to him. Blindman helps himself to another bag, chasing it down with some water.

Then a voice yells, "Hey mister, this might interest you!" Blindman looks in the direction of the voice. A slim, balding man stands in the doorway of the Quick Mart with a piece of paper in his hand.

"What the fuck is that?" asks Blindman.

"It's a wanted poster," the man replies.

"Well, read me the damn thing, I can't see worth a shit."

"Ok," says the man. "There is a reward of 100 cases of water for the head of El Roacho Rio."

"Who's payin it?" asks Blindman.

"Drunken Master, that's who," the man says.

"The Drunken Master, eh? Wonder where that limp dick cocksucker got that much water. So all I got to do to get it is cut the head off some spic bastard?"

"Well," said the man, "he's supposed to be the fastest gun in the Wasteland."

"Do I look like I'm just gonna walk up and hook and draw with the motherfucker? I can't see shit and I ain't been sober in months."

"No, this calls for some sneaky ass shit."

"Dog!!" he yells. "Let's go get us some head."

Laughing insanely, Blindman takes his haul and heads west.

2

BULLETS PINGED OFF the rusting hulk of a Ford Explorer. Four men had a young woman trapped, or so they thought. Nydia was half Mexican and half Irish and all mean. An inked up former punk rocker and roller derby queen, she wasn't drunk, but she was stoned on weed. Her choice, as she could function on that, not on liquor.

"C'mon bitch!" a shooter yelled. "Give us your water and some pussy and we'll call it square." He made the mistake of showing part of his head, and that got him a .22 slug from a Phoenix Arms automatic in his right eye.

"Fuckin cunt, you killed Ronnie!" a raider screamed. The guy charged toward the truck, firing two 9mm Glocks. He looked down in shocked surprise as a knife handle seemed to grow out of his chest. He took one step then collapsed face first in the dirt.

"Two down, two to go," Nydia muttered.

"You had your chance, cunt, now yer gonna die," yelled one of the two. Slugs peppered the rusting wreck like angry hornets. Nydia stayed quiet until one round nipped her shoulder. She inadvertently screamed in pain. One of the remaining raiders took that for a sign that she was hard hit. He ran right into two shots in the chest that punched his ticket for good.

"Maybe we can make a deal!" the last shooter yelled.

"Maybe you should go fuck yourself," Nydia shot back. "You opened this dance, so finish it."

"No, I'm finished." He threw a .38 in the dirt and stood up. "I give up," he said as he rose to his feet. He was a rat faced scarecrow, shaking from his intake of booze. He walked toward her, smiling. "I'm sure we can just work this out," he said as he got closer. His smile vanished as his hand reached behind his back. All of a sudden, he had two mouths, one spraying crimson high in the air. The .25 automatic dropped from nerveless fingers as he fell face first into the dirt.

Nydia wiped her knife clean on his dirty shirt. "Guess we'll call that working things out," she muttered. She picked up the two Glocks, the .38 and the .25. She went through the men's pockets for extra ammunition. She found some, a half a pack a smokes, a couple baggies of weed and a couple of pieces of paper. The papers were the reward posters for El Roacho Rio.

"100 cases of water, eh?" She packed up her gear and headed west.

3

COFFIN JACK WHITE WAS in a jackpot. He was playing poker for water and just got caught cheating. Jack was a former undertaker from Pittsburgh. He was a slender, frail looking man who had a bad case of the DTs when the booze ran out. Right now his luck ran out, not that getting in a poker game with four gangbangers was a good idea in the first place.

"You cheated, amigo," growled a huge black man with gold front teeth.

"No I didn't," Jack shot back. "You're just drunk."

"Not that drunk, motherfucker, now I'm gonna..."

Further conversation was useless as Jack had sneaked a double barreled .38 caliber derringer out and shot off the big guy's knee cap.

The big man screamed and fell clutching his ruined knee. One of the other men went for his gun and got the second barrel emptied in his left eye. A TEC-9 pistol fell from nerveless fingers. Jack scooped it up and stitched the other two men across the chest with it. The big guy reached into his shirt and Jack held the gun on him and said, "Don't."

"You fuckin honky faggot, you ruined me!" he screamed.

Calmly Jack said, "The luck of the draw."

"Weren't no fuckin luck, you cheatin bastard," the big man bitched.

"Maybe your luck just run out." Jack said, pointing the gun at the man's face. If a black man could turn white, this one just did.

"No, don't kill me! Look at this." The man pulled out a crumpled wanted poster. "Me and my boys was gonna go after this, but you take it."

Jack looked at the poster. "100 cases of water, 'eh, might be worth..."

The man made a grab for one of the discarded pistols. Jack pulled the trigger on the TEC-9, stitching the man across the chest. Blood splattered everywhere. Without a second thought, Jack put the weapon in his belt and searched the bodies for ammo.

Then he headed west.

THE THREE HAD JUST finished their brutal rape of a teenage girl. Her bruised and ravaged body was lying in fetal position in the sand. One of the three, a tall Latino, stood up and squeezed his crotch. "I'm getting ready again for you, mami." He broke into a gap-toothed grin as he rubbed himself. He kicked the girl in the side, rolling her on her back. Reaching down, he grabbed her ankles and forced her legs open.

Suddenly a massive hole appeared in his chest, showering his victim with gore. The other two looked up to see a moon-faced man in blue walking toward them. Edgar "Cop" Warren was a former police officer and a bad one at that. He was corrupt right down to his toenails. Shakedowns, extortion, brutality, rape and murder was Cop's game.

"You have the right to remain silent!" Cop shouted at the two men.

"Fuck this guy," one of them said, then raised his .38 at Cop. Cop was faster and expecting that move. Two shots from his Glock made short work of the two drunks. Cop walked over to the girl.

She looked up and said, "Thank you."

"For what?" Cop shot back. He reached down to seemingly help the girl up, then decked her with a hard right hand. He turned her over and dropped his pants. He brutally sodomized the girl, laughing at her struggles. "You have the right to remain silent!" he screamed at her before cutting the sobbing girl's throat. Cop kept kicking her, laughing as he did it.

Tiring of this, he searched the bodies of his victims. He found very little of anything. Then he found the poster. As he read it, a smile crept over his fat face. "100 cases of water, eh? Shouldn't be a problem."

Cop checked his guns and headed west.

4

RUBY WAS 300 POUNDS of trouble. The former owner of an S&M brothel, she supplied young girls to her twisted clients, most of them kidnapped runaways. Sometimes her girls didn't survive her 'sessions'. Ruby was a butch lesbian, a walking caricature with work boots, black jeans and a flannel shirt. She had a taste for young girls and she was brutal.

The end of the world was a great opportunity for her mayhem. She could grab girls at random and leave their ravaged, broken bodies rotting by the wayside. Ruby was ugly as sin with a porcine face and one eye covered with a makeshift patch. One of her 'lovers' had managed to gouge out her eye with a pencil before Ruby choked her to death.

Ruby hated men with a passion. She would call out anyone she came across to try their luck against her, either with guns or fists. Ruby enjoyed beating people to death with her fists. She was a sadist through and through with no conscience.

She was also very pissed off at the moment because she hadn't killed anyone in days. She saw a pickup truck in the distance that seemed to have someone sitting in it. Sensing a potential victim, she crept up on the truck. The guy she'd seen had a bullet hole in his head. Flies buzzed around his corpse. Disgusted, Ruby started to walk away, but then noticed the folded paper in the corpse's hand. "100 cases of water, eh?" she muttered. "I think this should be mine."

She started traveling west.

WONG DUCK WAS FROM San Francisco before the world went crazy. He lorded over the Tongs in the area. He got off the West coast with six of his trusted hatchet men, assassins that killed silently. He also had six Chinese girls that had been destined to work in brothels that The Tongs controlled. Wong was ruthless and completely devoid of any human emotion. He used the women to trade for water, guns, and anything else he wanted. When the men were occupied by the women, the hatchet men killed them.

He gave the girls just enough to keep them alive. If one fell behind, she was whipped and beaten. Wong despised white men as he felt they were weak and inferior to his race. When distracted by young girls, they were easy prey.

Wong and his entourage stumbled across group of bikers. The bikers had a lot of liquor, bottled water, and drugs. When Wong's group approached, the bikers eyed the women with open lust. Ever benevolent, Wong told the bikers that they would gladly share the women if the bikers would share their supplies. The bikers, lit up on drugs and alcohol, went for the deal.

They were brutal with the women, beating them when they refused some of the more perverted acts the bikers wanted. A nod from Wong Duck sent the hatchet men on the bikers. Blades and axes sent streams of arterial blood into the air. In under a minute the entire gang became slabs of cooling meat on the sand. The hatchet men quickly transferred the bikers' supplies into their packs. One hatchet man found the reward notice.

"Exalted One," the man said. "I found this on the person of one of the infidels.

Wong studied the notice. "We will go West," said Wong. "I will find The Drunken Master and take what is his."

5

THE DRUNKEN MASTER was with his massive bodyguard, Sluggo. Sluggo was a huge black man, about 300 pounds, with a shaved head and gold teeth. He was totally loyal to The Master.

The Master was a tall, almost emaciated man with a shaved, bullet head. He downed a big glass of scotch.

"Have all those posters been put up?" Master asked Sluggo.

"Yo boss, all done. I heard dem gunfighters are already bustin caps on each other."

"Amazing what effect greed has on the common man," The Master said.

Sluggo nodded. As a former high-ranking member of the Bloods, he knew all about greed firsthand. "If all dese bad asses kill each other, we got it all, don't we Boss?" asked Sluggo.

"Yes, my friend, that is the plan," replied The Master. "Since that piece of shit, El Roacho, ruined my hand, I need an edge. My edge is getting rid of all the big guns, the known names. In other words: eliminate all competition. Then no one can challenge me, ever."

Sluggo just nodded his approval.

NYDIA WAS TRACKING El Roacho, but the trail went cold when she came to a shanty town. She went into The Last Chance Bar, behind the bar was a huge, owl-faced man. "What's your pleasure, lady?" he asked.

"I'm looking for a man," she said.

"Got a couple of girls in the back, but no men to rent out," Owl Face replied.

Snarling, Nydia reached over the bar, grabbed his throat and screamed in his face. "Do you think I need to fuckin pay for a guy, you fat piece of shit? Do ya?"

A foul odor permeated the bar as Owl Face shit his pants. "No, no," he squealed. "I'm sorry, I'm sorry!"

"Stop crying, you fuckin pussy!" Nydia screamed in his face. "Where is El Roacho Rio?"

"In the cemetery," Owl Face blubbered. "He's buried in the cemetery behind the hill."

"How is it that he's dead? He was supposed to be a fast gun," asked Nydia.

"Oh, he was fast," said Owl Face, "but not very accurate. He got in a fight over a week ago. He lost, so we planted him deep."

Nydia let go of the sniveling Owl Face.

"Thanks," she said, and left the bar. Nydia walked to the cemetery. She found a fairly fresh grave with the marker:

El Roacho Rio

Hit What You Aim At, Fucker

Nydia was lost in thought. Obviously no one here knew about the reward or they wouldn't have planted him. *Now I have to dig him up,* she thought. *Can't do this without having someone watch my back. Who? Have to find someone I can trust, fuck!! But who?*

Then she had an epiphany. *If I found this grave, others will find it.* She tore down the marker. Finding another piece of board, she carved the name Arch Stanton on it and put it over the grave. *Hope this throws them off,* she thought.

6

JULIO AND MANUEL MARTINEZ were brothers and former members of The Latin Kings. When things went to shit, the two killed off their own gang. They found two other brothers, Stosh and Paul Rominowski, psychopaths who enjoyed killing. The Romonowskis became their 'soldiers', expendables that charged in at the bequest of the Martinez's orders. Julio and Manuel found those reward dodgers; they were determined to get El Roacho.

Julio was looking though a battered telescope. Scanning the burnt-out landscape, he spied two figures.

"Look at this," Julio said to Manny. "It's that crazy old pendejo, Blindman."

"T'ink he's knows about the reward?" Manny asked.

"Don't know, but I'm gonna cap his old ass."

Manny drew a bead with his rifle. "This will be quick," he said.

THE BLINDMAN WAS ONLY a few miles from that same shanty town. Walking across the desolate landscape, he was humming a tune, "Silver wings upon his chest/He is one of America's best. One hundred men will test today/Ninety nine will run away," he laughed at this, then saw the sunlight flash off of something metal. "Shit!" he yelled as he threw himself backwards. Not fast enough, as the bullet smacked into the meaty part of his thigh.

"God dammed limp dick motherfuckers!" he yelled, as he rolled down the incline. Hitting bottom, he yanked off his belt and tied it above the wound. Dog trotted over. Blindman grabbed the dog and whispered in his ear, "Find that fucker and do his ass in." Dog's ears went up and what could pass for a smile came across his face. He slunk off to do some damage.

Blindman looked at the wound. "Goddamn bullet has to come out before I do anything," he said. "I should see who fuckin shot me, though."

He fished a pair of binoculars out of his pack. He scanned the dunes until he saw a guy in camo fatigues with long blond hair. "Christ on a crutch," he muttered. "One of the Rominowski brothers. And where there's one, there's two. And these stupid polacks front for the fuckin Martinez brothers. Four cocksuckers I have to kill."

The Martinez brothers were total scum, rapists and murderers. They always used the Romanowski Brothers as bullet stoppers as the two were dumb as dirt and just liked to kill.

"I'm gonna have to punch someone's ticket so I can dig this slug out," thought Blindman. He took out an empty shotgun shell and slipped a sparkplug inside. *This*, he thought, *might just fuck up someone's day. Now to bait them.*

"Hey stupid!" Blindman yelled. "You guys still tossing Spanish salad?"

"You're dead, you old bastard!" one of the brothers yelled. "Stand up and take it like a man!"

Laughing insanely, Blindman yelled back, "Why don't you bend over and take it in the ass like you do for those spic bastards you work for?"

That had the desired effect. One of the brothers, Stosh, stood up screaming and shooting when a brown blur came up on his blindside and took him down. Dog ripped out his throat and arterial blood spurted three feet into the air. The other brother, Paul, screamed his outrage, stood up and drew a bead on dog. That exposed him to Blindman long enough for Blindman to get a shot. The sparkplug blew a bowling ball sized hole in his chest and pieces of his heart hit the ground behind him.

Blindman put his shotgun down and turned his attention to his wound. The slug had to come out before it got infected. He took out a knife and sliced his Levis open. It was slowly bleeding. Focused on the task at hand, he didn't hear anything until he felt metal against his neck.

"Don't be stupid," Nydia said. "You still have those two assholes out there."

"Ok, ya got me. What's your deal?" asked the surprised Blindman.

"We are both after the same thing and I know where it is," said Nydia.

"Well," said Blindman. "Why do you need me? I'm competition, why don't you just kill him yourself?"

"Because," said Nydia, "he's already dead and I can't dig his ass up by myself."

"Dead? Mister Fast Gun is dead? Excuse the hell outta me, but why didn't anyone claim the bounty?" asked Blindman. "Oh, by the way, you're covered."

Nydia turned around to see Dog glaring at her with blood dripping from his fangs. Genuinely frightened, she said, "Back him off or I shoot."

Blindman cackled. "You won't even get your gun up, he's that fuckin fast. Dog!" he yelled. "She friend, be nice."

The shaggy beast got up and walked toward her. "Easy girl," Blindman said. "This is make it or break it, he either likes you or he don't and if he don't you got a problem because you ain't gonna shoot him."

Dog walked up and sniffed Nydia, then circled her. After a few tense minutes, he started wagging his tail and licked her hand. "Well, I'll be a blind drunk son of a bitch, you made a friend," he laughed crazily.

"Now what?" she asked.

"Let's get the bullet out and kill these fuckers before they get their balls up enough to attack," Blindman replied. "Give me my knife and cut open one of these shotgun shells and give me the powder," said Blindman. "I need fire, too."

"What are you going to do?" Nydia asked, with more than a little fear in her eyes.

"Just watch," said Blindman, with a demented smile. Blindman stuck the tip of the knife in the wound. He plunged it in and twisted and the slug popped out with a spurt of blood. Nydia turned pale.

"Powder," Blindman said. Nydia gave him the open shell and he sprinkled gun powder into the wound. Smiling, Blindman turned to a shaken Nydia. "Got a light?" he asked.

Nydia tossed him a lighter and looked away. Blindman laughed and lit the powder. The smell of seared flesh filled the air. "Now I feel a lot better," he said.

Nydia looked at him in amazement. "You just cut a bullet out of your leg, then burned it shut, you are one chico duro."

"I need a drink." Blindman pulled a sealed pint of whiskey out of his bag and drained it in one gulp. "Good shit, takes the edge off another bad day. Let's flush those spic bastards out and be on our way."

"Not for nothing, you old bastard," said Nydia with considerable heat in her voice, "I'm half Mexican."

"Sorry," said a grinning Blindman. "Let's flush those limp dicked motherfuckers out and get this party started, that better?"

Nydia looked at him and thought, *maybe this was a real bad idea.*

"How do you want to do this?" she asked.

"Well, they don't know you're here and they do know I'm shot, so watch this," Blindman said with a grin.

Blindman started moaning and screaming. "Oh sweet baby Jesus, this hurts, this really hurts! Can't stop the bleeding, oh lord, just one more drink to kill the pain, I can't take it!"

Alternately screaming and crying loudly, Blindman looked at Nydia and said, "Lucy, I t'ink we got company. Shoot the bastards when they come over the top."

Blindman started gurgling like he was dying. The Martinez brothers charged over the top and a blast from the shotgun cut one completely in half. Nydia emptied a clip into the other one's chest.

Nydia looked at the mess the shotgun made. "What the fuck do you load that thing with?" she asked.

"Sugar and spice, but mostly things that ain't nice," replied Blindman. He checked out the other body. "Wow," he said. "You shot a smiley face right over this prick's heart, good thing I brought you along.

"Ok," he said. "Let's go find the grave and drop in on our old friend El Roacho."

Right about then Nydia was thinking, *what kind of lunatic did I hook up with? And can I trust him?*

7

BLINDMAN AND NYDIA started back to the shanty town. "How did you find out about El Roacho getting his ticket punched?" asked Blindman.

"I asked the fat bartender at The Last Chance Saloon," replied Nydia. "And he didn't know about the reward."

"Well that's a plus," muttered Blindman. "Those fuckers would dig up the whole desert if they thought they would find him."

They passed a turned over tanker truck. The truck was tricked out with turrets on top of it, obviously for guns. It was pocked by bullet holes and a few rotting bodies were scattered around it.

Blindman turned a body over. "These fuckers didn't get shot," he muttered. The corpse's face was contorted in agony and there were holes in the torso that looked like acid was poured on them.

"They drank something contaminated," Nydia stated. "That stuff eats you up from the inside out."

"Never did trust water," Blindman said. "It rusts out your insides, just like it rusts iron."

Nydia just stared at him. "That is one of the most fucked up statements I have ever heard," she said.

"I'll stick to liquor," Blindman said. "It keeps me sharp." Nydia just rolled her eyes.

It was getting close to dusk as they arrived at Shanty Town. "Let's just check out The Last Chance and see if word of the reward got here," said Blindman. The two entered The Last Chance, all the patrons were frozen with fear watching a guy dressed like a dime store cowboy. The 'cowboy' had a shock of red hair and buck teeth. He wore a black Stetson and a vest studded with silver conchos and a rig that held two chrome plated .44 magnums. He was screaming at a young kid.

"You don't fuck with Texas Red, you fuckin punk, now it's time to die!"

The kid said, "Mister, I didn't do anything. I'm not a shooter, leave me alone."

Red pulled a gun and blew the kid's kneecap off. The kid hit the floor screaming.

"Now, this is fun," laughed Red. He shot the other kneecap, then both elbows. The kid was flopping on the floor in agony. Red put his foot on the kid's throat and crushed his larynx. "That will teach you not to fuck with Texas Red," he cackled.

Blindman had seen enough. Nydia saw that he was about to buy into the game. "Don't," she said, putting her hand on his shoulder. But Red saw that move and a new victim.

"You want to try me, you old piece of shit?"

Before Blindman could answer, a voice boomed, "He might, but not before I get a piece of your chicken shit ass." The owner of the voice was a big man, well over six feet with a shock of black hair and a soup strainer mustache.

"And who the fuck are you, tough guy?" Red snarled.

"Blackjack Morgan, that's who," the man replied. "You're real tough with guys that can't fight. Want to try and shade me, you fuckin punk?"

Red went for his gun, but Blackjack was faster. The .45 automatic sounded like a cannon. The heavy slug caught Red right at the wrist. The hand, still holding the gun, hung by a strip of flesh. Blood spurted from the cut arteries. Screaming curses, Red tried to pick up his gun with his good hand. Blindman brought the butt plate of his shotgun down on the hand. The bones in the hand shattered like the sound of breaking sticks.

"So I'm an old piece of shit, eh?" Blindman snarled. He brought the butt down again and again until the hand was bloody pulp.

"Youse ruined me!" Red screamed. "Finish me off, I can't take the pain."

"Neither could that kid laying there, asshole," snarled Blackjack. "I'm not going to finish you, let someone you fucked over find you now, helpless. Just like that kid."

Moaning in pain, Red staggered out of The Last Chance.

"Nice shootin there, Mr. Morgan," said Blindman.

Morgan looked at Blindman, then at Nydia. "Thanks. But now a little business, as I think you two are looking for the same thing I am."

"And what might that be, Mr. Morgan?" asked Nydia.

"A certain gunslinger with a big price on his head," replied Morgan. "His trail turned cold here. Then you and this gentleman show up. Coincidence?"

Nydia looked at Blindman. "I need a drink," Blindman muttered. "Always fuckin complications. Morgan, have a drink with me."

"What about the lady?" asked Morgan.

"I don't indulge," said Nydia, "but I will roll one up." Nydia quickly rolled a joint.

"Hey Fatso!" Blindman yelled to the bartender. "Hook me and Morgan up with some hootch." The bartender hurriedly poured them shots. "Leave the bottle," said Blindman. "We got some parlaying to do."

THE OWL-FACED BARTENDER left a bottle and two glasses. Nydia sat back, smoking the spliff. Blindman tossed down his glass. He wiped the residue from his chin and looked at Morgan. "Ok, Blackjack, what's the deal?"

Morgan downed his drink. "100 cases of water split 3 ways isn't a bad haul," Morgan replied.

Blindman grunted, "Two ways is a lot more fuckin water. Why should we cut the pie 3 ways? What, pray tell, are you bringing to the table?"

"Another gun, that's what," replied Morgan. "This bounty has attracted every killer in the area, plus amateurs like Texas Red. We can cover each other, bring El Roacho Rio in, get paid, then go our separate ways."

"He has a point," Nydia interjected. "Getting El Roacho is one thing, getting him to the drunken douche bag is another."

"Yeah," mumbled Blindman. "We do have a lot of miles to cover and when word gets out, they'll be on us like flies on shit. Alright, Morgan, you just dealt yourself into the game."

"Good move," said Morgan. "This way we all make out."

"Groovy," said Blindman. "Another shot to seal the deal."

"Groovy?" said Nydia. "How the hell old are you, anyway?"

Cackling, Blindman said, "Old enough to have seen movies on a big screen, old enough to have seen the towers fall, old enough to see those fuckin Muslims overrun Europe, old enough to have seen all my friends die for nothing. Fuck this, I'm going to take a leak." Blindman staggered to the can.

"He's a little out there," Morgan said to Nydia.

"Yeah, he is," she replied, "but the old fuck is tough. I mean real tough. I saw him cut a bullet out of his leg and burn the wound shut. He's got this huge dog lurking around somewhere that actually listens to him and kills for him."

"Where's this dog now?" Morgan asked.

"Don't know," Nydia said. "It sorta just shows up."

"It didn't bother you?" Morgan inquired.

"Well, I had the drop on Blindman and it had the drop on me, but Blindman said 'She friend', so it let me alone. I'm sure things could have gone the other way if he wanted it to," she said.

Blindman returned to the table. "I think we have been here too long. Let's grab a couple of bottles, get El Roacho, and get truckin," he announced.

"Get El Roacho?" asked Morgan. "You mean you know where he's holed up?"

"Yep," said Blindman. "He's out back."

"Out back where?" asked Morgan. "Everyone with a gun is looking for him and he's hiding out back? What the fuck?"

Laughing insanely, Blindman said, "He's in the graveyard. Someone blew him away before the news of the bounty got out. The lady knows where he's planted, so now you two can dig him up."

"What do you mean *we* can dig him up, you old bastard?" Nydia shot back.

"My arthritis is acting up, my bowels are off, and I think I broke a nail. You should be kind to an old man in his declining years," replied Blindman.

"Now that's fuckin funny, Blindman. Tell you what, you dig him up and I'll give you a massage with a happy ending," said Nydia, with more than a trace of sarcasm.

"I say let's do this thing before someone else finds the grave," said Morgan.

"No chance of that," Nydia said. "I got rid of the marker. But you're right, let's get him and get going."

The three left the bar and walked into a wall of gunfire.

9

RED ROSE BLOSSOMS ERUPTED from Morgan's chest as the bullets threw him against the door of The Last Chance. The big man never even got his gun out. Blood gushed from Nydia's head as she took a hit. A bullet burned across Blindman's back as he hit the ground.

Blindman saw that Morgan was done. Nydia's face was covered in blood, but she was still breathing.

"Ambushing cocksuckers," Blindman muttered. "How the fuck did they know anything?" He grabbed Nydia and dragged her back into the bar.

"What the fuck is all the shooting about?" yelled the bartender.

"Ambush, that's what it's about!" Blindman yelled back. "Morgan's dead and she's hard hit." Aside from the bartender there were five drunks in the bar. "Any of youse got guns?" Blindman asked.

"Yeah," said a skinny blond-haired man. "We's all packin."

"Better get ready to use them," said Blindman.

"Ain't our fight," one of the barflies said.

"I don't think these guys care whose fight it is," replied Blindman.

Squinting out the window, he saw two things that really pissed him off. Texas Red was there; what was left of his hands were heavily bandaged. The other thing was Coffin Jack White. *Now I get it*, thought Blindman. *Morgan should have killed that redheaded prick. Jack must have found him, fixed him up and Red brought them here.*

Red was screaming obscenities about Morgan. "Fast draw, Blackjack. Ain't so fast now, are you, big man? Fuck with Texas Red and pay the price!"

I need another gun, thought Blindman. He belly crawled to the door; he needed Blackjack's .45 automatic.

Bullets whined over him as he crawled to Morgan's body. Morgan stared sightlessly into the desert. Blindman plucked the .45 from its holster. He searched Morgan and found a box of shells and four full clips. He reached up and closed Morgan's eyes. "You was game until the end, Blackjack. Shouldn't have went down like this. If I make it, I'll plant you proper."

Blindman crawled back into the bar. Nydia was stirring. "Stay down," Blindman said to her. "You got clipped in the head, bled a lot, but you should be ok. They think you're dead, we can use that." Nydia was still dazed, but nodded. Texas Red was still shrieking curses on Morgan.

Blindman searched his bag of shotgun shells until he found one with a black mark on it. "Texas Red needs my special blend," he muttered. Looking out the window he thought, *this will be a tough shot*. He looked toward the bar and saw a shotgun hanging on the wall behind it. It was a Remington Automatic with an extended barrel.

Blindman yelled to the bartender, "Let me have that shotgun." Owl Face was quick to comply. "Hope this thing don't blow up in my face," bitched Blindman. He broke the barrel and looked down it. No cracks, bore looked smooth.

He dropped the high brass round in it, then drew a bead on Texas Red. "Hey carrot top!" he yelled. "This is from Blackjack!" The Remington bucked and Red was turned into a gory red mess from his belly button to his kneecaps. He hit the sand, screaming in agony.

Owl Face looked like he was going to puke. "What the hell was in that?" he asked.

"Broken safety glass and pieces of barbed wire," replied Blindman. "He done Blackjack wrong, so I done his ass the same way." A single gunshot ended Red's screaming.

"That was a rotten thing to do to a man, you old bastard," someone said.

"Hey Jack, you albino looking piece of shit, go fuck yourself!" yelled Blindman.

"For an old man, you sure got a bad mouth!" yelled Jack.

"For a backstabbing card cheating low life, your posture ain't so bad!" yelled back Blindman. The dozen guys with Jack looked at him with WTF expressions on their faces.

"He's nuts," Jack said. "Stone bonkers, but he knows where El Roacho is. Look, you blind bastard, tell us where El Roacho is and I'll let you live".

"That's mighty considerate of you, Jack," snarled Blindman, "but that dumb fuck you hooked up with, Texas Red, just fucked you in the ass."

"How do you figure that?" Jack asked.

"That bucked toothed turd asked you to come in shootin. Well, you got Blackjack but you also got the girl and you got her before she could tell me and Blackjack where El Roacho is," said Blindman. Nydia looked up at him. "Yeah, Kid, you're my ace in the hole. You and Dog, if he shows up. There's a dozen of them and we are surrounded."

"You're lying!" Jack yelled. "I'm gonna beat the truth out of your blind ass."

"That means you'll have to get your hands dirty, Jack. If they can stop shaking. Need a drink, you fuckin alky? Got a whole bar here all to myself," Blindman laughed.

"You're dead anyway, you old cocksucker," a new voice yelled. "You killed my brother and you're going to pay."

"When, pray tell, did I do that?" asked Blindman.

"Remember a Quick Mart, you old bastard? A few days ago? You decided to play hero and you killed my brother. Here's news flash. We went back, we killed everyone there, raped the women and burned the place down. How do you like that?"

Blindman thought back and thought about the little girl that gave him supplies. A red haze enveloped Blindman's vision. He trembled from rage. He loaded the Remington with five shells, put the .45 behind his belt, and put two special shells in his sawed-off.

He stormed out the door screaming that he was going to kill every motherfucker he saw. Bullets buzzed past his head like angry hornets. The mouthy bastard and two others came at him, blazing away. A bullet burned his hip; he pulled the trigger on both barrels. The three men were incinerated. Dropping the sawed-off, he blasted another thug in the guts with the Remington. He heard a gun cock behind him, but a brown blur took down the gunmen with powerful jaws around his head. Dog was in the fight.

Nydia tried to stand up. She staggered and one of the barflies grabbed her. "You guys better start shootin'," she said.

"What the fuck was in that sawed-off?" asked the barfly. "He set those guys ablaze."

"Don't know and don't care," said Nydia. "What I do know is they'll kill us graveyard dead unless we start shooting back."

The men looked at each other, then pulled their guns. Each took a window. Outside it was bedlam. Dog had nearly ripped the head off the gunslinger.

Blood fountained into the air, covering the beast. Blindman was screaming for Jack to come out and die. He had several bleeding bullet burns on him but they weren't slowing him down.

Jack had lost four men. One ran toward the bar and caught a hail of bullets that cut him down like a scythe.

Blindman tossed the now empty Remington away. He broke open the sawed-off and thumbed two shells into it. A gunman tackled him. Blindman butt stoked him with the sawed-off and the thug went down, spitting out teeth. Blindman pulled out his 'nucks and caved in his skull.

Jack was down to six men. He screamed, "Let's rush the bar!"

No one moved. "Did you shitheads hear me?" Jack screamed.

"Fuck that shit, Jack," one man said. "We should pull back and get more guys."

"No time!" yelled Jack. "We can take them."

"Glad you think that because I..." his voice turned into a gurgle as Dog found him.

"I really need a damn drink," Blindman muttered. "I'm spent." He was also bleeding from the bullet burns. He had his back to a huge rock; he knew there were more guns than he could handle.

I fucked up, he thought, then thought again of the girl. A bullet pinged off the rock, bringing him out of his thoughts. He didn't know where the bar was in relation to where he was. *I'd have to stand up to see where the fuck I am, then bang, I'm dead.* He pulled out Blackjack's .45. "Well, fuck it," he said, and stood up.

The bar was off to the west and he saw no signs of life. He didn't see Coffin Jack or any of his shooters. "Aw, hell," he said. "Don't tell me they took the bar."

He sensed something behind him. Dog sat there, all bloody with what may have passed for a grin on his face. "Glad you're having a good day," said Blindman. "Now go flush somebody out." Dog's ears stood up and he ran off with his tail wagging furiously.

Blindman looked toward the bar, licking his lips at the thought of a bottle. He saw one of Jack's men crawling, belly down, toward the bar. Dog was following him. Dog slithered past him. The man reached a half-buried SUV and peeked over it. Powerful jaws clamped around his head and ripped his face off like it was a mask. The guy stood screaming. Before Dog could take him down, a shot from the bar punched his ticket.

Another shooter was dumb enough or drunk enough to stand up and shoot at Dog. His head exploded as the .45 in Blindman's hand spit death.

Jack was down to three very unhappy men. One said, "This ain't working, I'm outta here."

"The hell you are," snarled Jack, and shot him through the head. The other two turned on Jack. Jack shot one in the chest, but caught a bullet in his side from the other guy. Jack shot the guy in the brisket, but before the guy checked out, he shot Jack's left knee cap off. Jack screamed, lost his balance, and fell backward into a gully. He was directly beneath the big rock that Blindman was using for cover.

Blindman noticed that the big rock was sort of teetering on the slope. Jack was below it, screaming curses about his shitty luck. Blindman was determined to make his luck even shittier. He looked for something he could use to pry the rock loose. He saw something shiny and crawled over to check it out. It was the bumper from a truck. He dragged it over and rammed it under the rock. He crawled up on the rock, then dropped feet first on the bumper. The rock rolled free and down it went on Coffin Jack White.

Whistling a tune, Blindman checked on his work. Coffin Jack was trapped under the rock. It hadn't crushed him, but it pinned him to the ground.

"Still want to beat the truth out of me, undertaker?" Blindman asked.

"Get me out of here!" Jack cried.

"Naw," said Blindman. "You opened this dance, now I'm finishing it." Blindman then noticed that the sand was slowly trickling down into the gully, filling it up.

"You blind bastard, get me outta here! Get me the fuck outta here!" screamed Jack.

"No can do, Jack, looks like mother nature is taking a hand," said Blindman. He watched impassively as sand filled Jack's mouth, nose and ears. In a few minutes Jack was buried by the shifting sand.

"One less scumbag the world has to deal with," muttered Blindman as he limped off toward the bar.

10

NYDIA MET HIM AT THE door. "Drink," he moaned. "I need a drink." Owl Face quickly handed him a bottle and Blindman killed half of it in one gulp.

"Any of them left?" asked Nydia.

"No," replied Blindman. "I just buried Jack. Shame he was still alive when I did it." He laughed.

"What the hell was in your sawed-off?" one of the barflies asked. "You set them three guys on fire."

"Dragon's Breath," said Blindman. "Shotgun shells loaded with white phosphorus. I read they were considered inhuman for combat. Found them in a militia's hideout."

Nydia said, "I don't know what set you off, but you were awesome out there."

"They killed Blackjack, they almost killed you. Then that cocksucker mouthed off about the Quick Mart. I don't kill for fun, I kill to survive. I don't rob and rape people and I don't kill kids."

"Better let me clean those cuts," said Nydia. "Nice little speech, by the way."

"After you're done, I have to plant Blackjack. Then we'll dig up El Roacho," said Blindman.

Nydia cleaned his wounds with whiskey. Blindman sucked on his bottle until it was empty. "Let's go to work," he said. He squatted down next to Morgan and hoisted the big man over his shoulders. "We'll plant Blackjack first," said Blindman. "No reason he should share a hole with a guy with no head."

Blindman was drenched with sweat as he dug a hole close to six feet deep. They wrapped Blackjack in a tarp and put him to rest. "In another time and place we would have been friends, most likely," said Blindman.

"Yeah," agreed Nydia. "He wasn't a bad sort."

"Let's dig up our meal ticket." Blindman kicked away the marker and started to dig. "Did ya have to put rocks on top of him?" he bitched at Nydia.

"Hey, I just found the grave. I had nothing to do with planting him," she shot back.

A grueling thirty minutes later Blindman said, "You got a sack or something to put this head in?"

"Yeah," Nydia said. "I grabbed a flour sack from the bar."

Blindman moved the dirt away from the corpse's head. He stuck the shovel under El Roacho's chin, then stomped it with his boot. The head popped off with a dry crack. "Toss me the bag, Kid," said Blindman. He quickly bagged the head and tossed it to Nydia.

"Grab this," he said as he handed her the shovel, then pulled himself out of the grave.

She handed him a bottle of whiskey. "Here, have a drink, I'll fill in the hole."

He sat taking pulls from the bottle and watching her work. "You're not a bad lookin woman," he said. "If I was younger, I'd give you a tumble."

"In your dreams, Pops," she chuckled. "I'm not easy, but I can be made."

He laughed, but then cold steel jabbed his neck. "Now what?" He turned as he was poked hard. The owl-faced bartender and three of the barflies stood there with guns drawn. Owl Face had retrieved his Remington. Blindman snarled, "Oh, now you fuckers decided to grow a pair of balls."

"Calm down, old man," said one barfly. "Just give us the bag and walk away."

Nydia threw the bag in the air. Owl Face looked up and she swung the shovel like a scythe into his sagging belly. Owl Face screamed as gray intestines fell out of him like writhing snakes.

Blindman clawed out the .45 and shot the first barfly in the face, then he pivoted and shot another in the chest. The third one stared in horror at the handle of a knife that seemed to grow out of his chest, courtesy of Nydia.

"Nice move," Blindman said to Nydia.

"Wasn't there a couple more of them?" Nydia asked.

"Yeah, there *wuz*," retorted Blindman. "Let's find them before they give us another problem."

The other two barflies were sitting in the bar nursing drinks. "Those guys dead?" one asked.

"Deader than my cock," said Blindman. "Youse guys were smart to stay out of it."

"Mister," one said, "I just saw you kill a dozen men. Whatever you're after, you earned it."

"Well thank ye for that," said Blindman. "I'll tell you what, by the power vested in me, you two now own this place and all the bullshit that comes with it," proclaimed Blindman. "I'll just take these here bottles as a keepsake and me and the lady will be takin our leave, comprende?"

The two barflies, Leo and Knuckles, looked shocked. Happy, but shocked.

"We sure do, and thanks. You and the lady have a nice trip," said one very happy Knuckles.

"This trip ain't gonna be happy until it's over," muttered Blindman.

"How far is The Drunken Master from here?" asked Nydia.

"I figure about 50 miles or so due west," said Blindman. "Don't think it's going to be easy, either. Those two assholes will tell anyone who asks that we have the head and where we are going with it. I need your eyes, girl, mine aren't worth a shit."

"Ok," said Nydia, "but we need supplies."

"I got three bottles of bourbon from the bar. I'm good to go," he said laughing.

"We need something to eat. Jerky, canned stuff, whatever," Nydia said.

"Well forage something, but as long as I got liquor, I'm fine," said Blindman.

"I'll stick to the weed," Nydia replied. "I hate hangovers."

"Stay drunk and you ain't gettin no hangover," said Blindman. "But you have to be careful not to mix white liquor with brown liquor. Me, I stick to brown liquor. Gin tastes like shit, vodka you can use to remove paint and tequila gives me the drizzling shits. Now brown whiskey, bourbon especially, gives me energy. I did smoke weed, but it makes me sleepy and throws off my aim."

"What aim?" asked Nydia. "You can't see worth a shit."

"Yeah," muttered Blindman, "I know. Before the world went to shit, a prison doc told me I was getting Cadillacs in my eyes."

"He meant cataracts, you crazy bastard," said Nydia. "You need surgery to get rid of them."

"Fat chance of finding a doctor in this burg," mumbled Blindman. "Not that I'd let anyone with a blade near my peepers."

The two kept walking west, passing abandoned vehicles and a few bleached skeletons. Finally, they found a blacktop road, or what was left of one. They saw some buildings in the distance.

Blindman stopped and rooted though his rucksack. He pulled out a pair of binoculars. "Here," he said, handing them to Nydia. "Check out those building and see if anyone's lurking around."

Nydia scanned the area slowly. "I don't see anything moving," she said.

"Well," said Blindman, "let's check it out, maybe there's some eats stashed somewhere."

11

WONG DUCK AND HIS ENTOURAGE came within sight of The Last Chance. The two barflies had heard stories of the Celestials and what they were capable of. Wong Duck instructed one of his hatchet men to hail The Last Chance.

"We are weary travelers in search of some food and shelter. We will gladly let you use our women if you accommodate my master."

"Yeah, sure, then you kill us after," yelled Leo. "We heared about you. Unless you got a bag of egg rolls, you can fuck off."

The hatchet man screamed his outrage and rushed The Last Chance. A round from an AK-47 hit his head and he did a 360 spin before hitting the ground.

"We know what you fuckers want and we ain't got it!" Leo yelled from the bar.

"Tell us where it is and we won't burn this place down!" yelled Wong Duck.

"Like we would even let you get close, you yellow bastard. You want to see your ancestors? Cool, follow the tracks west," Leo yelled. "There's an old guy, a girl and a dog, they only killed about twenty gunslingers that we just planted."

"West?" asked Wong Duck.

"Yeah, west," Leo answered. "Better get moving before we start shootin again."

Wong Duck made a silent vow that he would return and these infidels would suffer the death of 1000 cuts. He signaled his men to back off. They went west and found the set of tracks.

"We will soon fulfill our destiny," Wong proclaimed to his men.

NYDIA AND BLINDMAN walked down what was probably the main street of a little town. The place was sun scorched, bleached almost gray. The signs of the stores were blasted from wind-driven sand. A few cars and trucks were scattered about, rusting hulks with a few skeletons in them. Bullet holes pocked the doors and windows of the stores. "Must have been some kinda fight here," Blindman mused. "Wonder if they left anything in these stores."

"Only one way to find out," said Nydia. "We search 'em one at a time."

The first place used to be a drug store. "Well," said Nydia, "I'll bet there isn't a fuckin opiate left here."

"No bet, that's a given," said Blindman, "but they might have left some antibiotics and that we can use." A search produced a bottle of amoxicillin.

"Better than nothing," Nydia muttered.

Another store had some clothing hanging on racks. "Need to find a liquor store," said Blindman. "My blood alcohol level feels low."

"Every town has a liquor store," said Nydia. "But in a little spot like this, it probably got cleaned out."

"Dash my hopes, why don't ya?" Blindman replied.

A couple of other stores were in shambles, nothing useable. They finally found a liquor store. It was a mess. Beer bottles had exploded, fermenting wine pushed the corks out of bottles and spilled onto the floor. The place just reeked of stale beer and wine.

"Gotta love that aroma," Blindman cackled.

"I might puke," said Nydia. "Looks like everything went to shit here."

"I'm gonna scrounge around a bit," said Blindman.

"Knock yourself out," said Nydia. "I need fresh air and a smoke."

Nydia rolled a joint and leaned against the building. It was twilight and the shadows were lengthening. *After he finds his liquor, we got to fort up for the night,* she thought. *No telling who's lurking around here.* Taking a pull from the joint, Nydia squinted as she saw something move toward the end of town.

"Blindman, better get out here, I think we got company" she said.

Blindman came out with a sack full of bottles. "What did you see?" he asked.

"Something like a moving black shadow, down toward the edge of town," she said.

"This ain't good," said Blindman. "Get those peepers and check it out. I'm not going to see shit, you be my eyes."

Nydia took out the battered binoculars and looked down the street. "See anyone?" Blindman asked.

"Yeah, a couple of people in black," she replied. "They're creeping up on us."

"Dog," Blindman whispered. "Get over here." The shaggy cur trotted over. Blindman grabbed the back of his neck and said, "Stay."

"Don't you think we should send him after them?" Nydia asked.

"No," replied Blindman. "I got a feeling them clowns are those chink killers, The Tongs. I'm not risking him, he's my friend, been with me too long. Those guys are professional assassins, they're real sudden. Let's get some cover."

Blindman kicked open the door of a small building. Dragging Dog, who wanted to go hunting, they got inside of what was a music store. "Seems like a solid place to defend," said Nydia. "Walls are pretty thick, should stop bullets."

"These guys don't use guns, they like to work close with hatchets and knives," Blindman said. "This is bad, real bad. Wish I had some dynamite, grenades, something where I could get 'em all in one shot."

"Maybe there's something in here," said Nydia.

"Yeah," Blindman said. "I can toss these records at them. All good stuff too, here. Frank Zappa, Lou Reed, Santana. Now, that was music. Not that hippity rappity crap. Damn, those were good times. I remember... Wait a minute, what's this?"

Blindman pulled a big dusty box from a shelf. "Piano wire!" he exclaimed. He had an idea. "Keep your eye out for those ninja looking pricks, I got some work to do."

A voice from outside called, "We have you trapped, Ancient one. Give us what you have and we will let you live."

"Yeah, sure they will," growled Blindman. "We give up the head, they turn us into sushi, fuck that. I know who that guy is, Wong Duck or something, real bad, really bad."

"Do you hear me, old man? Give us the trophy and the woman and you can go," shouted Wong Duck.

Nydia stiffened. "Fuck this guy, I'll just..."

"No," interrupted Blindman. "You won't. I need time. Keep the bastards occupied, insult them, throw a few shots at them, buy me a few minutes."

"Ok," said Nydia. "Do what ya gotta do. Hey, Go Fuck Ducks! You want this pussy? Try and take it!" Nydia let loose a volley of shots from her Phoenix Arms Automatic.

Blindman was working as fast as he could. He took two shotgun shells and cut off the ends. He spilled the double-aught buck pellets on the countertop. He pulled out a knife and split the shot almost in half. He pulled the piano wire out of the box. He closed the split shot over the wire at two-foot intervals. When finished, he stuffed it all back into the shells. He took a candle out of his pack, lit it, and used the wax to seal the shells. He picked up the sawed-off, broke it and put in the shells. "Moment of truth time, Kiddo," said Blindman. "If this goes bad, get Dog and get the hell outta here." Blindman picked up the bag and stepped out of the store.

"Hey Ducky!" shouted Blindman. "Tell you what, you take out your wok, whip me up some egg foo young, beef & broccoli, and moo shu pork and we'll trade. Got my order, you yellow bastard?"

Screaming their outrage, the five Tongs charged down the street. One old man with a shotgun might get some of them, but not all of them. Blindman stood impassively until they were about twenty feet away. Then he pulled the triggers. The shotgun roared and the air became a red mist. His tricked-out shot was like a scythe. The Tongs were reduced to a gruesome pile of arms, hands, legs, heads, and torsos. Blindman stood, surveying his work.

Nydia walked outside, her face white with shock. She looked at Blindman, awestruck. "I used to read a lot in prison," Blindman said. "I got that trick reading about the Civil War. Knowledge is good."

"Wow," she said. "Fuckin wow. That was incredible."

"Yeah," chuckled Blindman. "It was at that. But Duck fucker is still out there."

WONG DUCK COULD NOT believe his eyes when he saw his men almost disintegrate into bloody pieces. He had never been without minions to back him up. The cold fingers of fear were touching him. Duck shrugged it off. It was just an old man and a girl who stood in his way. After he claimed his reward, he could always find more disposable minions.

"Old Man!" Duck shouted. "You are a worthy adversary. I challenge you to meet me, one on one, to the death. Show your courage and accept my challenge."

"Sure I will," muttered Blindman. "When he stands up I'll just blow his head off."

"No," said Nydia. "Accept the challenge."

"Are you outta your mind?" said Blindman. "I don't know that chop socky stuff. I'll just shoot him."

"You don't," said Nydia, "but I do. I'll take him."

"What if you can't take him?" asked Blindman. "Then what?"

"I have to take him," said Nydia. "He's killed a lot of women, a woman should kill him."

"I ain't down with this, let me just blast him," bitched Blindman.

"I haven't asked you for anything so far. I'm asking you to let me do this," said Nydia.

"Alright," said Blindman, reluctantly. "Go for it."

"Wong Duck!" shouted Nydia. "There is no honor in defeating a blind, broken-down old man. I challenge you! You enslaved women, you used them like animals, then killed them. I want the honor of killing you myself. Or can you only deal with helpless women and children, you cowardly dog?"

Wong was now furious. How dare that bitch talk to him like this? Yes, he would face her, kill her. Then the old man.

Had Wong been a little more observant, he would have noticed that one of his women was listening very intently to Nydia's challenge. Wong stepped out on the street and motioned to the women that they should follow him. In Cantonese he told the women he would prove his superiority over a lowly female.

Nydia walked up to him and nailed him in the jaw with an uppercut. Staggering, Wong threw a roundhouse kick that missed. Nydia's didn't. Blood flew from Wong's smashed lips. Wong feinted, then hit Nydia in the ribs with a kick. Nydia went down but took Wong with her in the process with a leg sweep. The two were on the ground in a tangle of arms and legs.

Wong got Nydia into a head scissor lock, but Nydia sunk her teeth into Wong's thigh, drawing blood. That broke the hold, but Wong unleashed a backhand chop that knocked Nydia's front teeth out. Enraged and spitting out blood and teeth, Nydia uncorked a hard left hand that spread Wong's nose all over his face. Blood and snot flew into the air. The two were on their feet, glaring at each other, faces streaked with blood.

Blindman really was fighting the urge to just shoot Duck and Dog was growling, watching the fight.

Wong threw a kick that clipped Nydia's right knee. Nydia hit the ground and Wong launched himself at her. She rolled and Wong hit the ground hard, the wind knocked out of him. Nydia straddled him and started beating his head with a flurry of lefts and rights. Wong was getting the beating of his life. Blood started pouring out of his boxed ears. He grabbed a handful of sand and rubbed it into Nydia's eyes. Nydia stopped punching and clawed at her face. Wong jackknifed his body, throwing her off-balance. As she got up, Wong punted her head with a stiff kick.

Wong realized that he was outclassed. He pulled two knives out. Blindman brought up the shotgun yelling. "Real honorable, ain't ya?" But he wasn't fast enough. Wong threw a knife at him. The handle of the knife hit Blindman's wrist and the shotgun fired into the ground. Blindman's hand was numb. He looked in horror as Wong straddled Nydia, grabbed her hair and went to cut her throat. Dog streaked toward them, but not fast enough.

Wong's knife hand flew off as a hatchet slammed into it. Wong turned in shock and saw the six girls that he had abused for so long. They had all picked up the knives and hatchets that the dead Tongs had dropped. Wong held the stump of his wrist and looked at them. Terror was etched on his face. He said something in Cantonese, but it had no effect. The women fell on him, screaming like banshees. Knives and hatchets fell as gouts of crimson shot into the air.

Finally, the blood-splattered women backed away from Wong Duck, who now was sliced up like Peking duck. The women rushed over to attend to the uncurious Nydia.

Blindman, nursing his bruised wrist, walked over and spit on Wong's mutilated corpse. "That will teach you not to starch my shirts, you dry cleaning bastard," muttered Blindman.

The women had gotten Nydia up. "My fuckin teeth," she moaned. "What the hell happened?"

"The great martial artist couldn't handle you, that's what happened," said Blindman. "He was going to stab you, but then these ladies turned him into sushi."

Nydia looked at the bloody, but now smiling faces of the women. "What happened?" she repeated.

"You had him beat," said Blindman. "He cheated, pulled the knives. I tried to dust him, but the bastard threw off my aim. These ladies saved our asses, I think. What should we do with them?"

"I don't know," muttered Nydia. "We can't just leave them." She spit out some blood. "These teeth are ripping my tongue to shreds."

One of the Chinese girls spoke in broken English. "Me fix," she said, pointing to Nydia's bloody mouth. "You great fighter, you free us, you have our thanks." The two women huddled in conversation.

Nydia turned to Blindman. "I need a bottle," she said.

"You don't drink," said Blindman.

"I do now. Because Lee," she said, pointing to the Chinese girl, "is going to file my broken teeth down so I don't chew off my tongue." Blindman handed her a quart of whiskey.

Blindman decided to take a walk rather than watch the do-it-yourself dentistry. Dog trotted along. "Hell of a thing," Blindman said to Dog. "First it was just us, then Nydia came along. She's a tough little bitch; I actually like her. And now we got six more females. What the hell?"

Blindman further pondered the situation. "They're pretty good with them knives and stuff, maybe I could teach 'em to shoot." He laughed. "Great idea, being that I really can't see for shit... Nydia could teach 'em. After all, she great fighter," he laughed.

Now sweat and tears were running down Nydia's face as Lee filed the broken stubs of teeth.

"Can't leave 'em," thought Blindman. "Someone would get them and do 'em in. Now I got a fuckin conscience. Great."

Blindman sighed with resignation. "I better go look for supplies," he muttered.

12

BLINDMAN WALKED OVER to the women. "Any better?" he asked.

"Yeah," said Nydia. "You want your liquor back?"

"No, hang on to it," said Blindman. "You may need it later. I been thinking. We can't leave these girls, we gotta take them with us."

"Yes," said Nydia. "They are indebted to us, they feel, for freeing them. But if they didn't jump Wong we might be dead, so actually we sorta owe them."

"That's the way I figured it, too," said Blindman. "We're gonna need supplies. They don't drink, which leaves more for me." He chuckled at that. "But they need food. That girl, Lee, she understands English, right?"

"Yeah," said Nydia. "Not that great, but she gets it. Why?"

"I need you to tell her to have these girls tear this town apart for food," ordered Blindman. "Have them search every building, starting now. We have to get going before we run into any more assholes. We ain't out of dodge until we get that reward, if there really is one."

Nydia looked at him in shock. "What do you mean, 'if there really is one'?" she asked.

"Well," said Blindman, "I been thinkin on it. I know for a fact that El Roacho crippled The Drunken Bastard's gun hand. I also know that in a dying world, supplies are short. So follow my thinking on this. A lot of the gunnies out here are known names, like the old western gunfighters. Drunko was the baddest of the bad, but now he's declawed. He has his little kingdom, but now can't really defend it. Oh, he'll have some gunnies completely loyal to him, any little despot will, but all of us bad guys are a threat to him. So, why not come up with a scheme to pit us all against each other? That whittles down the competition. Coffin Jack White was a name, he's dead. This chink was a name, he's dead. So were the Martinez boys. Then you also have the fat cop and that ugly dyke. Get the picture?"

Nydia was deep in thought. "Damn," she said. "You might be right on with that. Names we know, and how many others have blown each other away that we don't know about? I don't know anymore," she sighed. "Maybe we should give it up."

"Naw," said Blindman. "I really need to see how this plays out. You can go if ya want, I won't fault you. You got sand, you're aces in my book."

Nydia pondered on it. "I've come this far," she said. "It isn't like I have anywhere else to go."

"Look at it this way," Blindman said. "If we can take him, we got it all. We can be set for a while at least, that's something to consider. Besides, if he's the lying cocksucker I think he is, I want a shot at him. Just for shits and giggles."

Nydia thought for a few minutes. "Alright," she said. "I'm in until it's over."

"Groovy," said Blindman. "I want you to teach those girls how to shoot. One of those stores was a gun shop, clean it out. You have a good eye, get those ladies up to snuff and we got a halfway decent chance of pulling this off."

SLUGGO HAD MADE THE rounds of The Master's compound. A few drifters had come begging for supplies. Sluggo had asked if they had heard anything of interest, like shootouts. What he learned put a frown on his ugly face. The Master wasn't expecting what had happened. Returning to The Master's lair, Sluggo found him nursing his second bottle of the day, and it was only 10am.

"Any good news?" The Master asked.

"No," replied Sluggo, "but a lot of bad news."

The Master was all attention now. "What bad news?" he snarled.

"Somethin we didn't count on," said Sluggo. "Dem drifters told me some of dem fighters teamed up."

"Teamed up!" The Master roared. "That's exactly what we didn't want. We wanted them all at each other's throats, not uniting forces. Goddammit! Who the hell teamed up with who?"

"The way I heard it made no sense," said Sluggo. "First off, dey was a lot of little fights between dem people. Lot of the suckers got killed. That old man, the one who's blind, he shot up a gang. Then he got ambushed by those Martinez boys and their crew. Dey had him until some bitch showed up and saved his ass. Then they hooked up with Blackjack Morgan. Coffin Jack's crew ambushed dem and capped Blackjack. The old man and da bitch wiped out Coffin Jack and all his boys."

"This is the last thing I wanted" muttered The Master.

"Dat ain't all dat went down," said Sluggo. "Dey got El Roacho."

"Are you fuckin serious, they actually killed El Roacho?" asked The Master.

"Somebody did him, dey got his head in a sack," said Sluggo. "The guy who ran The Last Chance and a couple of others tried to get the head. Dey didn't. Den they had a fight with dat ninja guy."

"Wong Duck?" said The Master. "They killed Wong Duck and his crew?"

"Yeah," said Sluggo. "Dem ninjas is all deceased."

"God fuckin dammit, those chinks were the ones I was really worried about. A half blind old man and some spic bitch took them out. Great. I gotta rethink this," bellowed The Master.

"Not to piss you off, Boss, but those chink women that Wong Duck used for bait, well now dey is with those two," added Sluggo.

"Having those women might slow them down," said The Master. "Bitches are useless except to fuck and trade for stuff. They won't be a threat."

Turning to Sluggo, The Master barked an order. "If they get here, you stop them, comprende?"

"Dey won't get by me, Boss, I'll waste dem all." Sluggo boasted.

13

BLINDMAN HAD TAKEN a snooze. Hot breath in face woke him up. Dog was staring at him, wagging his tail. "What the fuck do you want?" he asked the big cur. Dog sat and stared. Blindman pulled some jerky out of his pocket and tossed it to Dog. The mutt wolfed it down, then trotted off.

Blindman heard gunshots and walked over to see how shooting practice was going. Nydia turned at his approach. "How they shaping up?" he asked.

"Half and half," said Nydia. "Problem is they are frail, that duck fucker didn't feed them," she explained. "You give them a high caliber rifle, the recoil will break bones. I found a bunch of .22 rifles and magnum rounds."

"A .22 in the right place can do some damage," Blindman said. "Are they getting the hang of it?"

"Four of them are good, the other two suck," answered Nydia. "I found a couple of 20-gauge shotguns and a lot of shells. I got them practicing with those. If nothing else they can draw fire off of us."

"Good idea," said Blindman.

"Oh," said Nydia, "Lee told me something interesting. She said she heard Wong saying that he would team up with another group to take out The Master."

"What other group?" asked Blindman.

"She said he didn't care who it was, his trick was to use the girls to get guys in, use them, then dispose of them," answered Nydia.

"I wonder if Wong guessed what we sorta figured out," said Blindman. "I have the distinct feeling that if we just waltzed in with this head, looking for the payoff, the payoff will be in bullets instead of 100 cases of water. Let me ruminate on this," he continued. "We are still pretty far from The Master. Let's figure the reward is bullshit. There probably is water there, but he's not giving it up. He's shit scared of losing because he can't shoot anymore. That's why he wanted to get rid of as many of us as he could without exposing himself. He's probably got a lot of muscle protecting him, so we have another fight. We will more than likely run into more assholes out for the reward. Now we have two choices. We can forget about this and find a place to hide out. Or we take the fight to him," summarized Blindman. "What do you think, Kiddo?"

Nydia pondered the question. She looked at the ragged figure standing before her. "You got anything better to do, Old Man?" she asked.

"Not particularly," Blindman answered. "I'm not down with the odds, but we do have an edge."

"How do you figure we have an *edge*?" she asked.

"Simple," said Blindman. "They don't know that we know their plan. They expect someone to stroll in with El Roacho here, all fat, dumb, and happy, then they kill him. No more competition, they'll have it all," he explained. "Now, if we show up looking fat, dumb and happy, their guard is down and we might be able to take 'em."

Nydia thought on this. "What if we get there and they just come at us?" she asked.

"We are going there looking for a fight," said Blindman. "Like I just said, they don't know that we know what they are up to. We go in shootin."

"Makes sense," replied Nydia. "All we stand to lose is our lives, and without supplies, our lives ain't worth shit."

"That's the spirit," laughed Blindman. "If we pull it off, we're set for a while. If we don't ..." he trailed off.

"We are deader than shit," finished Nydia.

"Ok," said Blindman. "Let's get going. I'm going to take the point with Dog, we have to spread out just in case we run into more crap. You, Lee and two of the girls tag a little behind me. Put the other girls, the ones with shotguns, behind you. Tell Lee to tell them that if they see ANYTHING, start shootin and don't stop until we come runnin. We ain't gonna stop for anything."

"Ok," said Nydia, "I'll tell them."

Blindman and Dog took the point position. The sun had no mercy, but most were used to the heat. Little dust devils kicked up here and there. Dog loped out ahead of Blindman, looking for prey.

"Nice day for something," Blindman muttered, draining the last dregs of his bottle.

COP WAS DETERMINED to find El Roacho. He ran into a raggedy group of outlaw bikers, Sons of Satan. They had figured out how to keep their bikes running. Or sort of running. Using high proof liquor for fuel, the bikes coughed and sputtered, but would run. Cop snuck up on the group as they were sharing a girl they had captured. He had picked up an Uzi from one of his 'collars'. Cop walked right into the Sons' camp. Brandishing the Uzi, Cop announced, "You men are all under arrest."

The bikers stared at Cop in drunken amazement. "Who the fuck are you?" a biker growled, pulling a .38 from his belt. Cop stitched him from chin to crotch. Another biker grabbed the girl and held her in front of him as a shield. "Drop the gun or I'll do the bitch!" he shouted.

"No, you won't," said Cop. Cop shot the girl. The biker looked shocked. "Now you gentlemen are under arrest," said Cop. Too much liquor had dulled their senses. The gang didn't know how to react. "By the authority vested in me, I can offer you gentlemen probation if you cooperate," Cop told the gang.

"What kind of 'cooperation' do you want?" a biker mumbled.

"I have an arrest warrant for El Roacho Rio," said Cop. "I have to take him in, he broke the law. You men help me find him, I'll speak to the judge on your behalf."

A couple of the more lucid bikers figured Cop was crazy, but very dangerous. "So we help you find some spic and then we go our way, right?" asked a biker.

"Correct," said Cop. "El Roacho was last seen at a bar called The Last Chance. We will go there." The bikers, all nine of them, watched Cop straddle the dead man's bike. "Follow me, men," he ordered. Cop started the bike and took off.

One biker whispered to the others, "Play along with this pig until he lets his guard down, then we waste him." The others nodded their approval.

LEO AND KNUCKLES WERE enjoying a liquid breakfast. They heard some strange sounds in the distance. "What the hell could that be?" muttered Leo.

"Sounds like a bunch of chainsaws backfiring."

Leo looked out the window and saw the approaching bikes. "Knuckles," he said, "look at this, a bunch of bikers."

"This ain't good," replied Knuckles "Let's shut the place down."

THE BIKERS AND COP stopped a respectful distance from the bar. "You in there!" Cop bellowed. "I have a warrant for El Roacho Rio, send him out now."

"No can do, officer!" shouted Leo. "Number one, he's dead. Number two, he ain't here."

"That makes no sense," Cop yelled back. "Where is he?"

"His head's in a bag and a guy called Blindman has it," shouted Leo. "He left here two days ago, so you're two days late and two dollars short," he laughed.

"You think that's humorous?" shouted Cop. "You're both under arrest."

"For what, you dopey bastard?" shouted Knuckles. "In case you didn't notice, the world sorta ended."

"The law is the law," Cop shouted. "You broke it, aiding and abetting a fugitive, and serving alcohol on Sunday. Now lay down your weapons and come out with your hands up."

"This motherfucker is nuts," said Knuckles.

"I'm counting to three!" Cop yelled. "If you don't surrender by the count of three, we will open fire."

"He's serious," Leo said to Knuckles. "We can't hold out against all that hardware."

Cop counted off, "One, two, three! Men, open fire!" A barrage of gunfire erupted. Bullets cut though the walls of The Last Chance. Leo and Knuckles hit the floor.

"We're screwed!" Knuckles announced.

Leo thought a minute. "Didn't Owl Face say there was another way out of here, an escape tunnel or something?"

"If there is, we better find it quick," said Knuckles.

With bullets whistling overhead, the two men searched the floor. Leo crawled under the bar and saw a section of the floor that didn't look right.

Leo took out a folding knife and pried up a board. He smelled musty earth.

"Knuckles," he said, "I found it. Grab some guns and liquor and let's get the hell outta here."

The two men crawled into the tunnel. As they made their way down the long passage, they could see light shining through a wooden partition. They also heard the sound of a motor idling roughly. "Shitfire," said Leo. "They're out there."

"Might be just one of them," said Knuckles. "Maybe we can take him and get his bike."

"Good idea," replied Leo. He slowly pushed the wood out of the way. The backfiring engine covered any noise they made. The biker had his back to the hole. Knuckles crept up on him and clocked him with a vicious right hand. He grabbed the bike and told Leo to get on behind him. The two took off in a blast of sand and smoke.

Cop and the gang heard the bike blast off. The shaken biker was getting slowly to his feet. "Bastards snuck up on me," he said. "Stole my iron, too."

Cop looked at him in total disdain, then shot him in the head. Bits of skull and grey matter splattered on the sand. "You have the right to remain silent," Cop said. "Follow those two, men!" Cop shouted. "They will lead us to the fugitives and we will apprehend them."

The bikers took off in pursuit. To a man, Cop scared the shit out of them.

Leo and Knuckles stopped to fill the tank with 151 white overproof. "We gotta catch up with Blindman," panted Leo. "That Cop ain't gonna let up on us."

"You're damn skippy," agreed Knuckles. "If this piece of shit will keep running, maybe we can catch up to them."

Blindman heard something strange coming from their back trail. "Who the hell is using a chainsaw?" he muttered. A couple of shotgun blasts brought him running.

Someone was yelling "Don't shoot, don't shoot!"

Squinting, Blindman checked out the scene before him. The women had two men on a motorcycle surrounded. The men had their hands in the air. Blindman recognized the two barflies. "Business was that bad, boys?" he asked.

"The law shut us down," Leo snarled. "Do you know that fat bastard who was a cop?" he asked.

"I heard of the guy," said Blindman. "What happened?"

"The prick tried to kill us, that's what happened. Since you left, we had some ninja looking guys, now this cop. He was going to arrest us for having liquor on Sunday. He got some bikers with him and they shot The Last

Chance to pieces. He wants that head, and you," summed up Leo. "We got out and figured we'd warn you."

"How many men has he got?" asked Blindman.

"Maybe a dozen," answered Leo. "It's hard to count when someone's shootin atcha."

"How far behind you are they?" asked Blindman.

"I'd say about an hour," said Leo.

Nydia said, "It's going to be dark in less than that, maybe we can ambush them."

"Full moonrise tonight," Knuckles said. "If we stay out here we are going to be silhouetted, easy targets."

"You talk like you know somethin about tactics," said Blindman.

"I was in Iraq, Special Forces," replied Knuckles. "I'd say you should hunt a hole and stay in it until daybreak."

"Ok, now I got a question. Youse guys staying or going?" asked Blindman.

Leo looked at his partner, who nodded. "We'll stick," he said. "That pig will kill us just for the hell of it. Any chance we can get a little piece of that reward?"

"Well," started Blindman, "that whole reward thing is up for speculation at this point. Nydia and me think it might be bullshit, but we ain't gonna know until we play out the hand. Yeah, you guys help us, you're in. But we're going to have to fight for it."

"That's jake wit' us," said Leo. "You got two more guns."

"Groovy," said Blindman. "Now, how are these rice burners running? I know all the gas blew up with them solar flares."

"They are using the booze for fuel," Knuckles replied. "That's why you heard us coming. These things just spit, sputter and stall."

"Waste of perfectly good liquor if you ask me," said Blindman. "Knuckles, I got me an idea, do you think you can get everyone undercover for the night?"

"I think so, what do you think you're gonna do?" asked Knuckles.

"Try and scare the mortal piss outta them," replied Blindman. "Before the moon rises, I'm going to see if they decide to make camp or keep pushing on. If they push on, they get past us, then we are behind them and they won't know it. If they make camp, Dog here is going to make sure they have a night to remember."

"You sure about this?" asked Nydia, concern in her voice.

"Yup," said Blindman, "might even be fun." That comment drew curious stares from everyone.

"C'mon Dog," said Blindman with a chuckle. "We got some huntin to do."

Dog loped off with Blindman following. "You kids be good," he said. "We'll be back in time for the Continental breakfast."

"I honestly don't know what to make of that guy," Leo said.

"Yeah," replied Knuckles, "but after seeing him in action back at The Last Chance, I never want to get on his bad side."

It was near dark when Blindman heard the sputtering bikes. They stopped. Someone was shouting orders to make camp. "Good," Blindman said to Dog. "Let them get nice and comfy then we will piss on their parade."

A few hours went past and the camp was dead quiet. Blindman took out some jerky and let Dog get a whiff of it. Dog went for it, but Blindman pulled back. "You gotta earn it, make some noise." Dog looked puzzled, then whimpered. "No, Dog, talk to me," Blindman said, pulling the jerky away. Dog growled. "Don't give me shit, you fuckin mutt," he said. "You want this or not?" Dog stood up and let out a wailing, mournful howl. "Good boy," said Blindman, giving Dog the jerky.

The camp erupted in a flurry of gun fire. Someone screamed, obviously hit. "That's the ticket, boys," muttered Blindman. "Keep burnin up that ammo."

Blindman heard a stern voice yelling for the shooting to stop. *So that's the cop,* he thought. *I will own that pig bastard or die trying.* Blindman and Dog headed back to the others.

Dawn was breaking as Blindman and Dog found them. "It was swell," he announced. "I had the idjits shootin each other."

"We heard him howling," said Leo. "Did you train him to do that?"

"I never trained him at all," said Blindman. "He was locked up. I let him out and now I can't get rid of him," he chuckled. "I made him sing for his supper, shame those bikers didn't appreciate the tune."

"Think they are still coming?" asked Nydia.

"Oh, yeah, I heard that pig bastard trying to get them to stop shooting each other," said Blindman. "They wasted a lot of ammo and that's in our favor, plus with those shitty bikes a-spittin and a-stallin, we'll hear them way before we see them."

"How many are we facing?" asked Leo.

"I counted eight guys," said Blindman. "Plus the oinker. I'd expect them any time now."

Like it was on cue, they heard the sputtering of a badly tuned engine. One of the bikers, a skinny guy with sandy hair and a beard, had a white flag.

"Let me find out what bullshit this is," said Blindman. He walked toward the biker, carrying his sawed-off. "Close enough, Bro, something on your mind?"

"Officer Warren says you are all fugitives and are under arrest. He sent me to get his stolen property." The biker threw several pairs of handcuffs in front of Blindman. "Better put these bracelets on your people and give up," the biker said.

Blindman listened to the speech with an amused look on his face. Looking the biker over, Blindman thought, *This moron isn't even packin.*

"Youse guys are big bad outlaws, but you're kissing a cop's fat ass?" Blindman announced sarcastically. "Sons of Satan my ass, more like sons of bitches. Any respectable club would rip off those colors and wipe their asses with them," Blindman baited him. "You've kissed so much pig ass that your breath smells like bacon," Blindman snarled.

Then, in a complete insult, Blindman turned his back to the biker.

14

THERE WAS A LOUD POP and Blindman felt something bite into his shoulder. He turned to see the biker trying to unjam the .25 automatic that he had just shot Blindman with.

"You shot me with that piece of junk, a fuckin Saturday night special? Well, that just ain't gonna do it, sonny," said Blindman.

The biker was frantically trying to get the gun to work. Blindman raised the shotgun and said, "Adios, asshole." Then blew him off the bike with one barrel of the sawed-off.

Shots came from various places around the group. "That guy was a diversion," shouted Knuckles. "They're all around us."

"Well, let's not make it easy for them!" yelled Blindman. A biker roared toward Blindman, Nydia, and Knuckles. He had something sparking in his hand, a stick of dynamite.

Knuckles stood up, drawing a bead on the biker, but a bullet clipped his hip and he went down. As the biker passed a sand dune, one of the Chinese girls launched herself over the dune and onto the biker. The impact threw her clear, but the rider and the bike landed on the dynamite and went to hell in a ball of fire. Dog raced by and dragged the dazed girl behind a dune.

Nydia got to Blindman. "How bad?" she asked.

"Bee sting," he replied. "You got to cut it out before my arm cramps up." He peeled off his shirt and turned his back to her. "Do it quick," he said.

Cringing, she stuck the point of her knife into the wound until it hit metal. Sweat pouring out of him, Blindman said, "You got it, now pop it out." She pushed up on the knife and the piece of lead came out. "Pour some whiskey on it and yer done," said Blindman.

Knuckles was pinned down by two bikers. One of the Chinese Shotgun Girls was trying to stanch the bleeding hip wound and firing shots at the bikers. Leo and two of the other girls were swapping bullets with three other bikers.

Lee and the other girls were holding Cop and the other biker at bay. Cop gave the biker his Uzi and the guy charged at Lee's position. Screaming what he was going to do to those Chink bitches, he closed in.

Dog came out of nowhere with his huge jaws open. He slammed into the rider and clamped his jaws around his head. Dog's momentum caused the big cur to flip with the guy's head in his mouth. His neck broke with a dry snap. Dog tore out his throat and drank.

Knuckles got in a lucky shot that burned though the sand and hit a biker in his left eye, blowing his brains out. The other biker made the mistake of standing up and caught a shotgun blast in his barrel chest. The girl with the shotgun gave Knuckles a grin.

Blindman and Nydia crept up on the group that had Leo pinned down. "Time to end this crap," Blindman said. The two were directly behind the three thugs.

"Don't fuckin move a muscle," Blindman yelled. The three froze. "Ever wonder how fast you are?" Blindman asked Nydia.

"No, why?" she replied.

"Because those three fools are gonna pull on us," said Blindman. The three thugs stood up, their hands hovering over the guns shoved in their belts. Blindman dropped the shotgun and stood there glaring at the three. "It's good day to die," he told them, then pulled Blackjack's .45.

The three went for their guns, but were too slow. Nydia's knife seemed to just sprout out of a guy's throat. Blindman's borrowed .45 spit death. First shot took one biker in the forehead as a crimson mist appeared around his head. The last biker got off a shot that burned a furrow down Blindman's side. Blindman left pieces of the biker's heart on the sand.

"Let's get back to the others," Blindman said to Nydia. Slowly the group came together. Two of the girls had bullet burns and one was still loopy from the explosion. Knuckles had chunk of meat shot off his hip, but was up and walking. Leo was unhurt, as were Lee and the other girls. The girls tended to the others' wounds.

"We didn't get the cop," Blindman groused. "I really wanted a piece of him."

The sputtering of an engine drew everyone's attention. Cop was riding toward them on one of the bikes. "I can't believe the balls on this bastard," Leo said.

"Yeah," agreed Blindman. "There is a Santy Claws."

Cop stopped the bike and killed the engine. He dismounted like he was going to write a parking ticket. "You are all under arrest," Cop announced.

Blindman had a bemused look on his face. Dog growled. "Where is that animal's license?" Cop asked. "That mutt should be put down."

Cop started to raise his gun when Blindman said, "You're right, officer, we broke the law. I'm soooo sorry. Here, take my gun and put the cuffs on me."

The group looked on, astonished, as Blindman pulled out the .45 and walked toward Cop. "Here," Blindman said. "Take it, I give up."

Cop smiled and said, "I'm sure the courts will be lenient when I tell them…"

He never finished. Blindman shot his right kneecap off. Cop screamed and fell forward. Blindman punted him in the face with a stiff kick. He was on his hands and knees, spitting out broken teeth when Blindman kicked him in the ribs, breaking three of them. He turned to the group with a look of rage on his face. "Stay the fuck back!" he growled at them.

"Don't do anything," Nydia advised them. "I've seen him like this before. This is going be bad."

Blindman let Cop crawl a bit then started kicking him all over the desert floor.

"You'll pay for this!" Cop screamed. "You're assaulting an officer of the law!"

"There is no law, you worthless, raping, murdering bastard," Blindman yelled.

Blindman nailed him with flurry of hard kicks. Then he grabbed Cop's face and glared into it. "Do you remember a little shack by what used to be a river? Two 'hoors were using it, remember, you fat turd? They were just trying to survive, trading pussy for water, then you came along. Then I found what you left of them, you twisted piece if shit. They was friends of mine."

Blindman stuck the sawed-off under Cop's chin. Suddenly the air stunk. "Done shit yourself, 'eh officer?"

"Those women were breaking the law," Cop whined.

"So that gave you the right to rape, torture and kill them, all in the name of some perverse law that no longer exists?" snarled Blindman. "Well, now you have the right to remain silent…forever."

He pulled the trigger and Cop's head exploded. Blindman wiped the gore from his face.

Leo turned to Nydia and said, "Remind me again never to piss him off."

"I swear to Christ I think that gave me a woody," grinned Blindman.

"You really enjoyed that, didn't you?" Nydia asked.

"Kiddo, I been finding his 'arrests' all over this shithole," answered Blindman. "He was a psycho that was tolerated on the force, then you wonder why I hate cops. Those two 'hoors was bad enough. I found what was left of little girls that he took into 'custody'. I found whole families, just trying to survive, that he slaughtered. I'm glad I punched his ticket," summed up Blindman. "Truth be told, if youse wasn't here, I'd have made an entertaining day of killing his ass real slow."

"Can I ask you something?" asked Nydia.

"Sure, fire away." said Blindman.

"I know you're real near sighted and have them cataracts, but when we faced down those three, you just used Blackjack's .45 instead of the sawed-off. You didn't miss a shot."

"Sometimes I can see halfway decent, other times I just see shapes," answered Blindman. "I hit what I aim at, I ain't shittin anyone. With that sun the way it is, I'll be legit blind sooner than later. When that day comes, I'll take myself out. I won't be hobbling around here by myself trying to smell out liquor," he summed up.

"Maybe it won't come to that," said Nydia.

"Yeah," chuckled Blindman, "like the next drunk we find might be an eye guy. We just sober him up and have him fix my peepers. Hope springs eternal, right?"

15

SLUGGO HAD JUST FINISHED questioning a couple of gunnies who had drifted in. The news wasn't good and The Master was not going to be thrilled about the latest developments.

"Shoulda just let things be," muttered Sluggo. He went into The Master's quarters and found him on his third bottle, it was only 12pm. "Boss," said Sluggo, "we got us some problems."

"What now?" The Master spat at him. "When ya gonna give me some good news instead of this we got trouble shit?"

Sluggo controlled his temper. "Word is that the fat cop recruited some bikers. They went to that bar, The Last Chance. Dem barflies dat was there told them dat Blindman had El Roacho's head. The cop tried to arrest dem. They got away and joined up wit' da Blindman and dem women he got wit' him."

"Motherfucker," cursed The Master, "This isn't my fuckin plan. Those idiots are supposed to kill each other, not make friends. What happened to Cop and the bikers?"

Sluggo paused before he spoke, "All dead, Boss. Blindman's crew wiped them all out."

The Master jumped out of his chair screaming obscenities. "God damn motherfucking sons of bitches, this ain't happening. Someone has to stop them!"

Sluggo noticed that The Master was not only coming unglued, there was tangible fear in his voice now. "Calm down, Boss," said the massive bodyguard. "Dey ain't here yet. Let me t'ink on it and I'll make plans."

"You damn well better make good ones!" shouted The Master. "I'll not lose everything because you fucked up."

Sluggo held back a curse. *Miserable white boy fuck*, he thought. *Maybe your number is up. Maybe I should make sure of dat.* Sluggo knew there was a real good chance that he would have to deal with Blindman's crew. There were about two dozen gunnies loyal to The Master. *Hell*, thought Sluggo, *dey be loyal to whoever has the liquor. And dat someone will be me.* Sluggo decided to have a little 'meeting' with the boys.

RUBY HAD BEEN ONE BUSY bitch. She had already figured she needed some help to find El Roacho Rio, so she went out recruiting. She came across three old, hard-bitten hookers and a pimp, Jiminez. Jiminez would lure drunken gunnies in for a little fun with the women. The 'tricks' were murdered and robbed of anything useful, then dumped down an old mine shaft. The three skanks were Rose, Lisa, and Marie. Ruby walked up to a battered house trailer and yelled, "Anyone in there better get the hell out here!"

The skinny Jiminez came out grinning. "I don't think we can use another 'hoe," he snickered.

Ruby decked him with a stiff right hand. "Do I look like a whore, you spic bastard?" she yelled in his face. "What's your name?" she asked.

"Jimenez," he replied.

"Well, *Mayonnaise*," Ruby mocked, "I got a business proposition for you and your girls."

"An' what might that be?" asked the heavily made-up blonde, whose name was Rose.

Ruby looked at the trailer. Rose was standing in the doorway with a pump action shotgun with a pistol grip. "First thing," Rose said, "let Jiminez get up." The shaken man staggered to his feet.

Ruby looked at the three women. They looked as hard as she was. Rose looked at Ruby. "Now talk," she said. "And it better be something we want to hear."

Ballsey cunt, Ruby thought. She also thought she had better choose her words carefully. Predators, all of them. She discounted Jiminez, but the women had that look in their eyes that Ruby knew all too well. If they didn't buy her deal she would be history.

"Ok," said Ruby. "The Drunken Master has a bounty on El Roacho Rio, 100 cases of water."

"We knowed all about that," said Lisa, the bottle dyed, buck toothed redhead. "No one knows where El Roacho is hiding."

"That's the ticket," snarled Ruby. "He ain't hiding. His head is in a sack and that sack is being delivered to The Master by that blind guy. I need you four to take it away from him. Shouldn't be hard, it's only him and some chink girls."

"What's in it for us?" asked Jimenez.

"Equal shares, *Mayonnaise*, equal shares," said Ruby. "We grab the head, deliver it, and cut the cake. I'll even spice up the deal. We kill the blind guy, you take the chink girls and sell 'em. Sound good?"

The four mulled it over. It sounded too good. But greed overcame common sense. The had a little conference out of Ruby's hearing.

"I don't trust her fat ass at all," Jiminez stated.

"None of us do," said Rose, "but there's four of us. Once we get the head, adios fatso." Turning her head, she yelled to Ruby, "We're in!"

FIVE PREDATORS IN SEARCH of prey. Coming into view of The Last Chance, Ruby, sweating like a hog, said, "We can see if anyone there knows anything." Approaching the building, they saw it was pocked with bullet holes.

"Big fight here, it looks like," commented Jiminez. "Funny thing, no bodies."

"Yeah," said Ruby, her good eye scanning the area. "Something went down, this place is shot up to shit, ain't a bottle left in this joint."

They traveled a few miles more, then a horrible stench assailed them. "Damn," muttered Lisa. "Somethin sure do stink." They entered the little town and saw a pile of body parts rotting in the sun. Then they found what was left of Wong Duck.

Jiminez muttered to Rose, "I'm not liking this at all."

"If these guys have what we are looking for, it ain't like they are gonna give it up easy," answered Rose.

"Hey Ruby," yelled Rose. "A blind old man and a couple of girls did this?"

"They got lucky," Ruby shouted. "There's five of us."

"Yeah," Rose replied, "There was a bunch of these guys and they're dead meat. I think you know more about this bunch than you're telling, fatso."

Ruby snarled, "What did you call me, you cunt?"

"Clean the wax outta your ears, bitch," answered Rose.

Ruby screamed and launched all of her 300 pounds at Rose. Rose wasn't a small girl and met Ruby's charge. The two exchanged punches and rolled on the ground, gouging and biting. Ruby found a rock and slammed it into Rose's head. Rose was out cold.

"You fuckin whore!" screamed Ruby. "Now I own your ass, I own all of your asses! You're gonna get me that reward or die tryin, get it?"

BLINDMAN AND HIS CREW were about ten miles from that little town. They stopped and made camp for the night. The Chinese girls cooked up some food. Blindman took out a box of 12-gauge shells and was custom loading them. Nydia watched him with interest. "Sometimes double-aught buck just isn't enough," Blindman remarked as he inserted a sparkplug into a shell.

"Now, these things really make a statement." He put a roll of dimes in another shell. "At least I'll get my money's worth out of this one," he chuckled. Other shells he filled with rusty nails, bits of broken safety glass, pieces of barbed wire and other nasty stuff.

He fished a box of razor blades out of his pack. "Never tried this," he said, looking at the blades. They were the old doubled edged kind, used in safety razors. Blindman snapped them in half and stuffed the pieces into a shell. "Be interesting to see what this one does," he mused.

Nydia just had an amazed look on her face. "Nice to know you have some kind of hobby," she said sarcastically.

THE GROUP WAS STUNNED after seeing the huge woman demolish Rose. Lisa helped Rose to her feet. "Let's go," ordered Ruby. The group trekked on for a few more miles.

Then they found the remains of the motorcycle gang. "Jesus Christ," muttered Jiminez, crossing himself. "These are demons from hell."

Marie, the smaller of the three women, found what was left of Cop. "You better come over here and see what I found," she shouted. The four walked over and looked at the mutilated body of Cop.

"That guy was one bad motherfucker," Jiminez said. He turned to Ruby. "Cop was a stone-cold killer, and these bikers weren't no pussies. This is bullshit." Ruby decked him.

Frothing at the mouth, Ruby screamed, "No one is leaving, got it? You in this until I say different."

A low moaning interrupted any further conversation. "One of these bikers is still alive!" yelled Lisa. The group gathered around the fallen biker. He looked nearly dead. He had been shot about six times.

"Give him some water," Ruby ordered.

Lisa gave the biker some water. He gagged, spitting it up. Ruby got in his face. "What happened here?" she asked.

"The Blindman, that's what happened," the biker gasped. "That fuckin Cop thought he had all the answers, fuckin asshole got us all killed."

"One old man and a couple of girls did this?" Ruby exclaimed.

"Weren't that way at all," the biker said. "Cop thought the same thing. We chased them guys from The Last Chance, they hooked up with The Blindman and he had at least seven broads with him."

Rose glared at Ruby through swollen eyes. "This just gets better and better," she said, exasperated.

The biker coughed. "They fight like devils from hell, you ain't got a prayer."

"Neither do you, for that bad news!" Ruby roared. She grabbed him by the hair, pulled out a box cutter and slit his throat. "Let's go," she ordered.

"Wait a fuckin minute," Rose growled. "I'm not in a big hurry to die. This is a stacked deck, five against ten, ten that just killed a shitload of badass people."

"We can do this, they just been lucky," spit back Ruby.

"I'm with Rose," Jiminez said. "This is bullshit."

"Shut your greasy pie hole!" Ruby screamed, foaming at the mouth. "I know how to do this."

"Fuck you," Lisa said. "If you did, you wouldn't need us."

"You're dead, bitch," Ruby snarled, stalking toward her. A cocking noise stopped her. Rose, Marie, and Jiminez had their guns out and they were pointed at Ruby.

"Cool your jets, big girl, or we'll cool 'em for you." Ruby had no choice but to back down.

Jiminez said, "Now I got a plan, one that will work."

The four women listened. Even Ruby cracked a small smile.

16

SLUGGO HAD MADE THE rounds of The Master's compound. The Master had about two dozen gunnies lounging around. These guys may have been the dregs of humanity, but they weren't completely stupid. They had all the booze they wanted, water and food too. But they knew the boss had been coming unglued since he lost his gun hand. Sluggo played up that fact and let them know that if things didn't calm down, it might be time for a regime change. Most agreed with him; those that didn't were not so nicely asked to stay out of the way if something went down. Sluggo was pleased, looked like things were going the way he wanted. The Master was soused to the point of being incoherent. *Might not have to do anything,* thought Sluggo. *The booze might do it for me.*

BLINDMAN AND COMPANY made camp for the night. "Put a couple of the girls out on sentry, we'll switch off every few hours," he ordered. Two of the Shotgun Girls took position outside of the camp.

"I figure we are about a day from the drunken douchebag's hideout," Blindman informed them. "We're gonna have to have a plan. I know he's not just sittin there by his self."

"How many do you think are with him?" Leo asked.

"Maybe a couple dozen," answered Blindman. "If the reward's on the up and up, no worries, but I don't think it's legit. We go in ready and the minute that limp dick cocksucker tries to pull any shit, we blast him and his boys to hell."

"So we go in expectin a problem?" asked Knuckles.

"Yeah," said Blindman. "Better to be prepared than get out asses shot off."

A horrific scream ended any further conversation.

"What the hell?" exclaimed Nydia. A shotgun blast answered.

"Let's go!" yelled Blindman.

They didn't have to go far, one of the Shotgun Girls staggered into sight. Bleeding from a gash on her head, she chattered in Cantonese to Lee. "Some women and a man grabbed Ling," Lee translated. "They tried to take her, but she shot someone and then the man shot her."

Another horrible scream broke the night silence. "We gotta get her," Blindman said. "Let's go."

"No," said Knuckles. "It's a trap."

"How do you figure that?" said Blindman.

"The Taliban used to do the same thing," explained Knuckles. "They grab one of our men, gut him, and leave him screaming. When we tried to get him, they'd pick us off. We go out there, we are going to lose. Believe me, that's what they want."

More screams split the night.

JIMINEZ HAD BEATEN the girl and raped her twice. The three women had cut and burned her. Ruby was carving something out of branch she found. Marie was out of it, riddled by buckshot.

"They ain't comin, you stupid pimp," snarled Ruby. "Great plan, hope you enjoyed the takeout pussy because you ain't getting any more of it. Rose," Ruby ordered, "you and Lisa hold her down, I'm gonna have me some fun now."

Ruby had carved the branch into a crude dildo. She rammed the thing between the girl's legs. The girl howled mournfully. Rudy rammed it in and out until flesh ripped and blood gushed. Rose had a slack look on her face and drool dripped from the corner of her mouth.

"Getting turned on, aintcha?" Ruby snickered. "I knew you were as twisted as I am. What say we take a walk and enjoy each other?" Rose nodded. Ruby jammed the dildo in and left it. Ruby and Rose walked away as the girl continued screaming in agony.

NEEDLESS TO SAY, NO one slept in Blindman's group. He had been pacing all night. Nydia had a look of complete rage on her face. Dog was chomping at the bit to take off and hunt. The others were ready to go search for the girl.

"Let's not go anywhere yet," Blindman said. "They did that crap last night for us to come to them, now they can come to us."

The wait wasn't very long. "Hey you assholes! We got something of yours, wanna trade?" yelled Ruby.

Everyone looked at what was standing on a dune. Lisa and Ruby held the girl up. Her crotch was nothing but raw flesh; cuts and burns crisscrossed her body. She was barely alive.

"Give me that fuckin .45," Nydia snarled at Blindman. He didn't say a word, just took it out of his belt and handed it to her. Nydia sighted down the barrel and squeezed the trigger. The heavy slug crashed into her head, ending her torment. "This ain't gonna stand," Nydia growled. "Give me El Roacho."

Maybe it was the look in Nydia's eyes or maybe Blindman just understood the need for vengeance; he handed her the sack. "Hey man-bitch!" Nydia yelled. "You want this, you fat pig? Want it bad enough to fight me for it, mano a mano, or just bitch to bitch?"

Nydia walked away from the others and dropped the sack on the ground. She heard something behind her.

Lee walked up, her face impassive. "Me too," she said.

Nydia yelled, "Ok, Porky, bring your carpet munching buddy with you."

Ruby turned to Rose and said, "C'mon lover, we got us double date." The two stalked toward Nydia and Lee. "That was some sweet chink food last night, I do believe I'll be tasting..." Ruby's words were cut off as Nydia's fist crashed into her mouth, knocking her front teeth down her throat.

Ruby gagged and choked on her teeth. Nydia waded in, her fists beating a tattoo on Ruby's face. Ruby clipped Nydia's jaw with a stiff right hand; she shook it off and buried her fist into Ruby's ample gut. Her sour breath filled the air. Ruby kicked Nydia's knee out from under her. "Gotcha!" Ruby shouted. Nydia hit her chin with a hard uppercut on the way down. Ruby spit blood as she bit part of her tongue off.

Lee was just letting Rose exhaust herself. She sidestepped every punch Rose threw.

Nydia knew that going toe to toe would be a mistake with the larger woman. Slamming another punch to Ruby's gut was like hitting a slab of meat. Nydia caught a vicious backhand and tasted blood. Nydia's leg shot out and caught Ruby's knee, buckling it. Ruby hit the ground and Nydia was on her, beating her down every time she tried to get up. Nydia punted Ruby in the face, breaking her nose. Then everything went to shit.

Jiminez, Lisa, and Marie had been standing off to the side watching. Dog decided he needed a better look. Dog sat up and Jiminez shot him in the head. Dog flipped over, blood gushing. Blindman fired the sawed-off at Jiminez, it was the shell full of razors. Jiminez was turned into a screaming, bloody skeleton.

Marie got up with a shotgun, but her guts fell out on the dirt as her previous wounds ripped open. Lisa pulled out a snub nose .38 and aimed it at Nydia's back. Leo shot her in the nose, blowing her cheekbones out the back of her head.

Jiminez was flopping on the ground, still screaming. Blindman kicked him in the head as he ran to Dog.

Lee had let Rose wear herself down. Lee's educated feet nailed Rose three times on her left side, breaking ribs and bringing her to her knees. Lee looked at her, impassively. "You kill friend," Lee hissed. "Now you die." Lee kicked her right side in. Ribs broke and splintered, puncturing Rose's lungs. Rose choked as she tried to breathe through blood. It poured out of her mouth; her eyes glazed over and she hit the dirt. Lee spat on her corpse, then turned to watch Nydia.

Ruby was battered, bloody, and now desperate. The smaller woman was beating her to death. Ruby pulled out a straight razor and slashed at Nydia, cutting her left forearm. "Now you're playing my game, bitch!" Nydia roared, pulling out her 14-inch bowie knife.

"No matter what happens, stay out of it!" Nydia yelled to the group. The two circled each other warily, thrusting and jabbing. Nydia drew blood with every move, a nick here, a cut there. Ruby dripped blood from a dozen cuts, but none of them fatal. Ruby was also out of gas and knew it. She was sucking air and knew it was only a matter of time before Nydia wore her completely down.

Ruby went down on one knee; she grabbed a handful of grit and tossed it into Nydia's face. Nydia had anticipated something like this and ducked. She swung her blade up as Ruby rushed by and connected. A bloody 44D tit hit the ground.

Ruby grabbed her bleeding chest. "You fuckin cunt, you cut my tit off!" Ruby screamed. Nydia, now pissed beyond belief, picked up the bloody tit and started beating Ruby over the head with it. Each hit produced a sickeningly wet splat.

Ruby swung a wild punch that connected with the side of Nydia's head. She went down with Ruby on top of her.

Ruby's fingers found Nydia's throat and squeezed. Nydia gasped and heaved, but she couldn't toss the 300-pound woman off her. Blood roared through her head. Her fingers clawed the dirt and found something. She grabbed the object and drove it into Ruby's good eye. It was an aluminum gutter nail. Ruby screamed and rolled off Nydia. Blood squirted from her ruined eye. She staggered off, blood dripping from everywhere.

Gagging, Nydia got to her feet. Ruby was screaming for her now-dead companions for help. Nydia followed Ruby, who was now by a rocky outcropping, one that had about a 500-foot drop.

Ruby clutched her ruined face and bent down and Nydia booted her in the ass with a stiff kick. Screaming, Ruby plummeted down the slope, parts of her body tearing off as she bounced off the sharp rocks. She didn't stop screaming until she hit bottom. Nydia viewed her body and smiled a bit.

Nydia walked back to the group. She hurt, but walked proud. Lee hugged her. "Where's Blindman?" she asked.

"He's with Dog, over there," answered Knuckles.

Blindman had Dog's head in his lap. The big cur wasn't dead. "Bastard shot him in the head," Blindman told her. "Looks worse than it is; I thought I lost him. Used my best bourbon to clean this gash. He'll be ok in a day or so. Oh," he added, "just so ya know, I wasn't gonna stop your fight. But if that fat bitch won, I was gonna gun her on general principles."

"Thank you for that," replied Nydia. "She killed one of ours and that called for a woman to even it up. You understand that, don't ya?"

"Yeah," answered Blindman, "I do. Sisterhood and all that."

"Hey," yelled Leo. "This guy is still breathing." Leo stood over the mutilated Jimenez.

"Leave him," said Blindman. "Anyone who would shoot a poor, defenseless animal should suffer."

Dog actually looked up like he was taking umbrage to the 'defenseless animal' comment.

Jiminez gasped, then with a loud fart, died.

"Let's bury our friend," Nydia said.

"What about the rest of them?" Leo asked.

"Fuck 'em," she replied. "They opened this dance, but couldn't rock and roll."

"I got to ruminate on something," Blindman said. "I smell a trap. I need to get some idea of Drunkie's set up. The men, the buildings, you know. The more we know, the better we can deal with it."

Knuckles interjected, "Why don't all of you rest up for a bit? I'll go scout the place and see what we might be up against."

"You're up for that?" asked Blindman.

"Ain't like I haven't done this before. In Iraq, I'd sneak up on the rag heads and call in air strikes on them."

"Ok," agreed Blindman. "Just be careful, ok Sarge?"

Knuckles laughed, "Figured me out, eh, you old bastard?"

"Weren't too hard to figure, the way you carry yourself and all," chuckled Blindman. "Let's not lose any more of us."

Knuckles saluted. "Be back shortly, better let me take the binoculars with me."

"Take 'em, scope 'em out, then get back here and we'll make plans," said Blindman.

17

SLUGGO, ON THE ORDERS of The Master, sent one of his guys out to check what was coming. The guy, Eddie, had just returned. He was shaking badly from the DTs as he was told to stay sober for this job, or else.

"Well, what did you find, Eddie?"

"I need a drink, badly," Eddie said. Sluggo handed him a pint of rum. Eddie killed it in one swallow. "I fuckin needed that," he gasped.

"Talk," Sluggo barked.

"Alright," said Eddie. "We got about a dozen bad motherfuckers heading this way. I watched them take out that nasty, fat bitch Ruby. And Jiminez, you know, that greasy pimp, and his girls. It was a massacre."

Sluggo shook his massive dreadlocked head. "I ain't be too worried about old men who kill chicks."

"These weren't just chicks," Eddie blurted out. "They was stone killers, real bad people. Not a bunch of chicks. Less than a day from here. Whoever they are, they ain't going to be easy to kill."

Sluggo grabbed Eddie by the face. "Don't tell dis to anyone," he hissed. "I'll go talk to de boss."

As Sluggo walked toward the lair of The Master, The Master stumbled out and fell on his face. *Great*, thought Sluggo, *he be tanked already.* Sluggo walked over and helped The Master up to unsteady legs.

"Boss," Sluggo said, "you gotta straighten up, we got bad troubles headed our way."

"What troubles," The Master mush mouthed. "I don't see no troubles."

Sluggo exploded. "Dats because you're fuggin drunk, you been drunk ever since your 'accident', you fuck."

"You can't talk to me like that!" The Master roared back.

"The hell I cain't, you're just ignoring that you started a bunch of shit and dat shit's done blown up in your face."

The Master tried to interject, but was shouted down. "Shut up, white boy! You got a dozen stone cold killers less than a day away, dey didn't kill each other like you planned they would!" Sluggo screamed in his face. "Now youse gotta make a choice: pay the bounty or take them out."

"I'm not paying it," The Master stated firmly. "All of this is mine and they can't have it."

"Dats your deal then, you're gonna double cross dese people?" asked Sluggo.

"Kill them all," The Master replied.

"Done," said Sluggo. "Then half of all dis is mine."

The Master fumed, but just nodded.

"I'm going to prepare a welcome," Sluggo said. "You can go back to your bottle." Sluggo walked away from the seething Master.

Knuckles witnessed the entire confrontation from afar. There were four buildings, one built into the side of a hill. *I'll bet that's where his stash of water is*, thought Knuckles. He saw The Master go into one of the buildings. *Good*, he thought. *We'll know where to find him.* Knuckles tried to count up the number of men going in and out of what he figured were bunkhouses. "I'm gonna figure about two dozen," he muttered. "This won't be easy."

Knuckles decided to get gone before he was spotted. He went back to the others. "They know we're coming," he told the group, "and your suspicions are right, they ain't giving anything up."

"You know this for a fact?" asked Blindman.

"Yeah, I can read body language pretty good," answered Knuckles. "One of them was watching that dust up we had with those scumfucks. I saw him go report to this big black dude. Then the big dude has a screaming match with who I think is The Master, only it looks like he's got some sort of power struggle goin on. Make no mistake about it, they'll be waitin on us."

Blindman digested what Knuckles told him. "This ain't good," he said. "We walk in there, it's open ground. The fucker planned his hideout good, we can't sneak up on him. Ok, being that this was originally me and Nydia's deal, now you people hooked up with us," summed up Blindman. "We may all get out tickets punched on this one. Anyone want out?" No one answered. "Determined bunch, ain't we?" laughed Blindman. "Alright, we have to come up with an edge, something that will give us the advantage."

He thought on it a bit. "I got me an idea. Round up all the ammunition we can't use."

The group went through their equipment and dropped odd caliber shells into a pile. "Let's check the bodies," suggested Leo. The group emptied the odd assortment of guns.

Leo picked up an AK-47 that was in good shape and had five full clips. "Keep that for yourself," said Blindman. Leo nodded and started cleaning the weapon. "Crack open all these shells and dump the powder in here," Blindman ordered. He tossed them an empty coffee can. Blindman fished though his pack. "I found these in that gun shop." He had a can of black powder and a roll of fuse.

"I figure I can make about four nifty bombs outta this stuff," said Blindman. "Now, who's got a good pitching arm, as we all know I'm a tad limited?"

"I do," answered Nydia. "I pitched softball in high school."

"I figured as much," Blindman chuckled. "You just want to be close to me."

"Someone's got to watch out for your old ass," Nydia responded. "You grow on a person, sorta like fungus." That comment got a huge laugh from Leo and Knuckles.

Blindman cringed. "Terrible thing, to pick on a man in his declining years."

Blindman man pulled out four cans of beets. He opened them, careful not to break off the lids, then dumped the contents out. "I wasn't going to eat that crap and I'll wager neither was anyone else," he said. Blindman mixed the powder from the odds and ends shells with the black powder. He put nails, spark plugs, tips of barbed wire, coins and anything else he could find in his bombs. He packed them tight, then with a candle, used the dripping wax to seal them closed. "These are gonna have real short fuses, I don't want them getting tossed back at us," he said. "Now let's go see what the Drunken Asshole has in store for us."

The group checked their weapons and headed toward The Master's compound. Knuckles had paired off with one of the Shotgun Girls. Leo was paired with Lee. Nydia and Blindman took the point, and the three girls took up the rear position. Cresting a sandy hill, they had a complete view of The Master's compound.

"Ain't much cover," Blindman remarked. "Nor much activity."

Knuckles pondered the situation. "Fuckers are just waiting for us. When I saw them, they were just hanging around drinking."

Blindman spoke up, "Us four go in, the others hold back," he suggested. "This way they might get over eager and show themselves."

"So we enter the valley of death and just hope we are meaner than the motherfuckers who live there?" asked Knuckles.

"Unless you can think of somethin else," said Blindman. "They chose this place well, no way can you just sneak up on them. Let's go," he finished.

Knuckles thought a second and said, "Why not?"

The four spread out in a row and started walking toward the compound. "Be ready for anything," Blindman whispered.

They weren't. Three spider pits opened and three AK-47's chattered.

"Down!" screamed Blindman. He got off a lucky shot that hit a shooter in the throat. Arterial blood arced in the air as he fell backwards.

Knuckles and the Shotgun Girl were down. Blindman crawled over. "How bad?" he asked.

Knuckles groaned. "I'm done, gut shot. She's dead."

The girl had taken a round through her left eye. A tear ran down Knuckles' face. "She deserved better than that," he grunted.

Blindman motioned to Nydia, "Time for a no-hitter," he said. "I'll light it, toss it when I tell you." Nydia nodded nervously.

As Blindman lit the fuse they yelled "Charge!!!"

The two shooters stood up for the kill. "Now!!" Blindman screamed. Nydia tossed the bomb right between the two shooters. The blast shredded them to pieces.

Blindman turned to Knuckles. "Get me up and moving," Knuckles said. "I'll be fucked if I'll just lay here and die."

Blindman stuffed a piece of shirt in the wound to stanch the flow of blood. "What do you want me to do, Sarge?" Blindman asked.

"Get me over to that building where they are holed up. Wait a second." Knuckles fished though his pocket and came up with a vial. "I saved this for an emergency," he said. It was coke. Knuckles snorted the whole vial. "Now I'm good to go."

Blindman handed Knuckles the pump shotgun with the pistol grip. "It holds eight shells," Blindman told him. "Take these two Glocks, sixteen rounds in each clip."

Knuckles shoved the two pistols behind his belt. "Get me over there, I'm fading fast."

Blindman and Nydia got him up and ran for the building, dodging shots. Leo and the others laid down covering fire. Knuckles was standing next to the door "Youse two get outta here, I'll handle this," he told them. "Hey old man, I hope you and the rest make it," gasped Knuckles.

Blindman threw him a salute "Rock and roll, Sarge."

Knuckles grinned, the coke taking hold. "Oh, I intend to do just that."

Blindman and Nydia went on the attack. Knuckles sucked in a deep breath, "Coke," he muttered. "It does a body good." He kicked in the door and five gunnies turned to face him. "It's a good day to die, fuckers!" he screamed at them. He pumped the shotgun and pulled the trigger. The five were blasted to hell before they could get off a shot.

A hammer blow in his back dropped Knuckles to his knees. He felt his mouth fill with blood. He drew the two Glocks out and turned around as five more shooters rushed into the building. Knuckles screamed, "Just one ain't gonna fuckin do it, boys!" The two guns bucked in his hands. He soaked up bullets but cut the five men down with 32 rounds of 9mm death. The guns fell from nerveless hands as Knuckles hit the floor.

Sluggo had done his homework. Shooters were strategically placed, but their element of surprise was gone. Blindman and Nydia were trading bullets with four shooters that were holed up in a trench. Leo and the rest were keeping a withering fire on The Master's headquarters and the other building. It was a stalemate where neither side had the upper hand.

A huge black guy, well over six feet tall, charged out of the second building. He was swinging a machete and screaming curses. Blindman shot him in the stomach with the .45. The guy staggered, but didn't fall. "He's doped up on something," Blindman yelled.

Nydia took the guy down in a flying tackle and drove her Bowie though his skull. "I just ODed him!" she yelled. Bullets kicked up sand in front of her and she ducked behind a pile of broken bricks.

"We gotta shave the odds down some!" yelled Blindman.

"How?" asked Nydia.

"I'm gonna make those guys in that trench stand up," answered Blindman. "When I do, toss one of those bombs behind them."

Blindman threw the sack of bombs toward the pile of bricks. Bullets whined like angry hornets as she scrambled to get the bag. "Got it!" she yelled. "Now what?"

"I'm gonna stand up and draw their fire, you toss a bomb behind them," he ordered."

"You're cuttin it real close," she answered.

"We're running out of options," Blindman responded. "Just make it count! Here I am, you limp dicked cocksuckers!!" he yelled.

The four gunnies stood up for the easy kill. Nydia tossed the bomb in a high arc. It never hit the ground. It exploded about five feet in the air over the four shooters. Shrapnel tore through their heads and necks. The trench filled with their blood.

"How cool was that?" Blindman yelled.

The Master was in a complete panic. "This ain't working," he said to Sluggo. "We lost half our boys."

"Pick up a shotgun and help, you pussy!" Sluggo bellowed.

One guy made the mistake of showing the top of his head. Leo put a bullet through it. Blood and grey matter splattered The Master's face. He fell to the floor, puking up raw liquor.

"You make me sick," muttered Sluggo. Leo kept putting bullets through the window. Sluggo ordered one of the shooters to sneak out a back window and get the group in a crossfire. The guy was halfway out the window when a shotgun blast took his face off. The Shotgun Girl grinned, then threw a couple more shots toward the window. The bloody corpse fell back inside.

"They got us surrounded!" The Master yelled. Sluggo resisted the urge to put a bullet though his head.

Sluggo was trying to figure out how many men he had. Not a shot had come from the other building, so everyone must be finished there, he thought. He had three guys with him and five in the field. "Eight left out of twenty-five," he muttered.

The Master was curled up in fetal position on the floor. Sluggo looked at him with contempt. "Great plan, Boss, great plan." Sluggo kicked him hard in the side, cracking a rib. The Master yelled in pain. Sluggo grabbed him by the face and pulled him up until they were eyeball to eyeball. "I'm the fuggin boss now!" he yelled in The Master's face.

He turned to the three gunnies. "Any of youse have a problem wit dat?"

"Not at all," one of the men answered. "Let's wipe out these clowns."

Nydia and Blindman were figuring out their next move. "There's a bunch in that other building and some more in The Master's place," Blindman summed up. "Knuckles said he counted about two dozen, and he had to take out everyone in that building or they'd be shootin at us."

"So what's the plan?" Nydia asked.

"I'd really like to blow up one of those buildings, but I'd have to get real close to do it," answered Blindman.

"Problem is," said Nydia, "you can't run fast enough."

"There ya go again, damn it, no respect for yer elders," grunted Blindman.

"What about this?" asked Nydia. "You toss a bomb, I use the smoke to sneak up on the other one."

"That uses up all the bombs," answered Blindman. "But it may just cut the odds way the hell down. Just a sec. Yo, Leo! Hold off shootin until I tell you otherwise."

"You got it!" Leo shouted back.

Blindman handed Nydia a bomb and a lighter. "It goes like this," he instructed Nydia. "When it goes off, you take off." Nydia nodded.

Blindman lit the fuse and tossed it. It blew up with a huge puff of smoke. Nydia sprinted toward the building.

Blindman watched her run. "Gal's got a great pair of legs," he muttered.

Nydia made it to the building without being seen. She hugged the wall as gunfire erupted from the windows. She looked at the bomb and thought, *Really short fuckin fuse.* She crawled, still hugging the wall.

She felt the air of a bullet passing her ear. One of the guys in the other building spotted her. "Shitfire!" she yelled.

Blindman fired a high brass round filled with nails. The shooter's head disintegrated.

She lit the fuse and quickly shoved the bomb through the window. There was a loud but muffled thump. One gunnie staggered out, minus a left arm, but his right hand held a chattering Uzi. Nydia shot him though the head.

Another guy came out holding his intestines in with one hand and thumbing a 9mm with the other. Lee nailed him with one shot. It was now eerily quiet. A pale of gun smoke hovered over the area like fog.

"Nobody move," ordered Blindman. "Let them come to us."

18

SLUGGO WAS AMAZED AT the carnage. The Master was so scared that he was almost comatose.

One of the two remaining gunnies asked, "Now what?"

Sluggo shook his massive dreadlocked head. "Now dis," he said. He walked to a window. "Yo, Leroy!" he bellowed. "You want to settle up now, jist me and you?"

Nydia looked at Blindman. "What the fuck is that? You know that guy, Leroy?"

"Do you think my mother named me Blindman?" he said. "Yeah, I know him, he was a big man in The Bloods, we had a little problem in the joint."

"What kind of problem?" asked Nydia.

"Oh, I had a little run-in with three of his posse in the showers."

"You caught a beat down from them?" she asked.

"No," he answered. "They tried. I killed all three with a shaved down toothbrush handle. Being that he ordered the hit, it sorta pissed him off."

"Scuse me for being a nosey bitch," said Nydia. "But why?"

"I had a cellmate," explained Blindman. "Young black dude in on a bullshit charge. That big nigger kept trying to recruit him into The Bloods. Guy just wanted to do his time and get out; that scumbag had his boys gang rape him in the shower. They broke something inside him and he died. I knocked that asshole's teeth out with a food tray in the chow line. I got thrown in solitary, but I grabbed this toothbrush. I had a month to sharpen it. Guess he has a little grudge against me still."

"C'mon , you chicken shit old bastard!" yelled Sluggo. "How do you want it, fists or guns?"

"Knuckle and skull, that's how I want it, you black bastard!" Blindman yelled back. "Your people stay out of it, so do mine, winner takes this place."

"Ok, racist, anything goes," replied Sluggo. He walked out in the open. Eddie and the other gunnie followed.

Nydia said, "The bastard's huge, how are you going to beat him?"

"With my fists, that's how. And don't sweat the other two pricks, they're covered."

Blindman stood up and started walking toward Sluggo. Sluggo whispered to Eddie "If, on the off chance I start losing, gun the fucker and the others."

"You got it, Boss," Eddie replied.

Blindman looked at Sluggo. "Still think you're a bad ass, dontcha?"

"Bad enough to kill a pussy white faggot like you." replied Sluggo.

"Well, why don't you just shine my fuckin shoes, boy?" yelled Blindman and kicked Sluggo savagely in the balls. Sluggo screamed and bent down. Blindman grabbed his head and brought up a knee into the bigger man's face. He felt Sluggo's nose break. Sluggo caught Blindman with a backhand that knock him over. He got to his feet as Sluggo charged in. Blindman uncorked a stiff right hand into Sluggo's gut. It was like hitting aside of beef.

Sluggo grinned a bloody grin. "Dat all you got, you honky faggot?"

"Not even close, nigger, taste this." Blindman busted Sluggo flush in the mouth, knocking his teeth out. Sluggo spit out the bloody caps.

"Second time I did that," laughed Blindman. "You know why I call you a nigger? Because you're a fuckin disgrace to black people. Pieces of shit like you stand out because of the violent shit you pull, same as the way white trash does. No difference. Same crap, different skin color. Plus you all need a gang to back your sorry asses up."

Sluggo screamed curses and charged into Blindman, bowling him over. Sluggo grabbed a brick and tossed it a Blindman's head. It missed. Blindman grabbed big piece of firewood and slammed it into Sluggo's ribs. Sour breath rushed from his mouth. Sluggo nailed Blindman over the left eye and a curtain of blood gushed down his face. Wiping it away, Blindman saw Sluggo lumbering toward him. Blindman kicked a knee out from under the bigger man. A wild punch split open Blindman's ear. He went to his knees and Sluggo grabbed him from behind. Blindman swung his elbow into Sluggo's eye. Sluggo screamed in agony and let go.

Blindman, knowing that he couldn't keep this up much longer, waded in on Sluggo, throwing rights and lefts at his head. Blood flew as punches landed. Sluggo roared and grabbed Blindman in a bear hug, trapping his left arm. Blindman smelled his fetid breath as he started squeezing. Blindman knew he was screwed, his ribs and spine were starting to give. In a desperate move, he rammed his right fist into Sluggo's mouth.

Despite the broken teeth shredding his skin, Blindman forced his fist down Sluggo's throat. That cut off Sluggo's air. Sluggo chewed Blindman's arm, but Blindman kept shoving. Sluggo fell backwards with Blindman right on top of him. His feet started beating the sand in his death throes. His eyes were bugging out of his skull.

Then Eddie decided to make a move. Everyone was watching the fight and not Eddie. Eddie raised his gun.

Before he could take a shot, Dog lunged out of nowhere and ripped his hand off. The other shooter tried to get his gun out, but Dog streaked toward him and ripped out his throat. Eddie stared in horror at the blood gushing from his wrist. Dog turned to him, snarling, then pounced on him. Dog shook him by the neck until it snapped.

Sluggo finally went limp and died. A huge fart signaled his passing.

Blindman collapsed on top of him. "I can't believe you beat him!" exclaimed Nydia.

"I can't either," gasped Blindman. "I need a crowbar."

"What the fuck for?" asked Nydia.

"Because his teeth are clamped down on my damn arm and I can't pull it out." Blindman had his arm down Sluggo's throat up to his elbow.

Leo and the others walked up. "That was one awesome fight," Leo said.

"Just get my arm out of this bastard's mouth, he had bad halitosis and I might catch something," muttered Blindman.

"We could cut off his head," offered Nydia.

"No," said Leo, "I got a better idea." Leo found a garden trowel. He knelt down by Blindman. "I'm gonna break his jaws," Leo told him. "It's gonna hurt, just hang in there." Blindman nodded, his face etched in pain.

Leo put the point of the trowel where the jawbone connected to the skull. He used the butt of his pistol to hammer it. The bone broke with a wet cracking sound. "That fuckin hurt real bad," Blindman yelled. "Do the other side, quick!"

Leo switched positions and broke that bone. He pulled the jaws open and Blindman eased his lacerated arm out.

Nydia poured vodka into the open wounds. Blindman howled. "Jesus fuckin Christ almighty, that hurts!" Sweat poured down his face.

"I can't believe you did that," said Leo.

"You can't believe it, how do think I feel? I can't believe I did it either. I thought I was going to have to rip his heart out. I'm spent. I gotta..."

A shot rang out and Blindman twisted around, blood gushing from his side.

19

THE DRUNKEN MASTER stood in the doorway trying to re-cock his gun with a crippled hand. "You fucked it all up!" he screamed. "You ruined my plan! You can't have it, it's mine! Do ya hear me, this place is mine, all mine! Now get the..."

He didn't finish his rant because Nydia decked him. She kicked his gun out of reach. Blindman staggered to his feet, blood running out of his wound. "Save that cocksucker for me!" he yelled. Nydia had her foot on The Master's throat. Blindman dragged him to his feet and shoved him inside.

He got nose to nose with The Master. "The reward," he yelled. "Where is it?"

"You didn't earn it," The Master whimpered.

Nydia had enough. "Here's El Roacho," she said, holding up the sack. "He wants a word with you." Nydia started beating The Master with the sack full of head.

The Master screamed like a bitch. "Stop, stop, the shit's out in back!"

"Where out in back?" Blindman snarled.

"There's a shed built into hill," he sobbed. "Everything is in there."

"Go see what we got," Blindman told the group. "I got some unfinished business with the man who just killed me."

Nydia and Leo were about to say something when Blindman roared. "Go see what's there and shut the fuckin door behind you!" Grudgingly, they complied.

When the door clicked shut, Blindman turned to The Master and said, "Now it's just you and me, homeboy." The Master cursed, then lunged at Blindman, swinging a claw hammer.

NYDIA, LEO AND THE girls found the shed. It was padlocked. "I got the key," said Leo. He shot the lock off. Nydia yanked open the door. The shed went deep into the hillside. It was packed with cases of water, dried food, and liquor.

"We hit the motherload!" exclaimed Nydia. "We could live off of this for a long time."

"I hate to think how many folks died over this stash," said Leo.

All of a sudden there was a loud roar. The ground shook and everyone was knocked down. "Was that an earthquake?" Nydia asked.

"No," answered Leo. "That was an explosion."

BLINDMAN DUCKED THE swinging hammer. As he ducked, the hammer punctured a propane tank. The Master had Blindman backpedaling as he kept swinging the hammer in an arc.

"I'm gonna cave in your fuckin blind head!" he screamed. "You ruined everything!"

"You caused all this shit," Blindman yelled back. "You greedy gutless cunt, you got all these people killed. Now it's your turn."

Blindman pulled out the .45. A wild swing of the hammer knocked it out of his hand. The Master was closing in, an insane light in his eyes.

Blindman's legs backed into something at knee level. He fell backwards into an old bathtub. The Master stood over him ready to deliver a death blow. "Adios, you blind bastard!" he yelled.

Blindman fished a lighter out of his pocket. "Fuck you, it's Miller time."

The Master, a look of abject terror on his face, said, "Don't."

And the world exploded.

NYDIA, LEO, LEE AND the others looked at the smoking remains of The Master's former headquarters. The sandy hill had caved in on the place.

"What the hell happened?" asked Leo.

Nydia shook her head. "We used all the bombs. I know he said he was hard hit; I didn't see how bad it was. Christ," she said, exasperated. "We went through all that shit and he got blown to bits."

"The old bastard took the fight right to them, he never gave an inch," said Leo. "He deserves to be planted right, so does Knuckles and the girl."

"Yeah, he'd be real pissed off spending all eternity with The Drunken Douche," replied Nydia. "When that mess cools down a bit, we can dig him out."

Dog was running around the wreckage in circles. "What about doggie?" Lee asked.

"I don't know," said Nydia. "He listened to Blindman, I don't know how he's gonna be without him."

Dog was running back and forth along the ruined structure. "Look at him, either that head shot really addled him or he thinks Blindman is still alive," pointed out Leo.

Dog stopped short, he cocked his head, then his ears stood up. He started barking furiously as he sniffed a section of wreckage. All of a sudden, he started digging. Sand flew behind him as his huge paws tore at the earth. He stopped short, threw back his head and howled. Then he shoved his head into the hole he dug.

"What the hell is he doing?" Nydia asked.

Dog's back and neck muscles tensed, his legs dug in and he pulled.

"He's got something," Leo said.

"No, he got some*body*," Nydia gasped. The whole group ran to Dog. They recognized the blood-stained rust colored shirt. "Help him dig!" she yelled.

They widened the hole. Leo grabbed Blindman under his arms and pulled him out.

Blindman blinked the dirt out of his eyes. He looked at the group. "I could really use a drink right now," he said calmly. One girl handed him a bottle of water. "Not that crap, I need whiskey." Leo handed him a pint of Old Crow.

Blindman downed it with one gulp and belched. "Now I feel better," he said.

"How bad are you hit?" Nydia asked.

"Not sure," he muttered.

"Maybe you should look." Nydia turned him on his side and pulled his shirt up. He was hit low on his left side and there was a ragged exit wound out his lower back. It was oozing blood.

"I need to clean it. I don't think it hit anything vital. If it did, I'd be smelling shit, I don't smell anything," said Nydia. "You're not gonna like this." She poured vodka into the wound. Blindman howled so loud that Dog's ears went flat against his head.

"Now that really fuckin hurt," he gasped. "Shame you just torture a poor, defenseless old man like that."

"You're about as defenseless as a cobra," she shot back. "How did you blow yourself up?"

"Well, it wasn't like I planned it." he pouted. "I thought I was done in by the sneaky fuck and I wanted to beat the shit out of him. Silly me, all of a sudden he grew a pair and started swinging a hammer at me. He missed and put a hole in a propane tank. I got knocked over and fell in a tub. He was gonna cave my head in when I pulled out my lighter. I flicked it and bang. That's the last thing I remember. I figured I was done and I'd take him with me. Then this furry fuck rescued me," Blindman finished.

"We all thought you blew yourself up with him," said Leo. "We were in that shed when we felt the explosion."

"Speakin of that," said Blindman, "what was in it?"

"Enough water, food and booze to last quite a long time," said Nydia. "I think we'll be ok if we just stay right here."

"Ya all think we should stay here?" asked Blindman.

"Why not?" said Leo. "You got somewhere you have to be?"

"No," replied Blindman. "Might be nice not to have roam all over this shithole of a world trying to survive. Yeah, me and Dog will stay. Let's clear out these bodies, we got to do the right thing by Knuckles and the girl. They went out with both barrels blazing."

The group took the bodies of the shooters away from the compound. They rolled them into a ravine, then caved it in over them. They dug two graves for their fallen comrades. It was a solemn group standing by the graves.

"Do you think we'll be alright here?" Nydia asked Blindman.

"Maybe," he said. "Only time will tell. It's not gonna be like the old days, but it'll do. Hey Leo!" Blindman yelled, "I think it's time for happy hour."

The End?

Gunfighters of the Drunken Master
Book II: Unhappy Hour

1

About a week after the battle at The Drunken Master's compound, the survivors are still resting and healing their wounds, with the help of choice beverages. Leo had opened a bar in one of the buildings that hadn't been blown up.

The Shotgun Girls were tidying up the place by dragging the bodies away and dumping them in a ravine. They also made the buildings that were still standing into their living quarters. They rigged up a 'garbage' wagon so they could get rid of all the trash that was left lying around. Loads of empty bottles, cans, and other assorted crap was dumped away from the compound.

Nydia was nursing The Blindman back to health. The huge bullet wound in his side was painfully healing. But Blindman was restless, and drunk.

"I need to go for a walk," he groused.

"Maybe you should take it a bit easy," Nydia advised him.

"I should, but I have a restless nature," he replied. "How about we go check out those supplies we now own?"

Nydia thought about it. "Ok, but we take it real slow, comprende? You don't want to reopen that wound."

"Alright, I'll go slow. Anything is better than just laying around." Blindman picked up a pint of Old Crow and downed it. "Needed a little pick me up." Nydia just rolled her eyes.

Leo spotted the two and hailed them. "Where are you two love birds off to?"

"A cheap motel," shouted Blindman. "Any suggestions?" Leo laughed.

Nydia glared at Blindman. "If you weren't already hurt, you would be right about now."

Blindman laughed. "I'm the only eligible bachelor left."

"Thank Christ I still have my finger," muttered Nydia.

"Aw, that really hurt. And after all we have been though together," complained Blindman.

They reached the building that held The Drunken Master's stash of supplies. "We never got a chance to see how far this thing goes into the hill," Nydia said.

"Well, it ain't like we have anything better to do, so let's explore the whole shebang and see what we got," replied Blindman.

The place was packed with cases of bottled water, liquor, dried and canned food. "Seems this goes back a ways," said Nydia. She picked a bottle of water out of a case and opened it. "Now, what the fuck is this?" she said.

"What the fuck is what?" asked Blindman.

"See for yourself," said Nydia, as she tossed him a bottle.

Blindman caught it and opened it. "What did I miss that you didn't?" he asked.

"There should have been a little snap when you turned the cap. They aren't sealed," she replied.

Blindman picked up another bottle and opened it. "You're right, what the fuck is this?"

"Strange," she said.

"Yeah," said Blindman. "Real fuckin strange. We missed something. Or someone. Go get Leo and Dog, and something we can make a torch out of. Let's see what the hell we're dealing with now."

Nydia returned with Leo and Dog. "What's going on?" asked Leo.

"We don't know," said Blindman, "But none of these water bottles are sealed. We missed something. I say we follow this and see where it ends."

"I made a torch," said Leo. "Soaked it in 151 Bacardi."

"That's all that shit is good for," retorted Blindman. "Fire it up, but keep yer guns ready."

The three walked past cases of supplies, twenty minutes later they were almost a mile into the hill. "I had no idea this was as huge as it is," said Leo.

"For a fact," replied Blindman, "I didn't either. Is that light up ahead?"

There was a soft glow coming from around a bend in cavern. "I've seen something like this," said Nydia. "When I was a kid we went to some caves in Pennsylvania, they had a glow like this. 'Phosphorous', I think they called it."

"I think you're right," said Leo. "Ain't like there's electric on anywhere."

"You two hang back a bit," said Blindman. "Just in case we missed one of those cocksuckers. Let me see what we're dealing with.

He looked at Dog "You stay too, you might eat someone before I figure out who's who." What could have passed for a pout appeared on Dog's face. Blindman took the lead with Leo, Nydia and Dog about 50 feet behind him. He turned the corner and let out a scream.

2

NYDIA, LEO AND DOG took off after Blindman. They turned the corner to find Blindman in fetal position on the ground clutching his balls. The three stood in shock at the apparition before them. It was a man, but a man that was under three feet tall. He was filthy, hairy, and very pissed off. He was also chained to the wall of the cave by his ankle.

"Stay back," he hissed at them.

"What did you do to him?" screamed Nydia, pointing to Blindman.

"He kicked me in the balls," moaned Blindman. "I should feed him to Dog. Who the fuck are you?"

"My name is Angelo Settenbrino, I'm a scientist."

Blindman shakily got to his feet. "I'll bet you got one hell of a story to tell us, and it better be good," he said.

"I do," said Angelo. "But can you break this chain and give me something to eat? It's been a while since I've eaten."

"That might explain your belligerent attitude," muttered Blindman. He tossed Angelo a bag of jerky and a bottle of water. "Eat and then talk, after I hear your story I'll decide if I want you roaming around here," said Blindman, still massaging his sore nutsack.

The little guy polished off the jerky and the water in under a minute. "Thanks," he said. "It's been almost a week since they fed me."

"Ok," said Blindman. "We fed ya, now talk."

Angelo sighed. "Where to start... Like I said, I'm a scientist. Myself and four others were working here when the flares started. We had made a remarkable discovery, then those thugs showed up. They were going to kill us, then they found out what we knew. They started bringing all this food and stuff here. They would drop it in front and my people had to drag it back here. Pretty soon the place was loaded. Seems they found a Costco or something like that. They cleared it out. Then they took my crew out and shot them. Said they didn't want to waste food on pussies. They locked me up and just gave me enough to keep me alive.

"Then I guess a couple of weeks ago—forgive me as I have no sense of time from being down here—I heard a lot of shooting, then an explosion. I'm guessing it was you people. Now here you are."

"Yeah," said Blindman. "That wuz us. That Drunken Douchebag played a game and lost. We won, we took the place. Now, what wuz that remarkable discovery you said you made?" asked Blindman.

"Well," said Angelo, "I thought it would obvious by now. We found a subterranean lake."

All three looked at Angelo in astonishment. "You found *what*?" Leo had to ask again.

"An underground lake," said Angelo. "That's what's in the bottles. And that's why they didn't kill me. I rigged up a gravity feed to get the water out. Without me, no water, so the drunken scum kept me alive."

"Son of a bitch," said Leo. "A whole fuckin lake. Ok, Angelo, cover your ears." Leo took out a .38 and shot the chain off the wall. "We'll figure out how to get it off your ankle outside."

Dog walked up to Angelo, very cautiously. He sniffed Angelo up and down, then sat wagging his tail. "Looks like you made a friend," said Blindman. "And believe me, he don't take to many people. Let's get outside so Angelo can get some fresh air and clean up. This changes everything, we could probably survive a long time here if no one fucks with us."

Blindman picked up the chain, which was heavy. "Guess those guys were serious about keeping you around," he remarked. "This damn chain has to weigh about 50 pounds."

Angelo was temporarily blinded by the sun. "I never thought I'd feel the sun again, or breathe fresh air," he said.

"You'll be ok," said Nydia. "I saw something we could use in the bar, let me get it and cut this chain off." Nydia returned with a huge pair of bolt cutters.

Leo studied the situation. "It's a tight squeeze, let me get it in position so I don't hurt his leg." Leo adjusted the cutters, but couldn't bring enough pressure to break the bolt.

Blindman pondered it, then said, "I can break it, but it might hurt a bit."

"Just do whatever," said Angelo. "I'd rather deal with a wound than drag this around."

"Ok," said Blindman, pointing to a big boulder. "Get close to that rock. Leo, hold the cutters in position." Blindman climbed the rock, then dropped, feet first, on the cutters. The bolt broke with a loud snap.

"You alright, Angelo?" Blindman asked.

"Yes, I'm fine. It just pinched me, thanks," replied Angelo.

"Let's go get you cleaned up," said Nydia.

Going into Leo's Last Chance Saloon, Lee and The Shotgun Girls looked at Angelo in amazement. "Ok, ladies, this is Angelo," announced Nydia. "Let's get him settled and then I think we should have a little meeting and figure out some things." Chattering like magpies, the girls fretted over Angelo.

Blindman turned to Nydia and Leo. "We have to sit down and do some figuring. All of us thought that we could stay here until the booze and water ran out. Now, we could survive for a long time if we plan things."

"You really think that?" asked Nydia.

"Yeah," replied Blindman, "I do. We worked well together, we took out the baddest of the bad. It cost us, but we did it. Now we have to hold on to it."

"And it isn't like we killed off all the scumbags," interjected Leo. "We are going to have to plan some kind of defense to hold on to this place."

Blindman blurted out a big laugh. "Two men, six women, a dog, and a midget. What an army!"

3

"LAUGH, YOU OLD BASTARD. We already achieved the impossible." said Nydia. "We killed over 100 of the worst scum on the planet. It sucked that we lost Knuckles and the others, but we won, now lets keep it."

"Yeah," said Blindman. "Let's do that. But we need a plan, toss out some ideas."

"Get everyone together and meet in the bar," said Leo. "This Angelo guy has a lot of smarts, let's just lay everything out and make a plan."

The group gathered in Leo's bar. Blindman opened the meeting.

"When we took out The Drunken Master we figured we could survive on his stash for a couple of months," said Blindman. "Now we find out that if we play this right, we could last a few years. Angelo here is a smart feller, he found out that we are sitting on an underground lake, correct?"

"Yes," said Angelo. "We are. How long it will last, I can't say, but I concur that it could last for a couple of years."

"So," said Blindman. "We need a plan to hold on to it. We might have killed a lot of scumbags, but I'm sure there are more. There might even be some decent folk left. Sooner or later, they'll find this place."

"There is only one way in, unless you're a mountain goat," said Leo. "We need a 24/7 lookout. That way we can get ready for trouble."

Nydia brought up a point. "Do we let anyone join us?"

"We screen 'em," said Blindman. "Trash is trash and that will always show. Anyone who comes in has to contribute something, and has to prove themselves. The first thing anyone will see is the ladies, and that there's only me and Leo. If they have bad intentions, that will bring them out."

"We do lookout," said Lee, pointing to her Shotgun Girls. "You give looking glasses, we see who comes, we sound alarm, yes?"

"Yes," said Blindman. "But we do it in shifts so none of us are dog tired."

Dog looked up at that, wagging his tail. "You just want to go chew on someone, doncha?" Blindman said, scratching the big cur's head. "Dog will be an alarm, too, as you know he will get antsy if a stranger approaches. Well, let's get this in motion as sooner or later trouble will drift in."

Turned out it would be sooner than later.

4

IT WAS MIDAFTERNOON when the Shotgun Girl on lookout sounded the alarm.

"How many?" Blindman yelled. The girl held up four fingers.

"Shit," muttered Blindman. "Nydia," he said, "let's go up and see what we are dealing with."

Nydia and Blindman joined the lookout. "Lemme have those peepers," Blindman asked the girl.

Blindman squinted into the binoculars. He saw four men moving slowly toward the pass into the compound. Twisting the lenses so he could focus, he muttered a curse. "Motherfucker, this just fuckin figures."

"What's wrong?" asked Nydia.

"Everything," replied Blindman. "Here," he said, handing her the glasses. "Take a look."

Nydia took the binoculars. "I see four guys."

"Yeah," said Blindman. "And I know three of them."

"Old friends?" asked Nydia.

"I wouldn't go that far, but we all are graduates of the Gray Bar University." replied Blindman.

"In other words, they were on Riker's Island with you," filled in Nydia.

"You're sharp, Kiddo, that's why I like you," said Blindman.

"The dapper looking guy is Sal Deblasio, a former Mafia Don. That big guy, the one holding the baseball bat, is Sal's bodyguard, Home Run Eddie. The black dude is Blade Benson, knife artist. That tall, blonde guy I don't know," Blindman summed up.

"You had problems with these guys?" asked Nydia.

"Sal's an old school guy, a gentleman gangster. Eddie is an asshole and likes to swing that bat. He won't do anything unless Sal cuts him loose. Blade is a big mouth, but can cut your throat before you know it."

"Let's go see what they want," said Nydia.

"Yeah," said Blindman. "Before they see what we have. Just be ready for anything."

Blindman and Nydia approached the foursome. "I'd say it's nice to see youse guys, but I'd be lying," Blindman said with a laugh.

"Fuck you, you old cocksucker, I should take your fuckin head off!" yelled Eddie.

Blindman ignored him. "Sal, how are you doing?"

"Nice to see you again, Leroy," said Sal.

Eddie bellowed, "Don't ignore me you old piece of..."

"Eddie, shut up," ordered Sal. "We ran into a few 'survivors' of a little dust up you people had," he explained. "They claimed you wiped out The Drunken Master and his boys."

"Yeah," said Blindman. "Long story."

"Well," said Sal. "Scarecrow here," pointing to the tall blonde, "has a longer story that you really need to hear."

"You want to tell it over a drink?" asked Blindman.

"Hard to refuse any kind of hospitality these days," said Sal. "Lead on."

"Just so youse guys don't get any bad intentions," said Blindman, "aside from Nydia, there are five other women, all killers that will take no shit. Rule #1, unless they are interested, leave them alone."

"We will respect that," replied Sal. "Won't we?" he said, turning to the others.

"Speak for yourself," said Blade. "I'll do what I want."

"Cool," said Blindman, bringing up his sawed-off. "Then you can join the 50 or so other dumb fucks who played tough with us."

"Blade, back off," ordered Sal. "Don't cause problems, we have enough coming our way."

"That's what you want to parlay about?" asked Blindman.

"Yes," said Sal, "but let's have that drink. Trust me, you'll need one after you hear what Scarecrow has to tell you."

5

BLINDMAN AND NYDIA led the way to The Last Chance. Introductions were made and drinks were poured.

"Ok," said Blindman to Scarecrow. "Tell your story."

Blade snickered. "First I want to hear how the fuck you got out when the guards started killing the cons and left us to die."

"Oh, you want to have it out, Blade, do ya?" replied Blindman.

"He ain't the only one, you chickenshit bastard!" bellowed Eddie. "You were just for yourself and fuck anyone else."

"Not that I'm explaining anything to you two jerkoffs, but you were on the East wing of Rikers, I was on the West wing," said Blindman. "I heard those pricks blowing guys away, shooting shotguns through the bars. I was in the last cell, I got a toehold on the ceiling and fixed my bunk like I was still in it. When that bull shot up my cell, he opened it to see how bad he hit me. I dropped on him and shanked him. That's how I got this." Blindman patted the sawed-off. "When I got out everything was getting shot up, blown up or on fire. Sorry I didn't check on you boys, but I was saving my own ass."

"That's my problem with you," fumed Eddie. "You didn't give a shit about anyone but you."

"Not for nothin, asshole, you and I ain't exactly friends," Blindman pointed out. "You and Blade got a beef? Fine. Let's fuckin settle it now."

"Like you can take us, you blind piece of shit," Blade yelled.

"Yeah," yelled back Blindman. "All four of yas if you want to go that way!"

The air turned blue with threats and curses. Sal just watched.

Nydia turned to Leo and said, "It's really touching when old friends get together. Sorta brings a tear to your eye, don't it?" Leo just chuckled.

Nydia let go with a loud whistle. "Hey, being that you guys came from the same fraternity, I'm guessing you know a guy named Sluggo."

"Damn straight we do," said Blade. "Baddest motherfucker in the joint, had all the Bloods as his gang. Don't tell me—he's here?"

"Oh," replied Nydia, with a huge grin on her face. "He's here."

"Cool," said Blade. "Be good to see the brother, where's he at?"

"Out back," said Nydia. "We buried him with the rest of the trash. This 'old blind piece of shit' killed him with his bare hands."

"I don't believe you," snarled Blade.

Blindman rolled up his sleeve. "See these marks, big mouth?" he said, pointing to the still red scars on his right arm. "I shoved my hand down his throat and tried to rip his fuckin heart out. Now I'm sick of listening to your big damn mouth, you and this goon, so let's go end this shit right now."

Sal, who had been silent up until now, turned to Nydia and Leo. "He really killed Sluggo with his hands?" he asked.

"It was a fair fight," said Nydia. "And Blindman destroyed him."

Sal turned to Eddie "As long as you work for me, do not—I repeat, do not piss him off."

"Boss, I can't…"

Sal cut him off. "We both took an oath. You break your oath to me, you're on your own. Blade, nice knowing ya."

"What the hell do you mean by that?" said a shocked Blade.

"We are in a situation that we have to stick together. You want to fight Blindman, I'll be digging your grave," replied Sal.

"You serious?" asked Blade.

"Dead serious," replied Sal.

Blade looked like the air had been let out of him. He sat down muttering about bad luck, then got quiet.

"Hey Sal," said Blindman, "how did youse guys get out?"

"Sheer luck," answered Sal. "Those guards were killing all the cons, then there was an explosion. The back walls of our cells came down. We headed toward the East River. We figured we grab a boat and beat it out of there. We found a boat, problem was the river dried up. Fires were everywhere, so we went west. We had to kill a few punks who braced us, then we found a massacre. It was some kind of camp where survivors gathered. About 50 people had been there. All had their heads cut off. It was horrible, we figured an organized gang hit them. Then we found Scarecrow and his 'toy'. He told us the real story, and it's real bad.

"We were scrounging this town for some supplies when five guys dressed in black surrounded us," said Sal. "They were jabbering in some foreign language, then they charged us without saying a word. They had swords and machetes. We heard a shot and one guy's head exploded, then another one. Eddie hit a home run on one's head. One swung at Blade, Blade gutted him. I shot the last one. The one Blade gutted cursed us out, so Eddie finished him. Then Scarecrow here showed up with his 'toy' and told us what was going on. It isn't good, people." Sal summed up.

"OK, THE SUSPENSE IS killing us," said Blindman. "Tell us what's going on, Scarecrow."

The blonde man spoke with a nasal twang. "I was living near Memphis, Tennessee, had a little house there. Over the last few years there was a lot of Middle Easterners coming into the area. They all got jobs at this big meat packing plant. Then these mosques went up. They started buying out small businesses, then those places catered to just Islamics. They started pushing for their own holidays, preaching that Shira law crap and pretty much bought up a lot of property. They got real nasty with people who wouldn't sell to them, including me. They had meetings at this big mosque they built. What we didn't know was the mosque had a huge part of it way underground. Then the flares started.

"There was a brief alert telling people to get undercover. Then the airways went dead," Scarecrow continued. "Most of the Islamics were in that mosque. A lot of people hid in basements, afraid to come out. A few days after things died down they came out. They were all dressed in black, like those Isis fucks. They started rounding up people. Anyone who resisted, they shot. They missed me, as I was in my attic looking for this." Scarecrow patted the gun case. "It's my Granddaddy's Sharps. I had a couple of handguns and plenty of ammo. I knew I'd have to shoot my way out of town, but I wanted to take my sister and her family out with me.

"Everyone was herded into a courtyard. This guy, Kareem Mohammed, is their leader, along with his wife. They told the people that Allah caused what had happened to rid the world of infidels. Now it was Kareem and the others' job to convert the survivors to Islam. They had two ministers that survived. They sawed their heads off in front of the crowd. It was fuckin horrible, really bad. They said anyone who wanted to live had to prove their worth to Allah by turning over their women to the men. Some of these gutless cocksuckers did just that, including my brother-in-law. The women were dragged out and stripped. They were held down and gang raped by the men. The ones that really fought had their throats cut. So did the ones who were unattractive.

"The 'converts' were taken away to be 'enlightened'. The prettier women were also taken away. Then the slaughter began. It was sickening. They had a pack of their kids, young. They let them rape the women to 'get the hang of it for future conquests.'"

"You heard this?" asked a seething Nydia.

"Yeah," replied Scarecrow. "They were speaking English. Those kids took all the babies and toddlers from their mothers. They beat and kicked them to death as the men laughed. The rest of the afternoon they tortured anyone left. Then they slaughtered them with machetes and knives. I used the scope to see what was happening as I had gotten out of town. I was up on a hill watching. I couldn't do shit, but then I saw my brother-in-law give my sister to Kareem as a token of his loyalty."

"That must have been tough," Leo said.

"Yeah it was. Even tougher when I killed her," said Scarecrow.

The group was in shocked silence. "You killed your own sister?" Nydia stuttered.

"I had no choice. They put a dog collar on her, and they had beat her. What would you have done, let her be a whore to that Arab cocksucker?" The stunned looks on their faces were all the answer he needed.

"I tried to nail Kareem, but he ducked after the first shot. I took out a couple of them to keep them from following me. Make no mistake about it, they are going to scour this place and kill anyone they come across. They are finding pockets of survivors and wiping them out, like that camp Sal spoke of. But that ain't all they are doing. Sal, would you say those guys we killed were in pretty good shape?" Scarecrow asked.

"Now that you mention it, yes. They were," replied Sal.

"That's because they ain't missing any meals," said Scarecrow. "They are eating the people they kill."

No one said a word for a couple of minutes. "You're serious?" asked Blindman.

"I wish I wasn't, but I seen proof," replied Scarecrow. "We are scavengers, barely living off what we can scrounge. These bastards are well fed."

"I remember reading about the Japanese fighting on small islands in the Pacific," said Blindman. "Seems when they ran out of food, they ate their enemies, and sometimes their own fallen comrades. This is fuckin evil," he continued. "They gotta go, every fuckin one of them."

Leo, Nydia, and the rest sat speechless in stunned silence. "How many of these cocksuckers do you figure there are?" asked Blindman.

"Might be a few hundred," said Scarecrow. "I didn't take the time to count."

7

"A FEW HUNDRED?" SHOUTED Blindman. "Jesus H. Fuck, just what we need. As bad as we are, we can't take on a fuckin army."

"Maybe we can if we had more guns," said Sal.

"Yeah," interjected Scarecrow. "People will be driven this way, but these pricks are smart. They will try to plant turncoats among us."

"That's going to be a major problem, that and weeding out scumbags," said Nydia.

"A few hundred," muttered Blindman. "We really need a plan. Sal, you're a good judge of people. I want you, Leo and Nydia to really check out anyone who shows up here."

"What are you going to do?" asked Sal.

"Take the fuckin fight to them, slow the bastards down, hit and run, cut throats in the middle of the night, booby traps, that kinda shit," replied Blindman.

"All by yourself?" said Nydia "You're gonna get yourself killed, you crazy old bastard."

"What else can I do? I ain't gonna sit here and wait," shouted Blindman.

Scarecrow spoke up. "Might be another way," he said.

"What do you mean?" asked Blindman.

"Simple," said Scarecrow. "We go recruiting, get more fighters."

"There are a lot of crazy fucks out there, just keeping to themselves and killing anyone who bothers them," said Scarecrow. "They ain't exactly the kinda folks you'd want for neighbors, but maybe if we told them what's going on, they might help."

"Define 'crazy,'" Leo said.

"Well," said Scarecrow. "There's a guy called Firefly, he likes to start fires and he's got a tanker full of gas. Then you have a real head case, Reverend Hellfire and his 'nun' Sister Mary Gangbang. She's an ex-whore who 'saw the light'. Hellfire hates all us sinners, especially boozers. Then there's two real big guys, twin brothers, very unfriendly. Maybe a few more."

"Alright," said Blindman. "If Scarecrow can find these people, maybe we can convince them it's in their best interests to join the fight. Me and him will go, you guys start securing this place. After what we just heard, kill anyone suspicious that comes in. Remember, no fuckin mercy."

"Define 'suspicious'," asked Blade.

"Blade, you know the type. Nervous guys, maybe a really scared woman with a guy that doesn't match. Go with your gut, that's all we have," answered Sal instead of Blindman. "Go do what you do best," said Sal. "And we'll hold the fort."

Just then Angelo stepped out. "What the fuck is that?" asked Blade.

"That," said Nydia, "is a scientist who figured out how to get water from an underground lake. Meet Angelo Settenbrino."

Sal walked up. "Sal Diblasie, my friend, good to meet a pisano." Angelo shook his hand.

"Same here, my friend, a pleasure."

"Angelo," asked Blindman. "Do you think you could use your know-how and come up with some surprises?"

"Absolutely," Angelo answered. "I'm sure Sal has the organizational skills to put people to jobs they would be good at, so yes, you and Scarecrow go do some recruiting and we will secure this place."

"Ok," said Blindman, "but give me something to write with and write on. If we find anyone we think will be an asset to us, me and Scarecrow will check 'em out. If they pass the test we give 'em, I'll sent a note back with them."

"Good plan," said Sal. "That will save us the trouble of figuring out who we can trust."

"Hate to lay this on yas," Blindman said, "but if we ain't back in a week or so, you have to figure they got us."

That comment sobered all present. "Dog's coming with us. Get this place in shape, people," finished Blindman.

Blindman, Scarecrow and Dog armed themselves and left.

"How far out do you figure some of these people are?" asked Blindman.

"I figure they are spread out about 50 miles or so," said Scarecrow. "Firefly is about the closest, maybe 15 miles out."

"So he'll be our first stop," said Blindman. "Do you have enough shells for that Sharps?" Blindman asked.

"I keep the brass and reload them," said Scarecrow. "I can take the primers out of a 12-gauge shotgun shell. I know exactly how much powder to use for distance, and I have a bag of 50-caliber balls."

"If you run out, I may have some tricks you can use," said Blindman. "I have been making killer loads for my shotguns. I've used nails, barbed wire tips, sparkplugs, razor blades, broken safety glass, and dimes. They all have the desired effect," chuckled Blindman. "We should try a sparkplug in your Sharps, could be interesting."

"Wait until I'm completely out of ammo before we do that," said Scarecrow. "This Sharps is a family heirloom."

8

THE FIGHTER WAS TIED by his ankles to a scrub tree branch. His two companions were bleeding out into the sand with throats cut from ear to ear. A short, squat man, wearing jeans, a cut off levi jacket, and moccasins squatted down and looked the fighter in the eye. The fighter tried to spit at him, but choked back on the phlegm.

"Real tough when you're murdering helpless people," the man said. "You think you know torture, pendejo? My people invented it. Did you ever hear of The Apache?" he asked.

"More infidels we will crush," gurgled the prisoner.

"Not likely," The Apache said. "At least not you."

The Apache piled some dried sticks and branches under the prisoner's head. Then he lit the kindling and a small flame shot up. "It's a good day for you to die," The Apache addressed the man. "I doubt that you'll die well so I'll just leave you to the fire." He started lowering the man down to the flames.

"No, stop, have mercy, I'll tell you everything!" the man bellowed in horror.

"I already know everything, you and your people are vermin. Vermin that has to be destroyed," The Apache answered.

The man's oily hair burst into flames. The Apache tied off the rope and stepped back. The man screamed until his tongue burnt, his eyes exploded, his back arched and his bowels let loose. The Apache watched impassively.

"He didn't die well at all," he muttered in disgust. Then he walked back to camp.

APACHE'S CAMP WAS SIX motorcycles and six bikers. "Did he tell you anything?" one biker asked.

"What could he tell us, that we are fucked?" said Apache. "We have no gas, we are almost out of ammo and where there were ten of us, there is now six," summed up Apache.

A blonde-haired biker, Deke, spoke up. "So now what, just wait until they overrun us?"

"No, my brother," said Apache. "We keep fighting, this club will lay down for no one."

BLINDMAN AND SCARECROW had walked about fifteen miles. Night was approaching. Scarecrow muttered, "I'm just about spent, let's make camp somewhere."

"Not yet," said Blindman. "I want to talk to this Firebug guy. How close are we to him?"

"Not sure," replied Scarecrow, "but as soon as it's dark, you'll see where he's at. When the sun goes down, he lights up the sky."

Right after sundown the two saw a blaze of fire not too far off. "I'd say we found Mr. Firebug," said Blindman.

"It's Firefly," corrected Scarecrow. "No need to get on his bad side."

"Like he has a good side?" said Blindman. The two crested the hill and looked down at a man-made inferno.

Dog growled. "You stay," Blindman ordered.

A TANKER TRUCK WAS buried in sand, the back of it exposed. An open valve had poured raw gasoline down a culvert that ran to the base of a small valley. The gasoline was burning and a man sat on a rocky perch next to the tanker. It was impossible to tell if the man was black, white or whatever. He was covered with scar tissue from burns. One eye was seared shut and tufts of hair stuck out from his burned scalp.

"Right handsome devil, isn't he?" Blindman remarked.

They got within ten feet of Firefly. "She's beautiful, isn't she?" Firefly said without taking his eye off the flames. "She's the beast that can't be tamed," he continued. "I tried, but she bites me every time." He let out a maniacal laugh. Then his voice got hard. "Why are you here, disturbing me and the beast?"

Best we disturb you than some others roaming around here," said Blindman

"Oh, you mean those military people in black shirts?" Firefly asked. "They wanted to take her away from me," he rambled on. "They wanted me to convert to their barbaric religion. I let the beast embrace them." Firefly continued, "She is still embracing them."

He pointed down the valley where the fire raged. Blindman looked at the inferno, then realized something. To get to compound they would have to come through here. *Great place for a trap,* he thought, *now how to convince this crazy bastard to spring it.*

"You do know that more will be coming," said Blindman. "We got a place some ways back and we'd be obliged if you might help us out a little." Firefly stared blankly into the flames. Blindman went on, "We have food, water, liquor, smokes, anything you want." Firefly continued to stare into the flames.

Blindman turned to Scarecrow and shrugged. "Guess he ain't interested," he said.

Before the two could leave, Firefly spoke without taking his eyes off the flames. "Tell me something," he asked. "Can I set these people on fire?"

"That," said Blindman, "is exactly what we want."

"Sounds like a good time," said a more cheerful Firefly. "I'm in."

"Great," said a stunned Blindman. "We are going out to recon the situation, we'll talk more when we come back." Firefly just stared into the flames.

Scarecrow and Blindman used the glow of the flames to walk another couple of miles. "I wasn't about to camp near that crazy fuck," said Blindman.

"Yeah," said Scarecrow. "He's nuttier than a squirrel turd."

AS MORNING BROKE, THE two woke up to the sound of gunfire. Dog growled and ran to the top of a sand dune. Blindman and Scarecrow followed. Ten black-clad figures were pursuing a large man across the desert. They were shooting at his feet to keep him moving. One of the black shirts closed in on the man. The man whirled around, swinging something shiny. It was a three-foot-long meat hook. He hit the man in the right eye and the hook came out his temple. The big man jerked it and a big piece of skull flew off. A second man closed in, but the big guy was fast. He swung the hook up, catching the man under the chin. He jerked the man's lower jaw off. The man collapsed to the ground, blood pouring from the wound.

The remaining men surrounded him. "End of the line, jewboy!" shouted a man with a thick southern accent. "I jest know you want to get revenge for what we done to yer wife, she had good pussy 'til we ripped it up," the man laughed. "I done skinned her tit and made me a tabaccy pouch out of it. What do you think of it, jewboy?" The man took something out of his shirt. "See how hard I worked on it, now I'm gonna cut yer jew balls off for a trophy. Grab him, boys," he ordered.

Just then the man's left hip exploded in a shower of blood and shattered bone. "Nice shot," said Blindman, patting Scarecrow's shoulder. "Now let's finish them. Dog, hunt!"

Dog loped down the dune and knocked a fighter down, ripping out his throat. Blindman charged into the mix. A load of dimes caught one guy in the chest, erupting out his back in a shower of gore. The second blast of nails decapitated another fighter.

Scarecrow aimed the Sharps and blew a bowling ball sized hole though the guts of another man. Blindman didn't have time to reload, he ducked a swinging knife as he clawed out the .45 automatic. The knife swinger turned to catch a slug in his left eye, blowing off half his head.

A snarling Dog chased down the last fighter, ripping his arm off. The man bled out on the hot sands as Dog trotted up to Blindman and dropped the arm at his feet. Blindman looked at Dog, then laughed crazily. "Guess you thought I needed a helping hand."

Blindman and Scarecrow turned to the big man. "Sorry for buttin in," said Blindman, "but me and my friends didn't like the odds."

"Thank you," the man gasped. "My name is Goldstein, Arnold Goldstein."

A loud groan interrupted any further conversation. The man with the now shattered hip spoke. "Ya all gonna help me, I'm bleedin here."

Blindman looked at Goldstein. "We heard some of it, so I asked Scarecrow to fuck this traitor up. I figured you might have some unfinished business with him."

"He raped and killed my wife, he said he skinned her," snarled Goldstein.

"Hey, you two keep jewboy away from me and maybe I can get the boys to let you live. If you convert, that is," the man bleated.

"Arnold," said Blindman, "do what you feel is right."

Arnold nodded. He wrenched the meat hook out of the corpse and walked over to the prisoner. "So you wanted my balls as a trophy, how do you like this?" Arnold swung the hook in an arc and impaled the prisoner's scrotum. "This won't take long," he told Blindman. He dragged the screaming man out of sight. The screams kept up until a gurgling sound choked them off. Goldstein returned, covered with blood.

"You're pretty handy with that hook," remarked Blindman.

"I should be," replied Arnold. "I was a Kosher butcher before all this happened."

"We have a place aways back," said Blindman "We ain't lettin these cocksuckers overrun us. You interested in joining us?"

"If it means killing more of this filth, yes. I accept your invitation," answered Goldstein.

"Good," said Blindman. "Now I'm going to write you a note so you can get in. Ask for either Leo, Nydia, or Sal, they are in charge."

Goldstein took the note and put it in his pocket. "Thank you for this," he said. "I will defend that place with my last breath."

"Me and Scarecrow have some recruiting to do," said Blindman. "When you go back, I'd avoid a spot a couple of miles behind us."

"You mean that firebug with the gas truck?" asked Goldstein.

"Yeah," said Blindman. "He's on our side, but he ain't none too stable. We'll see you back there."

9

BACK AT THE COMPOUND a few stragglers had drifted in looking for sanctuary. "How many so far?" Leo asked Nydia.

"About a dozen," she replied. "All shit scared. We have to put some backbone to them or they'll fold."

Just then Sal and Angelo strolled up. "Angelo has an idea," said Sal. "Tell 'em, Angelo."

"There is only one way into this place, and it's narrow," Angelo started. "If they came at us, full force, they would get bottled up. And when they get bottled up, that's when we hit them hard. I propose we build a catapult; we have enough junk around her to build one." Angelo continued, "The faster we do it, we can figure out distance and elevation, then we can bomb them with whatever we can dream up."

"I like it," said Nydia. "I like it a lot. What would we need to make it?" she asked.

Angelo spoke, "The bed of one of these pickup trucks laying around here, then the springs. The bigger the truck, the bigger the springs. Then some ropes or cables."

"Let me talk to those new people that came in, they might have some skills we can use," said Leo. "I'll start with that guy." Leo motioned to an emaciated man, dressed mostly in a frayed black suit.

"I don't know about him," said Sal. "He came in late yesterday, asked if he could stay the night. He coughs a lot and don't look too good."

Before they could act on that, one of the Shotgun Girls yelled, "Men's coming!"

Leo picked up the field glasses and looked. "Don't like the look of these guys, they have outlaw biker written all over them."

"Let's reserve judgment until we hear their story," said Sal. "None of us are exactly members of the clergy, either," he chuckled.

Five filthy, stinking men came into the compound. They wore tattered 'colors' of some kind of gang. Leo and Lee confronted them, the others stayed back to see what would play out. "You guys lost?" Leo asked.

One of the men, with matted red hair and beard said, "This is your lucky day, brother. We came to protect you from those evil sand niggers."

At the word 'nigger', Blade got up and walked toward the group. Nydia blocked him. "Let them make the first move," she hissed. Blade nodded.

"Yeah, youse people are lucky we's found you," continued the redhead. "We'll save you, and all we need is a little pussy," he said, reaching toward Lee.

"Oh," said a smiling Lee, "you want to play with kitty?"

"That's right, baby," he said, reaching for her. "Now get naked and show me some lovin."

Lee's educated foot caught him under the chin and Red's neck snapped with a dry crack.

"You're dead, bitch!" one biker yelled as he went for his gun. All the bikers pulled firearms.

Leo and Lee went for their guns when a voice rang out. "She ain't dead, but you fuckers are." The man in black was standing with his coat drawn back. The four bikers turned with their guns out. "Remember me, boys?" The man asked. The bikers looked perplexed. "Card game in Vegas, you gentlemen were sore losers. You came back and robbed the game. You killed a friend of mine in the process, now it's payback time."

One biker laughed. "Sure, old man. Our guns are out, stupid. Now you can die."

Leo, Nydia and the others would swear they never saw the man draw, but four bikers, spouting gouts of crimson, lay dead and dying in the dirt. The man just stood over them, holding two smoking pistols.

"So sorry to cut in," the man said, "but I've been tracking these crud for weeks."

"Who the hell are you?" Nydia asked.

"Ace Scanlon," the man answered. "I guess you would say I'm the fastest gun alive. I had an act in Vegas, using these babies." He patted his six shooters. "Trick shot stuff like shooting a cigar out of someone's mouth, putting a hole in the ace of spades, that kind of show. Then I had a run-in with these assholes right before everything went to shit. They killed a friend, so now I'm even."

"We can use your gun if you want to stay," offered Leo.

"I figured you might," chuckled Ace. "But my time is short, I'm loaded with cancer."

"Aw Christ, man," said Angelo. "Anything we can do?"

"I've been taking drugs from some of these cretins," Ace said, pointing to the dead bikers. "If you have any drugs that would help. The pain is real bad. I wish for death, but I can't do it. I'd rather go out with both barrels blazing than let this eat me alive."

"We have some Vicodin, things like that," offered Leo. "You're welcome to them."

"Thanks," said Ace. "I can't pull the trigger on myself, but taking on these scum, well, I'd rather go out taking as many of those pricks as I can."

"I'm sure we'll all be doing that sooner rather than later," Angelo summed up.

10

KAREEM MOHAMMED SURVEYED his latest 'conquest'. His followers attacked a group of ten people. The men were slaughtered, and the few women were now being raped by the fighters.

His wife, Sylvia, ordered the men, "When you are finished with those cows, cut their throats and bleed them out." She turned to her husband, smiling. "Now we have some fresh meat," she said. Sylvia may have been the worst member of this extremist group. Haughtily beautiful, she had used many a man, then cast them aside. Her perversions bled into her extremist beliefs. She had her own 'stable' of prisoners, young captured children who she abused at will. When her 'pleasures' got out of control, another tortured body would be left on the sand.

Kareem turned to his Captain, a man called Hussan. "We sent men out after that jew and others after those bikers, have they returned yet?"

"No, Exalted One," replied Hussan. "No one has returned."

"Then send some of our 'converts' out to search for them. I won't waste our own people, we need them for our ultimate victory. Our sacred jihad will destroy these American dogs as we drive them into the sea."

Hussan thought, *What sea?* but wisely didn't speak on it.

Kareem continued, "We are herding the infidel pigs to slaughter. Soon they will have nowhere to run and we will earn our 77 virgins in the afterlife."

Sylvia interjected "There are stragglers hiding out in the hills ahead. One of our scouts has reported small groups." She continued, "They have to be destroyed or they may unite their forces against us."

"Only fools would try and stop the forces of Allah," bellowed Kareem.

"There are two men that refuse to join us," said Sylvia, "and a priest with his church that is in our path. They need a lesson in Islam," she finished.

"Yes, my princess, you are right," he said. "Hussan, send out two death squads of five men each. Make examples of these unbelievers."

"Yes, Exalted One," replied Hussan. "It will be as you wish."

Hussan picked ten men. "You five will go visit the fat men, the other five will go tell that priest that there is only one religion now and he must pay for his blasphemy. Now go," he finished.

11

DOG HAD BEEN LOPING out ahead of Blindman and Scarecrow. He came charging back, barking furiously.

"Looks like he found something," said Scarecrow.

"Yeah," replied Blindman, "and I'll bet it ain't good. I need an eye opener." He took out a pint of Old Crow and drained it in one gulp. "That hit the spot."

Scarecrow threw him a dirty look. "I guess sharing the wealth ain't in your vocabulary," he groused.

"I'm sorry, man. Here." Blindman handed Scarecrow a pint. "Been solo for so long I done forgot my manners."

"Thanks," said Scarecrow, taking a healthy slug.

"Now let's see what Dog is so riled up about," said Blindman.

Dog led them to Apache's handiwork. "Someone had a barbecue," remarked Blindman, looking at the hanging corpse with its head burnt up.

"Two more over here," said Scarecrow. "Throats been cut."

"Look at those tracks, moccasins tracks," said Blindman. "Burning that guy's head over a fire is an Indian trick."

"You think we are near a reservation?" asked Scarecrow.

"Maybe," replied Blindman, "but whoever did these guys had a real mean on and we can use a guy like that. Let's follow these tracks."

They had gone about a mile when Dog stopped in his tracks. His hackles were up and he started growling. Blindman shouted, "We know yer watchin us so come on out and let's parlay."

Apache showed himself. "Who are you?" he asked.

"They call me The Blindman," he yelled. "My buddy is called Scarecrow and he's Dog."

"I have heard of you," said Apache. "Follow me, our camp is over this hill." They followed Apache to the camp where the other five men waited.

Blindman noticed the death's head insignia on the cutoff levi jackets. "Youse guys are HA, ain't yas?" asked Blindman.

"Yes," said Apache. "Meet Deke, Denny, Lobo, Marty, and Jones. We are all that's left of our chapter."

"I did time with some of your New York boys," said Blindman. "Honorable guys, we were cool with each other and watched each other's backs. I seen your handiwork a mile or so back."

"That was mine," said Apache. "They didn't die well."

Deke interrupted. "Hate to break up this mutual admiration society, but what do you guys want? We ain't got shit, no gas and running out of ammo."

"Well," said Blindman, "a proposition. We took out The Drunken Master and we have his place. We got water, liquor, food, smokes, and shelter. We also got that fuckin army of Islamic scumfucks heading this way. Being that they are killing anyone in their path, we thought you gentlemen might be interested in joining us."

"Those black shirted cocksuckers killed more than half of us," said Deke. "Apache is our Pres, so if he says yeah, then we're in."

Apache replied, "I say yes, but we have no fuel, no water, no nothing. We've been stuck here and they have been picking us off."

"What do you need?" asked Blindman.

"Gas, 9-millimeter ammo, water, etc. We are sorta fucked," answered Apache.

"Maybe not," Blindman said, rummaging through his pack. He pulled out two boxes of shells. "Here, take these. I use .45s, grabbed these by mistake".

"We found a guy with a tanker full of gas," said Scarecrow.

"Yeah," said Denny. "We know all about that nutty motherfucker, he'll burn anyone who gets close to his 'treasure.'"

Blindman laughed. "Yeah, he would do that, but we sort of recruited him. Seems they tried to convert him and it didn't go too well. For them, that is. I think he'd be willing to give us some gas. Scarecrow, feel like takin a walk back and make Firefly a little trade for some fuel?"

"I'm game," said Scarecrow. "What are you going to trade him?"

Blindman pulled three bottles of vodka out of his pack. "These should do it." Turning to Apache, "You got any gas cans?"

"We have three 5-gallon cans," answered Apache.

"Ok," said Blindman. "One of you go with Scarecrow, he can't carry that much back by his lonesome."

"What if he don't want to trade?" asked Denny.

"Oh, he'll want to, trust me on that," said Blindman. "He'll drink, but he won't leave his gas stash to find any. But if he gets stupid, walk away."

"Ok, I'll go with Scarecrow," Denny said.

"Good," said Blindman. "I'll hang out here and we'll make some plans by the time you get back."

12

NYDIA WAS LOOKING OUT into the desert when Leo strolled up.

"I'm guessing you're worried about him," said Leo.

"Yeah, I am," she replied. "He's one bad hombre, but you know there's always someone badder."

"I guess you two got pretty close during that little war we had," said Leo.

"We worked well together and we saved each other's asses more than once." Nydia turned to Leo. "It's not like I'm in love with him, I just care about the old reprobate," she summed up.

Sal wandered up, wine bottle in hand. "Angelo got his catapult ready to test out," he announced.

"What has your buddy, Eddie, been building over there?" Leo asked, pointing to the huge man standing back looking at a small structure.

"An outhouse," said Sal. "Eddie wanted his own crapper, he's always been strange like that, he needs privacy to poop."

"Why the hell did he build it out there?" asked Nydia. "It's right where those fuckers will storm us."

"I didn't ask," replied Sal. "When Eddie gets it in his head to do something, there is no reasoning with him."

"It's ready," Angelo announced. Angelo had drafted the burly ex-butcher, Goldstein, to be his muscle and drag the parts Angelo needed to build his contraption. Angelo took huge springs from an old dump truck, then the bed of a pickup truck. They tied it back with thick, metal cables they had scrounged. Goldstein muscled a huge rock in the bed.

Angelo made some calculations. "Alright, Arnold, release the pin," he ordered. The cables were hooked up to a device that would release them when the pin was pulled. With a loud twang, the device fired the rock and that rock took the roof off of Eddie's crapper.

Eddie stood looking in horror. "You sawed-off little SOB, you wrecked my crapper!" he yelled. Eddie stormed up to Angelo, cursing him out. "All that fuckin work, now look at it," Eddie groused.

"Who the hell told you to build it in the line of fire, you cretin?" Angelo yelled.

"No one," Eddie shot back. "I liked the view."

"The view of what, you moron, the desert?" Angelo shouted.

"Fuck this, you need an ass whippin!" Eddie screamed back. Eddie ran toward Angelo, but the little guy stood his ground. Eddie towered over him, then Angelo punched him in the side of his knee.

Eddie dropped to his knees and Angelo bored in, swinging like a windmill. His small fists beat a tattoo on Eddie's astonished face.

"Oh fuck," said Sal, "He'll kill him." Sal moved in to break it up, but Eddie clamped a huge hand on Angelo's head.

Angelo kept swinging his fists, but Eddie held him at arm's length. "Enough!" Eddie bellowed.

Angelo stopped swinging and stood there panting.

"For a little bastard you sure got a huge fuckin pair of balls." Eddie walked over to what was left of his crapper. "Alright," he announced, "I'm moving it back there and none of you fuckers better mess with it." Eddie bear hugged what was left of his outhouse and dragged it behind Leo's Last Chance Saloon.

Sal walked up to Angelo "Pisano, you took one hell of a chance with Eddie."

"Not really," said Angelo. "We either work together or die together, that's our options."

"He's been with me for years," said Sal. "He's completely loyal to me. I do think that you earned his respect by standing up to him, Angelo."

"I learned a long time ago," said Angelo, "never to back down, never let anyone get the upper hand on you."

13

SCARECROW AND DENNY approached Firefly's camp cautiously. "Wonder where the hell he is," said Denny.

"Probably sleeping," answered Scarecrow. "The fucker spends the night burning shit up."

The sound of a gun cocking had both men turn. Firefly stood behind them, a rifle in his hands. "Problems?" he asked.

"No," said Scarecrow. "Blindman sent us back to ask for a favor. He held up the gas cans. "We need some fuel so we can take the fight to them."

Firefly stared at them for a minute then said, "And I get what for filling those cans?"

Scarecrow pulled the three bottles of vodka out of his pack. "Blindman sent you these."

"Well," Firefly said, his burned features softening "That's right decent of the old feller, I been dry for too long. Let's go over there and I'll fill those right up for yas."

Firefly was downright cheerful as he filled the cans. "When do you think those Arabs will be coming?" he asked.

"Hopefully not too soon, we gotta get ready for them," said Scarecrow.

"Well," snickered Firefly. "Just give me a heads up as to when to start the barbecue."

"I'll be coming back this way after me and Blindman finish talking to some people, so I'm sure he'll tell you when," said Scarecrow. "Just let Denny here and his buddies pass on through, as they're with us.

"No problem," said Firefly as he opened a bottle of vodka. "Thanks for the juice."

BLINDMAN HAD BEEN DISCUSSING strategy with Apache. "I figure we could trick out your bikes with guns," said Blindman. "We got a few TEC-9s, we got a real smart feller back at the place, a guy named Angelo. I'll wager he could put them on your bikes."

"I like that idea," said Apache. "In fact, I like it a lot."

Just then Scarecrow and Denny got back. "These fuckin cans are a real pain in the ass to carry when they are full," Denny bitched.

"I'm guessing Mr. Firefly went for the trade," said Blindman.

"He was downright hospitable when I pulled out the booze," said Scarecrow. "Oh, I told him youse guys would be coming and not to bother you," he said, gesturing to Apache. "The crazy fuck is just chomping at the bit to torch those fuckers."

"Groovy," said Blindman. "Apache, here's a pass to get you in. I left two guys, Leo and Sal, in charge. Ask for them."

"What about this Angelo guy?" asked Apache.

"Ok, just so your mind don't get blown, Angelo is a midget. But he's a scientist, tell him what we talked about and let him figure out how to do it."

"Do you want me or one of the guys to go with you? A little insurance, maybe." offered Apache.

"Nah, but thanks for the offer. Us three can handle it," replied Blindman.

"Three?" questioned Apache.

"Yeah, three," answered Blindman, then he whistled. Dog came bounding over a sand dune. "He's our insurance."

The six bikers looked shocked. "You mean that's been watching us all this time?" said Denny.

"Yeah," said Blindman. "He's real sneaky like that. You guys stay still. Dog!!" Blindman called. Dog trotted up, cocked his head then walked to the bikers. "Let him get your scent so he knows who you are," said Blindman.

Dog sniffed all the bikers, but then sat down in front of Apache. "Pet him," Blindman said.

Very cautiously, Apache rubbed Dog's head. Dog wagged his tail, then licked Apache's hand. "I'd say you made a friend," chuckled Blindman.

"I have never seen a dog this big, he's got to weigh about 150 pounds. What breed is he?" Apache asked.

"Don't really know," answered Blindman. "When I busted out, I found him a few days after, locked in a cage. I let him out and he's been with me ever since. But he's a killer, for a fact, you move on me or a couple of the women back at the compound and he'll tear you apart."

The bikers primed their bikes with the gas. "See you back at the camp!" shouted Apache as they took off.

14

AFTER WALKING ABOUT ten miles, Blindman spotted a small plume of smoke. "We better see where that's coming from," he said. Blindman handed Scarecrow the glasses. "What's it look like?" he asked.

"Weird," Scarecrow said. "Really weird, looks like a cemetery. There's a bunch of crosses, but I can't see it clear. That smoke is coming from a little shack."

"I smell a trap," said Blindman. "You lay back, I'll go in. You keep me covered, don't kill anyone unless you have to. These may be some of the people we are looking for."

"Ok," said Scarecrow. "But I think this might be where that crazy priest is holed up."

"Well," said Blindman, opening a sealed pint, "I'll just bring him some holy water."

BLINDMAN MADE NO PRETENSE about sneaking up. He just walked toward the crosses. When he got closer he saw rotting bodies on the crosses. Most were wearing the black outfits of the jihadists. Five of the bodies looked fresh. They *were* jihadists. Their eyes had been gouged out, kneecaps and elbows shattered, and roofing nails were driven though their arms and legs into the rough wood. One of the bodies moaned. "Fuck," said Blindman.

He raised the .45 to end its misery when a voice boomed out loudly, "Drop your weapon, sinner, and take your penance." Blindman turned to see a tall man dressed in a priest's garb, complete with a clerical collar. He had a shock of long white hair and his eyes burned with the light of a fanatic. He was holding two cut down .20-gauge shotguns.

"You must be the Reverend Hellfire," Blindman said.

"You have heard of me," said Hellfire. "Good. A man should know who will send him to hell."

"Piss off, Padre, your ass is covered." Blindman waved his hand and a bullet hit the sand about six inches from Hellfire. "Next one takes off your head, preacher."

The door to the shack was kicked open and one of the ugliest women in the history of western civilization stepped out holding a shotgun. She was under five feet, weighed about 300 pounds, had a big, hooked nose and a pockmarked face. She was dressed like a nun.

"Drop it, Sister, or I'll plug the Padre here," ordered Blindman.

Hellfire was losing control. "Do as he says, Sister. The Lord will protect us," he ordered. She dropped the gun.

Hellfire snarled at Blindman. "You're a drunkard, a fornicator, and a thief," he yelled. "You're doomed to burn in the pits of hell!"

"And you're a self-righteous asshole," Blindman spit back.

Blindman decked Hellfire, knocking him to the ground. Sister went for her gun, but Dog had sneaked up on her. Dog launched at her, knocking her down, then pinning her with his paw on her chest.

"You flinch, bitch, and you're history," Blindman snarled. By that time, Scarecrow had caught up.

"I thought we might need these two sorry pieces of shit, but now I'm not too sure," Blindman said to Scarecrow.

"What do you mean, 'might need us'?" asked Hellfire, wiping some blood from his smashed mouth.

"You see these bastards you got nailed to these crosses? Well, there's a fuckin army of them that will be heading this way shortly," said Blindman.

"They are unbelievers," said Hellfire. "They worship a heathen god, a false god, a usurper. They sent people to convert us, but we showed them the light," he finished.

"Well, you've done right well with a few of them. Now you got a few hundred coming this way," said Blindman. "Think you can handle those?"

"The Lord will provide," snarled Hellfire.

"Amen," muttered Sister.

"Maybe he will, probably he won't. But I can," Blindman told them.

"How so?" asked Hellfire.

"How you fixed for ammo, Padre?"

"We'll get by," said Hellfire.

"No, we won't," interrupted Sister. "We are almost out."

"I'll tell you what I'll do," said Blindman. "You want to send these sinners to hell, I'll give you the means to do so."

"What can a drunkard like you do for the righteous?" snarled Hellfire.

"I'm really wanting to beat the *righteous* piss out of you," said Blindman. "But I'll wait for that. I can have ammo and a few more guns dropped off to you. Then you can continue your crusade. Oh," he said, "if the guys I send don't come back and I find out you killed them, what you did to these fucks on the crosses will be a day at the beach compared to what I'll do to you. Comprende, you sanctimonious shithead?"

"Your men will have safe passage, then after the unbelievers are dealt with, I'll be taking down your little Sodom and Gomorrah."

"You'll try," said Blindman. "And I'll bury you. Do we have a deal?"

"Bring me guns, and I'll show these heathens the error of their ways," finished Hellfire.

15

HUSSAN WAS TROUBLED. He had done what Kareem had asked, but none of his men had returned. Hussan really believed that the survivors would not resist. Some had given up, others put up a vicious fight until they were put down. Kareem was on a high with all of this killing. Hussan enjoyed torturing and killing Americans because of their invasion of the Middle East. But Kareem took it to another level by having them eat the flesh of their victims. Hussan also didn't trust Sylvia. Her perversions overrode what the teachings of the Prophet had laid out. He would have given her captured children to the young shock troops to practice their killing skills on. One of his troubles sprang from a recurring dream where a fiery demon dragged him to hell. But he knew this would never happen because he was promised 77 virgins in the afterlife.

The voice of Kareem interrupted his musings. "Have your men returned yet?" he asked.

"No, Exalted One," Hussan answered. "I fear those converts weren't up to the task."

"You mean to tell me that our soldiers couldn't kill these infidels?"

"Sadly, Exalted One, that seems to be the case," Hussan replied. "And that group of bikers, they're gone."

"How could they be 'gone'?" bellowed Kareem. "They were trapped, cornered by our brave soldiers. How did this happen?"

"I'll tell you how," a female voice cut in. The two men turned as Sylvia walked up to them. "They had help."

"Who would dare help our enemies?" shouted Kareem. "Who would oppose the will of Islam?"

"Two men and a dog," Sylvia replied. "If you two had bothered paying attention to little details, you would have listened to the rumors. These men seem to be gathering people to stand against us."

"The dog must be the eyes of Satan; all dogs are in league with Satan. That's why we destroy them," said Kareem. "Satan must be rallying his forces against us."

"Then we should seek out and destroy these minions of his," said Sylvia. "But don't send converts, they lack the courage to do what's needed. Send out your trained assassins."

A beefy man with a shaved head and a thick southern accent marched up to the three. "I hate to bother y'all with this, but we had an escape last night," he said. "That black girl you gave to us to fuck, well, she found out that last night was it for her. One of my boys was finishing up with her, she gouged his eye out and took off." He laughed. "Guess she got a tad upset when we told her she'd be on today's menu."

"So she was on your watch when this happened?" Sylvia asked.

"Yeah, well y'all said we could do whatever we wanted with her," he said. "Guess she didn't cotton to where we put it," he laughed.

"You think this is a laughing matter?" Sylvia said, motioning to Hussan. "You were given a sacred trust and you failed."

"Bitch won't last a day out in that desert," he said. "But I'll get some of the boys and run 'er down."

"No, that won't be necessary," she said, giving Hussan a signal. Hussan swung a machete into the guy's neck. The man looked shocked as Hussan proceeded to saw his head off. Blood spurted in an arc, drenching Hussan as he finished cutting the head off. "He can take the woman's place at the dinner table," Sylvia said. "Hussan, get six of your best assassins," she ordered. "I want four heads before me by sunrise tomorrow."

"Four heads?" questioned Hussan.

"Yes, get that woman who escaped first, then go after those rallying against us."

Hussan nodded and went off to get his men.

16

TAMERA WAS SCARED OUT of her wits. She had been a captive for three weeks, raped and tortured. Then they gave her the to the redneck 'converts' as a toy. They constantly raped her, then branded her like cattle. When she found out that she was to be killed, she ripped the eye out of her rapist's head and took off into the desert. Now she had no idea where she was, but she knew they were not about to let her get away. Stumbling in the darkness, she was terrified. She tripped in the darkness. She pulled herself up, then saw a shape blocking her path. She started to back up, then the shape growled. Something metallic touched her back. "Don't move," a voice rasped.

Tamera froze, waiting for the steel to cut into her neck.

"Turn 'round real slow like," the voice ordered. Tamera turned around looked at the source of the voice, a beard stubbled, craggy face with milky eyes. "You with those cocksuckers or runnin from them?" he asked.

"I escaped from them last night," Tamera gasped. "I was with a group of a dozen or so people. We were trying to find a safe place when they hit us." She continued, "They killed all the men outright. They gave the children to these child soldiers who used them for knife practice. It was awful. They raped two women to death, then took me and three others captive. I was the last one," she finished.

"What happened to the other three?" Blindman growled.

"After they got tired of torturing and raping them, they killed and ate them," she said. "Last night it was going to be me. I saw a chance to get out and took it. The bastards branded me like I was a cow," she sobbed. She tugged her jeans down over her butt and a crude raised fist was burned into her flesh. "They used an old metal coat hanger to do this," she said.

Blindman fumed. "We are going to kill every last one of these pieces of shit," he said. "We have a place a ways back," he told her. "We have people there that are going to fight. You want in?" he asked. "Or do you want to keep running?"

"I want in," she said. "If I gotta die, at least let me take some of these fools with me."

"That's what I wanted to hear," said Blindman. "Scarecrow, Dog, c'mon out," Blindman shouted. "I'm The Blindman, he's called Scarecrow, and the dog is Dog."

"I'm Tamera," she said.

"You know how to use a gun?" Blindman asked.

"No, not really," she admitted. "My life was a bit sheltered before all this."

"Well," said Blindman, "I'll be thinking it's pretty unsheltered right now."

"I can't send you back there, we are too far out. You'll have to tag along with us until we go back," said Blindman.

"They are looking for me," said Tamera. "They send out execution squads to kill anyone who escapes."

"Then let's make the bastards feel right at home," said Blindman. "They can die here. Scarecrow," he said, "I'm going to be the bait for a trap. You take Dog and Tamera, hide behind those rocks."

"What are you going to do?" asked Scarecrow.

"I'm gonna sit here, have me a drink and catch some rays until the bad guys show up. You just follow my lead. When it goes to shit, and it will, start killing the fuckers."

The three took cover behind the rocks. Blindman sat on a big rock and took out a pint of Old Crow. "Nice day for something," he muttered under his breath. As it would turn out, it was a real bad day for someone.

The six assassins followed Tamera's tracks in the sand. The tracks led into an arroyo. As they turned the corner, Blindman was waiting. "You gents lost?" he said, smirking.

Their leader, a hook-nosed man with a scar across his face, spoke. "You have a black bitch that is our property, where is she?"

"Oh, she's just fine. A little banged up after what you pig fuckers did to her, but fine."

"Give her to us," the man barked, "and we will kill you quickly."

"Now, that just upsets the hell out of me, you threatening a poor defenseless old man," remarked Blindman. "You a tough guy, camel fucker? How's about you and me have it out, winner gets the girl. Or do you need these five goat fuckers to back you up because you ain't got the balls?"

"Get ready to die, infidel pig!" the man snarled and charged Blindman.

Blindman just stood his ground. When the man was upon him, Blindman kicked his balls into his belly. The man fell to his knees, clutching his balls. Blindman bored in, his hard knuckles breaking the hook nose with a loud crunch.

Scarecrow turned to Tamera. "I heard he gets like this and there's no stopping him."

The other five men stood back in a slight depression in the ground. Blindman was destroying the killer. A looping right hand broke the man's jaw. Teeth, like bloody Chiclets, flew out of his ruined mouth. Blindman started pounding on his ribs, feeling them crack. Finally, the killer couldn't take the humiliating beating any longer. Backing up, he pulled out a knife. Scarecrow's Sharps send a 50-caliber slug into his chest in a burst of blood and ripped flesh. The man's body flew back and hit the ground hard. The ground caved in as the other men lost their footing and fell into what appeared to be a sinkhole.

A loud buzzing noise came from the hole. Scarecrow and Tamera joined Blindman, who stood staring at the hole. "What the hell is that noise?" he asked no one in particular. Two of the other fighters clawed their way out of the hole covered with snakes that were biting the hell out of them. "Jesus H Christ on a crutch," yelled Blindman. "It's a fuckin rattlesnake den!"

The five men, turning bluish-black from the massive amount of venom in their systems, convulsed and lay twitching in their death throes. Hundreds of angry snakes poured out of the hole.

Dog growled and started toward the snakes. Blindman grabbed him and pulled him back. "Run!" he yelled. The four took off running, but the snakes were in pursuit. "Fuck this," said Blindman. He pulled out the Remington automatic. Eight blasts of buckshot blew the hell out of the snakes. They slithered back to the hole.

"Of all the goddamn motherfucking things to survive an apocalypse why did it have to be snakes?" bitched Blindman. Scarecrow and Tamera were shaken, Dog still wanted to fight. "Scarecrow, hold Dog back," ordered Blindman. "I want to get a dead snake to bring back."

"Why," asked Scarecrow, "do you want to do that?"

"I want to show it to Angelo, maybe he can make sense as to why these fuckers survived." Blindman took out a laundry sack.

Scarecrow handed him a machete. "Cut its head off just to be sure," he said.

Blindman went to the nearest dead snake. It was almost seven feet long. "You'd make a nice pair of boots if I was inclined to be a shoemaker," Blindman said to the dead snake. He severed the head, the body convulsed.

"Guess you don't know you're dead," he muttered. "Brr, I really hate these fuckers," he said, as he stuffed the twitching body into the bag.

17

THE BIKERS FOUND THE compound and showed Leo the pass from Blindman. They met Sal, who introduced them to Angelo. Apache told Angelo about Blindman's suggestion to mount TEC-9s on their bikes. Angelo took Apache's bike to work his magic on. The newcomers busied themselves by building shelters to live in.

Ace Scanlon was standing in front of the one he built, nursing a bottle of his homemade pain killer. "Mornin, Ace," Sal said as he walked up, carrying a small box.

"Morning to you, too," Ace replied. "What do you have there?"

"Something that might interest you," answered Sal. "When I was up and coming, I was a button man. An old timer showed me a trick using these." Sal opened the box. It was full of brass thumb tacks.

Ace was intrigued. "Thumb tacks, eh, what do you do with them?"

"Let me have one of your guns," asked Sal. Ace pulled out one of his six guns and handed it to Sal. "Nice piece," said Sal. "Now watch this." Sal took out a bullet, then jammed a tack in the head of it. "See that old cactus over there?" Sal pointed to a huge, dead, cactus about 100 yards away. Sal fired one shot and dust flew from where the bullet hit the dead plant. "That's your ordinary bullet," said Sal. "Now here's the special one." Sal fired again; this time the bullet hit the cactus dead center and exploded the plant in half.

One of the bikers, who was watching, said, "Holy shit, that was fuckin awesome."

"We used to call these dum dums," said Sal. Sal handed the gun and the box of tacks to Ace. "Use them well, my friend."

"Oh, trust me, I intend to," replied Ace. Ace unloaded his guns and started putting the tacks in his bullets.

"Peoples coming!" yelled one of the Shotgun Girls, who was on lookout.

Leo and Nydia came running up. Nydia had the binoculars. "How many?" asked Leo.

"Looks like a couple dozen," replied Nydia. She squinted for a better view. "Something strange about this, there's a couple of hard looking characters sorta hanging back," she said.

"Alright," said Leo. "Let's do a meet and greet. Ace, me, you and Nydia, let's check them out." Leo addressed the rest of the group. "Hang loose and be ready," he said.

The group was ragged, some looked half starved. Mostly women, a few older men. Then Nydia noticed something. "A few of these guys look pretty well fed," she muttered to Ace and Leo.

The two men took a hard look. "Yeah," said Leo. "Be ready for anything."

Anything didn't take long. A tall, blonde woman suddenly yelled, "It's a trap!" The man behind her stabbed her and pushed her to the ground.

Nydia's bowie knife spouted about an inch above his belt line. He hit the ground screaming as four other men pulled out pistols and started shooting.

Ace took a graze across his left hip, but drew and shot. Two attackers' heads exploded in a shower of gore and grey matter.

The other two, their element of surprise gone, tried to retreat. Denny was running one down with his bike. The shooter turned and fired, hitting Denny in the shoulder, throwing him off his bike. The out-of-control bike hit the shooter dead on, crushing the life out of him.

The last shooter made it past Leo's Last Chance Saloon, but the door to Eddie's crapper flew open, knocking the man to the ground. Eddie, his pants half down, stood over him with his bat. "It's the bottom of the ninth!" he yelled. "The bases are loaded, he swings, he misses! Strike three, motherfucker, you're out!" Eddie swung his bat, crushing the man's skull. "Hell of a thing," he muttered. "Man can't even wipe his ass before he kills someone." Eddie went back into the crapper to clean up.

Nydia was standing over the man who had her knife in his guts, Denny was more concerned about his bike than his wounded shoulder, and Ace was stanching the blood flowing from his grazed hip.

Nydia grabbed the knife and twisted it. "Talk, fucker," she barked.

"You're all going to die!" he screamed. "The Exalted One knows of this place and he will make it his kingdom after all you infidels die."

Nydia twisted harder. "How many of you trash are there?" she snarled.

"Enough to wipe all of you out, you worthless cunt," he screamed.

A look of rage came over Nydia's face. She slid the knife up to his breastbone and he screamed as his intestines fell out on the sand. "One thing I hate is being called a cunt," she said.

Leo looked at her and smiled. "You been hanging around Blindman way too long," he said with a chuckle. A moan interrupted any further conversation.

The woman who had been stabbed was still alive. Ace was kneeling over her. Nydia and Leo walked over to them. Ace shook his head. "It's real bad," he said. The knife had punctured her lung, pink froth was on her lips.

She reached up and grabbed Ace by the shirt. "Those bastards have children, two are mine. That Muslim bitch has them as slaves." She pulled Ace closer to her face. "Promise me you'll find them, please give me your word."

Ace looked pained, but he said, "You have my word, I'll find them."

"Thank you," she said. Then her eyes closed forever.

Ace stood up, shaken. Most of the group had gathered around and had overheard. Ace spoke. "If she didn't warn us, a few of us might be laying here. I'll find them kids. I gave my word and I'll do it."

"Before we do anything," Nydia said, "let's have a little Q&A with the rest of these people." There were seventeen of them, beaten down and defeated. Nydia, still livid, took over. "Anyone else in this group we have to kill?" she asked.

An older man answered. "No, they were it. They told us that if we tried to warn you, they would gun us down."

"So one woman had more balls than all of you and she's dead because of it," she snarled.

"You don't know what we've been through," the man said.

"I don't really give a fuck!" she yelled. "Everyone here has been though some horrible shit, but we don't give up, we fight. Question right now is are you willing to grow a pair and fight, or do you want protection?"

One woman spoke up. "All of us are not fighters, we need help."

"Oh," said Nydia. "You need help, but you're not willing to help yourselves." She slapped the woman in the face. "Like that?" Nydia snarled, slapping her again. "Do you like it?" She kept slapping the woman until she had her back to the wall.

Finally, the tearful woman threw a punch. Nydia blocked it. "That's what I wanted to see," she said. "I just made my point, you get backed into a corner, ya fight your way out. We can teach you. You have two choices, you stand with us and fight, or you leave right now," Nydia summed up. "Ace," she said, "you and Denny better go let Angelo dress those wounds."

"I'm ok," said Denny. "I just hope the cocksucker didn't bleed all over my bike."

Ace grabbed Denny by his good arm. "Let's go get fixed up, your bike isn't going anywhere."

"We'll clean it up for ya, Bro," Deke assured him. "Go get patched up."

18

BLINDMAN AND COMPANY were about 50 miles from the compound. "If we don't find them two guys today, I say fuck it and let's head back," Blindman said. "I've been making a map so we know where things are. I don't need snakes and I don't need that altar boy fucker either."

"He really got under your skin, didn't he?" needled Scarecrow.

Blindman shot Scarecrow a withering glance. "Break my balls all you want, you earned that, but I'll tell ya something. He lives though this and we live though this, I'm gonna punch his ticket," said Blindman. "Just the way he said he'd take us down means he's trouble and you can't trust a man that don't drink."

Tamera interjected, "You guys talkin about Hellfire and that crazy bitch?"

"Yeah," said Blindman. "You know him?"

"No," she said. "But word's out, he's as nuts as the people we're dealing with. Kill or convert, no middle ground."

"Great," muttered Blindman. "I should go back and just shoot him on general principles."

All of a sudden a voice cried out. "Oh, you're still alive. Well, you won't be in a minute."

The three gave each a what the fuck look. "It came from over that ridge," said Tamera.

The three climbed to the top of the ridge and looked down at a heap of carnage. Broken Jihadist's bodies were strewn about, four of them fresh. A huge man had one of them held over his head. He viciously slammed the man on some concrete steps. The man's back snapped in about six places.

Blindman applauded. The man looked up, hate in his eyes. He was huge, about 400 pounds. His face and arms were covered with mottled blotches. "You're fuckin next!" he yelled and started to climb up the ridge.

Blindman aimed the sawed-off at him. "Not a real good idea, big boy," he said calmly. "Now back up and let's talk a bit."

"We got nothing to say to you bastards," another voice cut in. Another man, almost identical to the first, came out from behind a huge rock.

"Nothin to say? Well I think we do. We have the same enemies," said Blindman.

"Hold up a minute," said Scarecrow. "I recognize you guys, you're wrestlers, you used to do those death match things."

The two behemoths looked at each other. "Yeah," one said. "We're pros. I'm Manny, he's Juan, we used to be a tag team called the Heavy Hitters. Now we're just dead men."

"You look alive to me," said Blindman.

"We are both dying," Manny said. "Our kidneys are shot. We were supposed to go on dialysis, then the world went to shit. See these blotches? It's poison in our systems killing us slowly. If that isn't bad enough, we have to deal with these fucks," Manny said, kicking one of the corpses in the head. "We beat every one of them to death with our hands, and they keep coming. We ain't going out without a fight," he summed up. "But this is a real shitty way to die, poisoned by our own bodies."

Blindman was silent for a moment. "How would you boys like to go out in a blaze of glory?" he asked.

"What do you have in mind?" Manny asked.

Blindman told them of The Compound and his plans to defend it. "I honestly wish I could help you guys, but I don't know anything medical except cutting bullets out of people, and we don't have a doctor."

"You got liquor?" Juan asked.

"That we have," answered Blindman. "Ok, here's what I can do, I can have someone come back here with booze and guns, does that work for you?"

"You're serious, you'd do that for us?" asked Manny.

"I will, because any of these bastards you kill will take the load off of what we have to deal with when they reach us," said Blindman. "Plus I hate to see real men just die just because their bodies gave out. Deal?"

Manny and Juan walked up to Blindman and shook his hand. "Yeah, we got a deal," Juan said. "I'm partial to tequila, and so is Manny."

"I'll send some your way, and a bunch of guns too. Some bikers will drop the stuff off after we get back," Blindman told them.

Scarecrow spoke up, "Got a question for you guys. When these dirt bags show up, which direction do they come from?"

"Right over there," pointed Manny. He motioned to a pass between two mountains. "Reason they never got us was because we always saw them way before they saw us."

"Be a wonderful thing if we could catch them in that pass and drop the whole mountain right on them," said Blindman.

"You serious?" asked Scarecrow.

"Dead serious, we could end all of this right there. I got to ponder on this, run it by Angelo," said Blindman.

"Who's Angelo?" Manny asked.

"Oh, he's a right smart feller that The Drunken Douchebag had prisoner. He's with us now."

19

HUSSAN WAS DEEP IN thought when he was interrupted by Sylvia. "Hussan, where are your men?"

"They haven't returned as of yet, my Queen," he said haltingly.

"They won't be returning, Hussan, they have been destroyed," she said. "I had a vision of a blind man and a dog. The dog is his eyes and all dogs are the eyes of Satan," she stated. "We have to kill the dog and capture the blind man," she said. "With him as our prisoner, the others will lose heart and surrender," she finished.

Hussan thought of his vision of a fiery demon, but knew better to speak on it. "You know the man called Cal, a brave convert and fierce fighter?" she asked.

"Yes," said Hussan. "He is the one who willingly gave his wife to The Exalted One."

"Yes, and her brother killed his own sister so she couldn't serve our great leader," she said. "This man is with the blind man and the dog. I believe we should send Cal to do this job as his heart is filled with vengeance toward this man," she finished.

"It will be done as you asked," said Hussan.

Sylvia went looking for Kareem. He was 'interrogating' a female prisoner. The woman's body was covered with bloody welts after Kareem had beaten her with a belt when she tried to refuse his more perverted desires.

"Leave this cow," Sylvia ordered. "We have matters that need to be discussed."

Kareem kicked the weeping woman in the ribs. "We will finish this when I return," he snarled.

Kareem and Sylvia went where they could talk in private. "Speak," he barked at her.

"Don't get an attitude with me, Exalted One," she said with a smirk. "While you're indulging in carnal pleasures, we have a real threat ahead of us."

"You have no place to talk to me in such a manner!" he shouted at her. "You're doing a lot of 'indulging' yourself," he finished.

"Be that as it may," she shot back, "forces are organizing against us. Allah is guiding us," she said. "He will make us prevail."

"Spout that line of crap to the fools who believe it, you and I know better," he spat at her. "Do you think some kind of 'god' would allow us to do what we are doing? What would you have me do?" Kareem asked.

"Pay attention to what's going on," she said. "The infidels are rallying around someone, this blind man. Those bikers are gone, that black girl escaped, everyone we sent out hasn't returned. Worried a bit now, my dear husband?"

"Why should I be? The Americans are like sheep, and sheep get sheared," he answered.

"Yes," Sylvia said. "They are, for the most part, but some aren't. Like cowboys, they'll fight."

"So what is the solution to this problem?" Kareem asked.

"Simple," answered Sylvia. "We have to capture this blind man. Without him, they will fall."

20

BLINDMAN, SCARECROW and Tamera headed back to the compound. "We'll stop and chat with Firefly about things," said Blindman.

"What about Hellfire?" asked Scarecrow.

"Fuck him," spat Blindman. "He's just as bad as those Islamics. If we didn't need him for cannon fodder, I'd put a window in his head."

"Yeah, I agree," said Scarecrow. "He's a fuckin fanatic. I think that crazy bitch keeps him sorta in check though."

"Probably," agreed Blindman, "but if he survives this thing, I'm going punch his ticket for him. Can't abide by a man who don't drink. I get the feeling these bastards know about us by now," he said. "Between the bikers, the brothers, Hellfire, and us, we killed a lot of them. I suspect they are going to try and overrun us," finished Blindman.

"Too bad we can't blow up that pass with them in it," said Scarecrow.

"I been thinking on that," said Blindman. "That would end it."

"Can we do it, though?" asked Scarecrow.

"I'll run it by Angelo," said Blindman. "We'd need a shitload of explosives to make that happen, but I'm down for it."

The three avoided contact with Hellfire as they skirted his camp. Around dusk, they arrived at Firefly's camp. "This place looks deserted," said Scarecrow.

"Nah, he's here someplace," retorted Blindman.

"Ah, my friends have returned from their quest," a voice said. Firefly came around the side of the tanker. "I gave your friends what you needed." he said. "Now do you have any more liquor you could donate to the cause?"

"Not with us," answered Blindman, "but I'll have a case delivered to you shortly, what's your preference?"

"Vodka would be nice," said Firefly. "When do you think those *visitors* will be arriving?"

"I'd say sooner than later," said Blindman. "I got a plan to sort of thin the herd, but I have to run it by the others. I'll bring you back your hooch and then we will figure out the best way to kill these assholes."

"Have a safe journey," said Firefly. "I have to talk to the Beast, tell her she will be needed shortly."

"You do that," said Blindman. "I'll see you in a couple of days."

Tamera shuddered. "He's one scary SOB," she said.

"That's for sure," said Blindman, "and we need that kind of scary."

The trio headed back to camp. "Good thing we mapped this out," said Blindman. "We have to make three deliveries of booze and weapons, and we have to avoid those snakes, and Hellfire."

"Hellfire and snakes are about the same thing," said Scarecrow.

"Yeah," chuckled Blindman. "For a fact, they could be cousins." Scarecrow suddenly stumbled. "You ok?" Blindman asked.

"Yeah, I'm alright, I just tripped on this thing," Scarecrow held up a hunk of metal with a hole in the center.

"Lemme see that," asked Blindman. Scarecrow handed the hunk of metal to him. "I think this was the head of a pickaxe," said Blindman. "See these knobs on each side? Looks like they got melted down. I have a use for this."

"You do?" asked Scarercow.

"Yeah," chuckled Blindman. "A gift for someone special."

21

IT WAS DUSK WHEN BLINDMAN and Scarecrow got back to the compound.

"Looks like they have been busy," said Blindman as he noticed the fortifications that were built in his absence.

"Welcome back," called Nydia as she, Sal, and Leo waved Blindman into The Last Chance.

"Looks like you guys have been busy fixing the place up.

"Yeah," said Nydia, "and not without a few complications."

"What happened?" asked Blindman.

"One bunch of no-goods came in, we buried them," said Nydia. "A group of refugees came in, but had infiltrators. We punched their tickets too. We got maybe another 150 stragglers and survivors all scared shitless, but they will fight. We dug pits with punji stakes in them, Angelo got his catapult working, and the Apache's group now has TEC-9s on their bikes."

"Great," said Blindman. "Now I got Firefly, that nutty preacher, and two wrestlers out in front. I need to talk to Apache and Angelo."

"I'll go find them," said Sal.

"What's going on?" asked Leo.

"I made some promises to those guys out there," said Blindman. "They need supplies or they won't be any good to us. Plus," he added, "I might have an idea to take them all out at once."

Sal returned with Angelo, Apache, and Eddie. "Ok, boys, we gotta go over some shit that needs to be done," announced Blindman. "Apache, I need your boys to make a couple of deliveries."

"Whatever you need, we'll take care of it," said Apache.

"Ok, first a case of vodka for Firefly," said Blindman. "Then a couple of cases of 20-gauge shotgun shells, two AK-47's and a couple of handguns for the reverend shithead. Oh, and if that fucker gives you any shit, just turn and leave him," he growled.

Apache chuckled, "Guess you didn't like his sermon."

"If he lives through this, he won't live long," snarled Blindman. "He's just as bad as the Islamics. Last stop is a case of tequila and guns and ammo for the two brothers," finished Blindman.

"Now right where those two brothers are is a pass between two mountains that these black shirts have to come through. Now here's a thought, if we could get most of them in that pass and bring the mountain down on them, well, it would be a beautiful thing," said Blindman.

"If that could be done, it would pretty much end it," said Angelo.

"My thoughts exactly," said Blindman. "Oh, Angelo, can you explain this?" Blindman dumped the dead snake on the bar.

"Holy fuck!" shouted Eddie. "That was alive?"

"Yeah," said Blindman. "And a lot more where this one came from."

Angelo examined the snake. "Somehow they survived," Angelo said. "But how?"

"Does it matter?" said Denny, who caught the end of the conversation. "Why don't we use them against these fucks?"

"How do you figure that?" asked Blindman.

"Easily, that's how. You know where they are, right?"

"Well, shit yeah," said Blindman. "I drew a map so we could stay the fuck away from them."

"Well, me and Lobo could go back there, get these fucks to come after us, and lead them right to where that den is," said Denny.

Blindman pondered that thought for a minute, then smiled. "I like the way you think, Bro. Yeah, if you got a bunch after you, you guys could jump your bikes over that area. A big group running over that place would cause the ground to cave in. Yeah, I like this idea a lot," finished Blindman.

"Then there's nothin to it except to do it," said Denny. "I'll go see if Lobo is down with it."

Denny left to find Lobo. "Hey Eddie," said Blindman, "I don't want you to feel left out, so I got ya something to improve your swing."

"What the hell are you talking about, you old bastard?" growled Eddie.

"This," said Blindman. He tossed Eddie the pickaxe head they found. "Slide it over your bat and you'll see what I mean."

Eddie slid the piece of metal up to the head of the bat. "This is awesome," Eddie said as he hefted the bat. "You found this thing and thought of me busting some scumbag heads."

"Yeah," said Blindman. "We all need a little edge in this fight."

Eddie extended his hand. "Sal was right," Eddie said. "You're one stand up motherfucker."

Blindman shook his hand. "Let's send these cocksuckers to paradise," he said.

22

BLINDMAN WAS DRAWING a map for Denny as to where the rattlesnake den was. Angelo walked up and sat down. "I was thinking about your plan to trap them in the pass," he said. "How would you set off the charges?"

"Well, a remote detonator would be nice, but we don't have one," Blindman said. "So the only way it would work is that we set up the explosives where we know they would bring the mountain down, then have Scarecrow set them off with his Sharps."

Angelo pondered this. "That would solve the situation if you trapped most of them in that pass," he summed up.

"Lotta 'ifs' in this equation," Blindman pointed out. "They will get past Manny and Juan, that's a given. Hellfire will stand and fight, but they'll overrun him. Firefly could cook a bunch of them, but if any get by him, they will hit us big time," Blindman summed up.

"Don't forget the snakes," said Angelo.

"Yeah," said Blindman. "I'm not forgettin about them at all."

"Then we have to concentrate on bringing that mountain down on them," said Angelo.

"Fuck it," said Blindman. "I'm gonna round up some dynamite and start the dance."

"What if something goes wrong?" asked Angelo.

"Then it's on youse guys," said Blindman. "You got the best here, so use them."

"You know Ace made a promise to that woman who warned us," Angelo told Blindman. "He's going to find those kids the minute shit starts. He's determined to do it," said Angelo. "He's getting weaker every day, but this seems to keep him going."

"This sucks," muttered Blindman. "He's sick, those two brothers are sick, be nice if we had a doctor."

"But we don't," injected Angelo. "And going out in a hail of bullets seems better to those guys than letting the diseases eat them up."

"For a fact, you're right," said Blindman. "Now I'm going to get busy."

HUSSAN BROUGHT CAL to see Sylvia and Kareem. "Calvin!" exclaimed Sylvia. "You have become a magnificent soldier of Islam."

Calvin, a big six foot something with a shock of long blonde hair, stood motionless. "We have a special task for you," she continued. "And revenge for your sister's murder." Cal's eyes bugged open at that. "Your brother-in-law is traveling with an enemy of Islam, a blind man and his dog. Your mission is to capture that blind infidel. Kill the dog, for it has the eyes of Satan, and kill your brother-in-law." she finished.

"Thank you for this honor, my Queen, I will take care of this right away," said Cal, practically salivating at the chance to kill again.

"Take some of your men, Calvin, and don't fail us," ordered Kareem.

Sylvia caught up to Cal outside. "You must succeed in your mission," she said, her hand rubbing his crotch. "The rewards will be many, including my own gratitude."

"Show me how grateful you can be. In other words, I want a taste," said Cal with some authority in his voice. Sylvia pulled down his filthy jeans and Cal's erect cock sprang out.

"Now you can give me that taste," Cal groaned. Ignoring the smell of piss and sweat, Sylvia gave Cal a very wet blowjob. Cal tensed up before warning her. "I'm gonna cum." Sylvia took his spunk on her face.

"There's your taste, Calvin. There will be more when you complete your mission," said Sylvia.

"You suck cock like a pro," said Calvin. "You can be bettin I'll be wanting some more of that." Cal went to round up his men.

Sylvia watched him walk off, then spit disgustedly in the sand. "This will be you last mission, infidel. Hope you enjoyed that because it was the last *taste* you'll ever have."

BLINDMAN WAS TALKING to Scarecrow about blowing up the mountain. "The way I figure it, we set up the charges, then let them see one of us," said Blindman. "I lead them into the pass, then you start shootin."

"It will be close," said Scarecrow. "Real close."

Tamera walked up to the two. "I need to do my part here," she said. "Who can teach me how to shoot?"

"I'd say Ace would the one," said Blindman. "Besides, he needs something to keep himself occupied. C'mon, I think I know where he is."

Ace was sitting on a chair in front of The Last Chance. "Hey Ace," shouted Blindman. "You feel like showing this lady the finer points of marksmanship?"

Ace chucked, then went in a coughing spasm. "Sure, isn't like I have anything better to do."

"Groovy," said Blindman. "Ace, Tamera. Tamera, Ace," he said in way of introductions. "Now I gotta go blow up a mountain and get this dance started."

"That's the plan?" asked Ace.

"Yeah," replied Blindman. "Time to cut down the odds bit. I'll be back after I finish that landscaping." He went off to get ready.

"I'll bet you never even held a gun," Ace said to Tamera.

"Yes, you're right, never have. But now I have to," answered Tamera.

"No shit," said Ace. "We fight or we die." Ace handed her one of his pistols. "See that dead tree about 50 yards out?" Ace said, "Point the gun at it and squeeze the trigger."

Tamera jerked the trigger and the bullet pinged off the roof of Eddie's crapper. "Next one who shoots at my shitter is a fuckin dead man!" Eddie bellowed.

"I think we better try this somewhere else," Ace said. Tamera was horrible with the pistol. After an hour, Ace decided to try something else.

"Let's go see what other weapons we have, you're not getting anywhere with this one," Ace summed up.

They went into the cavern where they stored the extra weapons. Leo was cleaning some of the guns. "Target practice didn't go so well I see," remarked Leo.

"No," said Ace. "I think the lady needs something lighter than my hand cannon."

"How about this Uzi?" Leo suggested. "It's light. Here, try it." Leo handed the Uzi to Tamera.

"It is a lot lighter," she agreed. "Let me try it out."

Leo gathered up some empty bottles. "Let me set these up and we'll see if you and Mr. Uzi are a match," said Leo. He set up the empties.

Ace stood behind Tamera. "Hold it like this, it's going to spray bullets," said Ace. "Try to control the rise of the gun when it's shooting." Tamera held the gun waist high and squeezed the trigger. The first burst hit the sand, but Tamera controlled the rise of the weapon and burned down the row of bottles. Ace grinned at Leo. "I think we have a winner," he said.

Leo said, "Let me show her how to take this apart, clean it, oil it up, you know. Let her learn her gun, then go back to practicing."

"Yes," said Tamera. "I should know all of this, let's get started."

Ace nodded. "I'll be back later and you can practice your shooting."

Leo spent an hour going over the gun with Tamera. Then Ace took over for another hour. "Now here's the real test," said Ace. The Uzi was disassembled and Tamera was blindfolded. "Now put it back together," Ace ordered. Tamera's hands moved over the parts and within a minute she had the Uzi back together. "Great job," Ace complimented her.

"Ace," she said, "I heard you're going after that bitch who has the captured children."

"Yeah," said Ace, "I made a promise I intend to keep."

"Want some help with that?" Tamera asked. "I know that bitch, Sylvia, and she always hangs back when there is fighting."

"That's good to know. And you're on, I can use your gun," answered Ace.

23

BLINDMAN, SCARECROW and Dog started back to that mountain with enough dynamite to take it down. "Let's bypass our friends Firefly and Hellfire," Blindman said. "I don't want them to know that we ain't in the camp."

"You think they might try something stupid?" Scarecrow asked.

"Not Firefly, but Hellfire just might," answered Blindman.

It took 3 days before they got to where Manny and Juan were. Both brothers were sipping tequila. "Thanks for the refreshments, boss," Juan shouted.

"Cheers, boys, you guys enjoy while I blow up that there mountain," said Blindman.

"You're gonna blow up that mountain," said Manny. "What the fuck brought that on?"

"I figure that will slow them down a lot," said Blindman. "Might even catch some in the pass with their pants down."

"Good luck with that," said Juan. "We'll just stay here and see how it plays out."

"See yas later," said Blindman.

Blindman and Scarecrow scoped out the terrain. Finding a couple of places that would cause a lot of damage, they planted two huge charges of dynamite.

"What do you think, Scarecrow, can you hit these from that ledge we scoped out?"

"Piece of cake, my man, piece of cake," answered Scarecrow.

"Now we just gotta get these clowns movin," said Blindman. "Hey camel fuckers, you lookin for me?" he yelled. "C'mon, you miserable bags of shit, you want a fuckin jihad? Come and get it!"

Black-clad figures began filling the pass. "That's it you dumb fucks, you want those 77 virgins? That just shows how dumb you really are. Better off with ten working girls but you camel fuckers wouldn't know a real woman because you're too busy tossing each other's salad. There ain't no fuckin virgins waiting for you, there ain't no paradise for you baby killers, there ain't gonna be nothing after we kill your worthless asses."

The pass was teeming with fighters shouting obscenities. "Ok, Scarecrow, open this dance," Blindman ordered.

Something slammed into Blindman. "Scarecrow, what the fuck are you...goddamn it." He looked at Scarecrow's severed head, his mouth open in a silent scream. Cal was standing there with a bloody machete. "You fuckin traitorous piece of shit!" Blindman yelled, bringing his shotgun up.

A rifle butt hit Blindman between the eyes. The shotgun discharged, taking Cal's leg off at the knee. Fighters closed in on Blindman, but Dog jumped into the middle of them biting and slashing to keep them off of his friend. A swipe of a claw took an eye out and left the fighter screaming as it dangled on his cheek. A fighter pulled out a pistol and lost his hand at the wrist. Dog's massive jaws ripped flesh from arms and legs. Finally, a fighter scored a hit on Dog. Dog yelped and took off, bleeding from his hip. Bullets buzzed after Dog like angry hornets.

The fighters tied up the unconscious Blindman and dragged him off. Dog tried to follow, but another barrage of gunfire burned his flanks. Dog followed at a respectable distance. Something clicked in his canine brain. He turned and started running at a lope back to the compound.

JUAN AND MANNY HEARD the barrage of gunfire. "Looks like our liquor supply has dried up," muttered Manny.

"Either way, we're dead," said Juan. "I was sorta hopin he'd bring that mountain down on them."

"Well, he didn't," said Juan, taking a gulp of tequila. "So we best get ready for these fucks."

Just then a blood-streaked Dog charged past them. "Could he be going for help?" Manny wondered out loud. "Might be too late for that."

BLINDMAN AWOKE TO THE stinging slaps to his face. He couldn't see at all. A boot to his side cracked two ribs. "Where is your camp?" a voice with very foul breath screamed in his face.

"Fuck you, sand monkey," Blindman croaked.

Hussan punched Blindman in the face. "Every insult you spew will get you more of this," Hussan snarled. "Now, tell me where your camp is."

"Same answer, camel jockey, you fucks blinded me so I can't even draw you a map, not that I would anyway."

"You'll talk," Hussan said, "Get ready to waterboard this infidel."

At that moment Kareem entered the room. "Did you get him to tell you where his camp is?"

"No, Your Excellency, but he will. His government was so fond of waterboarding our brave soldiers that I will do the same to this old dog."

"Do not waste our water supply on this worthless pig," ordered Kareem.

"I had no intention, your excellency, I am going to use these." Hussan held up two half-gallons of Russian Treasure vodka.

Kareem sought out Sylvia. "We captured The Blindman," he told her. "He severely injured our brave Calvin, he's in the infirmary missing a leg."

"Did you find out where his camp is?" Sylvia asked.

"No," answered Kareem. "It seems he went totally blind during his capture. Hussan is trying to extract information from him."

"If we can't make him talk, he is useless to us," Sylvia said.

"Not really," Kareem answered. "We cut off his head, mount it on a pike and let his followers see that he has fallen to Allah."

"Perhaps Hussan will be able to make him talk," said Sylvia, savoring the thought of more victims to play with.

24

DAWN WAS BREAKING WHEN Dog limped into the compound. He sat in the center of it and let out a mournful howl. Apache had been on guard and sounded the alarm.

Nydia was the first to reach Dog. "He's been shot!" she shouted to Leo. "Get Angelo now!!"

Leo ran off to get Angelo. Dog laid on the sand with his head in Nydia's lap. Angelo came running with Sal, Ace, and Leo. "He's been shot," said Nydia. "And where are Blindman and Scarecrow?"

At the mention of Blindman, Dog sat up and howled. Angelo checked his wounds. "He got hit high in his hind leg, but it went through, the rest are just grazes," Angelo said. "I'll clean them up."

Dog rose to his feet and barked at Nydia. "He's trying to tell you something," Leo said.

"Maybe they are alive," said Nydia. Dog took her hand and pulled on it. "He wants me to go with him, I think," she said. Dog started barking again, then ran out a bit and looked back at her.

Nydia stood transfixed for a minute. "I need a bike and weapons," she announced. "I'm going to find them."

"Alone?" Angelo asked.

"Yeah," she replied, "but not alone. I got him."

Apache chimed in. "I'll go with you."

"No," Nydia replied. "You're needed here, they may be using Blindman and Scarecrow to draw us out. "This is personal, I have to know what happened."

"Nydia, Blindman, and Dog were together before we took out The Drunken Master," said Leo. "They have a bond, let her go find him."

"Then take my bike," said Apache. "And I hope you bring them back."

Nydia nodded, then picked up an AK-47. "Dog," Nydia ordered. "Find Blindman." Dog took off and Nydia followed on Apache's bike.

"TALK, DAMN YOU!" HUSSAN screamed at Blindman.

Blindman was shitfaced drunk as he tried to drink the vodka Hussan was using to waterboard him. The two half gallons were gone and Hussan was livid. He slapped Blindman viciously across the face.

"You don't talk now, you die tomorrow!" Hussan screamed into Blindman's face.

"Go brush your teeth, camel fucker," Blindman slurred. "You got the zacklies, your breath smells ex zackly like your ass."

Hussan punched and kicked Blindman until he was panting from exertion. "You die tomorrow, old man." Hussan shouted as he left the room.

"Good thing I'm drunk or all that might have hurt," muttered Blindman. "What the fuck, now I really can't see a damn thing. I hope I killed that fuckin Cal, I really do. Hope Dog got away, fuck this shit to hell goddammit, had to fuck up my eyes so now I'm fuckin done and I can't fight back. Next bastard that comes near me, I'm gonna make him kill me, I..." Blindman felt a hand on his shoulder.

"Listen to me," a faintly accented voice said. "I can get you out of here, but you have to take me with you."

"Who the fuck are you?" Blindman muttered.

"I'm a doctor, my name is Patel. These savages keep me alive to treat them when they are wounded."

"You ain't part of this bunch?" Blindman asked.

"No, not in any way. They stormed my clinic, killed everyone but me. I hate them. When they conquer your people, they will get rid of me," Patel said.

"Hate to tell you Doc, but even if you walk me out of here, I can't see to find the way back to anything," said Blindman.

"I can fix your eyes. Well, at least one of them," Patel said.

"How?" asked Blindman.

"I can cut out one of those cataracts as I have one lens that I can put into your eye."

"You're serious?" asked Blindman.

"It's risky, but what choice do you have?" answered Patel.

"Not much," muttered Blindman.

"We have to act now," said Patel. "I'll do the surgery, then get us out of here. We will have to hide out for a couple of days, then I'll take the bandages off. You will have one good eye."

"Let's do it then," said Blindman. Being that a blind man is not a threat, no guards were posted.

Patel helped Blindman to his clinic. "You have a lot of alcohol in your system," said Patel. "I'll numb your eye. You have to lie very still, do you understand?"

"Yeah," said Blindman. "Go for it."

Patel was very good. Thirty minutes later he was finished. "Now we must go while the darkness is still our friend," said Patel. He got Blindman to his feet.

"Wait up a minute." Blindman asked, "The guy who brought me in, that redneck, is he here?"

"Yes," said Patel, "but we don't have ..."

"Take me to him," Blindman barked. Patel steered Blindman over to Cal's bed. Blindman grabbed Cal's face. Cal awoke with a start. Blindman's hand clamped his mouth shut. "Remember me, hillbilly bitch? This is for Scarecrow." Blindman twisted Cal's head until his neck broke with a dry snap.

Patel looked on in horror. "He pissed me off," said Blindman. "That's what happens when you piss me off."

25

BLADE WAS SHOWING LEE some of the finer points of knife fighting. "It's all in the balance," he told her as he put a knife though an ace of spades they were using as a target. Lee matched Blade as her knife hit right next to his.

"You're a quick learner, Mama. If I was a bettin man I'd…"

Blade was interrupted by one of the bikers, Denny. "Hey man, Sal and Leo just called a meetin, looks like it's gonna go down."

"Shit," muttered Blade. "We're coming."

There were too many to crowd into the bar, so they all stood in front of it. Sal opened the dance. "With Blindman, Scarecrow and now Nydia gone, we have to assume the worst. They'll be coming at us, so we best get ready. Lobo and Denny, you guys said you do the snakes, right?"

"Damn right," snarled Lobo. "Give us the map, we'll leave at daybreak. Me and Denny will wait until they come out of their holes, then we'll fuck with 'em."

"Ok," said Sal, "but tip off that fire guy on your way, just so he's not sleeping at the switch."

"Done," said Denny. "He'll recognize the cut."

"Ace," Sal said. "You still set on trying to find those kids?"

"I gave my word, Sal. You of all people know what that means."

"Yes," Sal said solemnly. "I do. I'd suggest you get out and come in from behind them. It's a cinch they won't be dragging kids with the fighters."

"They could use them as shields," Apache chimed in. "They are that low."

"I wouldn't put anything past them either, but they think we are demoralized without Blindman," said Sal. "They think this will be easy."

Eddie smacked the bat in his hand. "Fuckers will bleed for every inch of ground they take."

"Angelo and Goldstein will man the catapult," Sal said. "If they can keep dropping all kinds of hell on them, we should be able to cut a lot of them down. Eddie and I will be in that building on the right. Blade, you and The

Shotgun Girls take the one on the left so we get them in a crossfire. Leo, you got The Last Chance and that is our last line of defense."

"Right," said Leo, "but I'm rigging my place with some of that dynamite we have left. If we get overrun, I'm blowing the place up."

"Apache and his guys will play hit and run with the TEC-9s," said Sal.

"Everyone else find cover and get ready to fight. Remember, they have no mercy, so we should have less. Burn every one of these bastards down." A cheer went up after that statement.

NYDIA WAS CLOSE TO the pass when the bike sputtered to a halt. "Goddamn fuckin piece of shit," she snarled, beating her fists on the handlebars.

Dog grasped her hand in his mouth and started pulling her. "Alright, I'm coming," she said. She followed Dog up a small trail and found what was left of Scarecrow. "No," she moaned. "Fuck no."

A few days in the sun had dried out the corpse. "Bastards just left you here," she muttered, sobbing a little. "They musta got Blindman too." She started scooping out a trench in the sand. "At least I'll give you a decent burial," she said. Dog trotted over and started digging furiously, then backed off, barking furiously.

"What the hell got you so riled up now?" she asked. She looked where he was digging and saw a metal tube. Pulling it out of the sand, she recognized Scarecrow's Sharps. "They just left this here," she muttered in surprise.

Nydia rooted around in the sand and found the bag of shells. "I'll just take this with me, maybe I'll blow some big holes in some assholes," she said.

Dog had been sniffing the ground, but all of a sudden the hair stood up on his back. He stood looking toward part of the mountain, then his tail started wagging. Nydia strained her eyes, but could not see what Dog was seeing. Then she remembered that the Sharps had a scope on it. She picked up the rifle and looked through the scope, then gasped. Two men were on a narrow ledge. A slightly built smaller man was helping a larger man whose face was heavily bandaged. The Blindman.

"He's alive," she said, starting to tear up.

PATEL HAD HIDDEN BLINDMAN in a cave for two days. Blindman got some of his strength back and decided to try and make it back to the compound. With all of his injuries and no liquor to dull his pain, it was slow going. Blindman was leaning heavily on Patel. Patel stopped suddenly.

"There's a wolf coming this way," he said, fear in his voice.

"Shit," said Blindman. "Stop and don't move. No, fuck that, get behind me. Dog!" Blindman yelled. Dog stopped in front of him. "Stay behind me, Patel," said Blindman. "He don't know you from the others."

Blindman held out his hand, Dog trotted up and licked it. Seeing Patel, a low growl came from Dog's throat. "No, Dog," Blindman ordered. "He's a friend."

"He better be, you old bastard, or he's history."

Nydia rushed up and threw her arms around him. "I thought I lost you," she said.

"Close, but no seegar," Blindman said. "Scarecrow's brother-in-law ambushed us.

"I just buried him," she said. "They just left him to rot in the sun."

"Scumbags," muttered Blindman. "They fucked me up, I went totally blind. This fella here is Doctor Patel. He fixed one eye, but I won't know how good until I take these bandages off."

"You're really a doctor?" asked Nydia.

"Yes," replied Patel. "I was their prisoner, too."

"Did you really fix his eye?" asked Nydia.

"Yes, it should be fine in a day or so."

"We have to get back to the others," said Nydia. "I had Apache's bike, but it crapped out on me."

"We'll hoof it," Blindman said. "With these busted ribs it's going to be a slow walk unless..." A loud chanting cut off further conversation.

Nydia looked toward the pass. "They are on the move. Jesus, it looks like ants streaming out of a nest. Damn, I wish I could shoot this rifle."

"What rifle?" asked Blindman.

"I found Scarecrow's Sharps," answered Nydia.

"Any ammo?" asked Blindman.

"Yeah," said Nydia. "Got a bag of bullets."

"Doc," snapped Blindman. "Get these bandages off me."

"It's too soon," said Patel. "Your eye may not have healed."

"Right now I don't give a shit," said Blindman. "We got to slow these fuckers down and I know how to do it." Patel reluctantly started removing the bandages. Blindman's eyes were shut. He slowly opened them. One eye was hazel green, the other clouded over. "Damn, Doc, you done good. I can see," complimented Blindman. "Give me that rifle."

Nydia handed Blindman the Sharps. Blindman sighted through the scope and muttered "You pricks want to go to paradise, allow me to send you there." The Sharps barked once and a huge explosion brought half the mountain down on the black-clad jihadists.

"Holy crap," said Nydia.

"Not done yet," said Blindman. He fired the Sharps again and more of the mountain buried the fighters. "Too many got out," he groused. "Let's get outta here, we're gonna have to fight our way back."

Dog led the way off of the mountain. It was slow going because Blindman was in extreme pain from the beatings he received. "No one thought to bring any liquor," Blindman muttered disgustedly.

"I was more concerned about saving your old ass," said Nydia.

Dog came to a halt and started sniffing the ground. "Now what the hell does he smell?" asked Blindman. The question went unanswered as the ground gave way and all were plunged into darkness.

LOBO AND DENNY HEARD a huge explosion and saw clouds of dust rise into the air. "I do believe that The Blindman has risen from the dead," said Lobo.

"Now for some payback," snarled Denny. "Let's ride."

Manny was on the verge of nodding out when the earth shook him awake. "I'd say The Blindman just started the war," Juan announced.

"Good timing because the tequila is almost gone." Manny squinted as he looked into the distance. He saw a horde of black-clad figures fast approaching.

"Here they come," said Juan, finishing off the last bottle. "Viva la Raza."

The two brothers stood shoulder to shoulder, the AK-47's spitting death into the horde of jihadists. Blood spurting fighters lay dead or dying as the brothers mowed them down. Finally the ammo ran out and they were overrun. It was hand to hand. The brothers took hits, but kept on smashing skulls with the empty guns. Juan grabbed a fighter and broke his back over his knee. Manny was throttling a fighter before a huge knife cleaved his skull in two. Juan grabbed his brother's killer and gutted him with the same knife. Another swing of the blade took an arm off. Juan was holding a guy by the throat when the fighters surrounded him. Using the guy for a shield didn't help as Juan was shot to pieces.

Hussan arrived to view the carnage. At least thirty or more jihadists lay dead or dying. "Two men did all this," muttered Hussan. Doubt entered his mind, as well as a chilling vision of a fiery demon.

26

DENNY AND LOBO WAITED until a group of jihadists passed their position. They fell in behind them and opened up with the TEC-9s. Bullets cut the fighters down like a scythe. The two bikers blasted past the fighters. Screaming curses, the fighters charged after the bikers.

"Getting close to the snake den!" Lobo shouted over the roar of bikes and gunfire. "Time to jump."

The two bikes went over a dune and were airborne. The jihadists scrambled over the dune and the ground collapsed. A very loud buzzing started as the rattlesnakes poured out of the den, biting anything in reach. Jihadists opened fire on the snakes, but it was too late. The snakes covered the fighters, pumping their venom into their bodies.

"Die, motherfuckers!" Lobo shouted. Lobo kept raining curses on the fighters, but one got clear of the snakes and got off a shot. Lobo flipped off his bike, shot though the head. Screaming obscenities, Denny cut the fighter's legs out from under him. Snakes slithered after the fighter and started striking him. Full of poison, the fighter's face turned a dark shade of purple before he died twitching on the sands.

Lobo lay on the sand, brains leaking out of the side of his head. Denny looked down at him. "Sorry, Bro. I'll come back and plant you if I live though this." Denny turned his bike back toward the compound.

BLINDMAN WOKE UP IN a world of hurt. Dog limped over, grabbing his hand and tugging it. Blindman stood up and saw that Patel and Nydia were buried under a pile of debris. Blindman and Dog dug them out. "Any broken bones?" he asked.

Nydia and Patel were banged up, but no broken bones. "What the hell happened?" asked Nydia.

"I don't know, seems the ground just caved in," said Blindman. "At least there ain't any fuckin snakes this time."

"Look here," said Patel. "These are walls. Walls built out of cinder blocks."

Blindman and Nydia looked at what he was talking about. "Yeah, for a fact someone built this." Further down the wall was a tunnel. "Well," said Blindman. "It may be a way outta here."

"Then let's check it out," said Nydia. The group walked slowly down the tunnel.

"You smell that?" Blindman asked Nydia.

"Smell what?" she replied.

"Gun oil, gun grease, cosmoline," he said.

Nydia sniffed the air. "I do smell something chemically," she said.

"Yeah," said Blindman. "It's getting stronger." They followed the tunnel in almost total darkness. The tunnel ended in a huge, cavernous area.

"Now what the hell is this?" Blindman ran his hand over something. "Anyone have a match, a light? Nydia, you smoke, you gotta have something."

"Let me see if I have a lighter." Nydia fished though her pockets and came up with an old Bic lighter. "Here," she said, handing the lighter to Blindman.

Blindman flicked the lighter and said "Well I'll be damned, it's a fuckin jeep."

Just then the area was flooded with a bright light. A voice shouted, "Turn, I'll kill you!"

Blindman, Nydia, and Patel froze like statues. "We ain't looking for trouble," Blindman said. They heard footsteps behind them.

A man in an ill-fitting uniform faced them. He was a military man, sergeant stripes were on his uniform. His eyes were sunken into his face and were bloodshot. It was obvious he had been drinking. He held a .45 automatic in his hand. "So if you're not looking for trouble, what the hell are you looking for? the man asked.

"Help," replied Blindman.

"Why do you need help?" the man asked, looking confused.

Blindman was trying to think quickly. "Because our country has been invaded.

"What do you mean 'invaded'? No one invades the United States of America," the man asked, with some heat in his voice.

Blindman studied the man. "Who are you?" he asked.

"Gunnery Sergeant Frank Monroe," he answered. "I'll ask you again. Invaded by who?"

"Terrorists," said Blindman. "A whole army of them. We have a group of true Americans back in the hills that will fight them to the death. These bastards have slaughtered innocent people and they have to be stopped."

Blindman noticed the Sergeant had blank look on his face. "Sergeant," Blindman snapped, "What are your orders?"

"My orders," muttered the Sergeant, "are to secure and defend this depot."

"What about defending your country, aren't you supposed to defend that too?" asked Blindman.

"Yes," said the Sergeant. "It's my sworn duty."

"Then you gotta help us." Blindman summed up.

"You're right," said the Sergeant. "What do you need?"

"I need a damn drink right now, do you have any liquor?"

"Sure," said the Sergeant. "Follow me."

They were led to what had been the Officer's Club. Blindman helped himself to a bottle of Maker's Mark. "That hit the spot," he said, as a warm glow spread though his body. "Sarge," he asked, "any of this old shit you have here actually work?"

"Most of it," said Sarge. "The jeep is in fine shape and the guns are all good."

"What's the biggest gun you have here?" asked Blindman.

"I have an operational 50-caliber machine gun," Sarge said, almost proudly.

"Well, that just gives me a wonderful idea," said Blindman. "Let's mount that sucker on the jeep and go on our own jihad. How are you fixed for fuel?" Blindman asked.

"The gas I have is stable," Sarge said.

"Well then," said Blindman, "let's fix up this hotrod and get ready to rock and roll. Any chance you might have a shotgun around here?"

"You lost your sawed-off?" Nydia asked.

"I didn't 'lose' anything, those fucks took everything I had. The sawed-off, the Remington, even Blackjack's .45." summed up Blindman.

"There's a double barreled 12-gauge fowling piece back here," said Sarge. "The Colonel stationed here liked to duck hunt."

"Lemme see it," Blindman asked. It was a magnificent gun with long barrels. "I'll have to cut it down a bit," muttered Blindman.

"Here's a couple boxes of shells," Sarge said, putting them on the bar.

"Birdshot," said Blindman. "I'll have to modify them bit."

27

BLINDMAN WENT LOOKING for a hacksaw. "What did he mean by 'modify' the shells?" Patel asked Nydia.

"Well, little pellets aren't going to hurt anyone," she answered. "He'll put screws, nails, coins, broken glass, just about anything that will kill in them. The results are pretty nasty."

Blindman returned. "I'm going where the tools are, I found a vise I can use to hold this while I cut 'er down to size," he said. Sarge, can you mount that 50-caliber on the jeep? Nydia and Patel will help you."

Sarge shook his head like he was clearing out the cobwebs. "Yes, Sir," he said. "I'll get right on it."

The three went off to mount the gun. Blindman cut the shotgun down to a two-foot length. He took a file to the rough edges. He looked at the finished product. "Might be better than the old one," he muttered.

Now he went to work on the shells. There were two dozen. He cut them open and dumped out the birdshot. He found a box of #2 sheet metal screws. "These will work," he said. He filled about a dozen shells with the screws. "Now what else do we have that will make a mess?" He found two sparkplugs, some roofing nails, and a roll of barbed wire. "This will do," he said to himself, then went to work.

Sarge managed to mount the huge gun on the jeep. He fed an ammo belt into it, then loaded some more cans of ammo on the jeep.

Patel and Nydia went exploring. Patel called Nydia. "I found something I think will be useful," he said.

"What is it?" Nydia asked.

"A case of grenades," answered Patel. "It says 'firefrag' on the case."

"They are like mini claymore mines," said Sarge. "Very effective at close quarters."

Blindman caught the tail end of the conversation. "Load 'em on the jeep," he said. "Now let's get going."

"Why not?" Nydia replied.

HUSSAN AND HIS MEN reached the snake den. Over 50 fighters lay dead on the sand, snakes still slithering over the poison bloated corpses. "This can't be," muttered Hussan.

Kareem and his Honor Guard arrived. "I see we are making progress," he said to Hussan.

"Progress?" gasped an astonished Hussan. "Almost 100 dead believers and you call that progress?"

"Sacrifices must be made to earn our places in paradise," Kareem told him.

"These aren't sacrifices," Hussan barked with considerable heat in his voice. "They are slaughtering us like we have been slaughtering them."

"You doubt the word of Allah?" Kareem screamed, frothing at the mouth.

"No!" shouted back Hussan. "I doubt your word."

Kareem exploded. "For that, I will make an example of you after we dispose of our enemies!" he screamed, then stormed off.

"I seriously doubt there will be any of us around to make examples of, shortly," Hussan muttered in disgust.

BLINDMAN ROUNDED UP a few more guns to add to the arsenal in the jeep. "Ok, Sarge, get us out of here." Sarge went to a panel and flipped a switch. A loud groaning was heard as part of the wall opened up. Sarge started the jeep and they roared out into the desert.

Blindman surveyed his handiwork. "Looks like I brought the mountain down on a bunch of them," he said. "But a lot of them got out, and we got to kill them."

They reached the first line of defense and saw the carnage. Blindman found the two brothers under a pile of dead jihadists. "They went out with both barrels blazing," he said sadly. "I ain't gonna leave them to rot out here. Help me drag them over to where that ledge is jutting out." The group muscled the bodies under underneath. Blindman took a grenade and tossed it on the ledge. The explosion brought a rockslide down, covering the bodies.

"Best I can do for yas," muttered Blindman.

Moving out, the next thing they came across was the snake den. Patel turned to Blindman with a horrified look on his face "Snakes?" he asked.

"Yeah," answered Blindman. "I don't get it either, but I'd say they came in pretty handy."

"Look," said Nydia. "There's a bike and a body over there."

"Shit," said Blindman. "Let's see who it is." The jeep pulled up to a sprawled-out body. "Damn it, they got Lobo," he snarled. "I'm not leaving him here." He got a blanket and wrapped up the body.

"Nydia, can you ride that bike?" Blindman asked.

"Yeah," she replied. "I rode Apache's bike out here."

"See if it starts," asked Blindman. Nydia righted the bike and hit the starter. The engine roared to life. "Ok," said Blindman. "Let's change up a little. We are hitting them from the rear. If you can keep a cover fire on me, I can do a shitload of damage."

"Consider it done," said Nydia.

HELLFIRE WAS PACING back and forth in front of his 'church'. He had heard the two explosions and the gunfire. He squinted in the harsh sunlight as he saw the jihadists in the distance. "Ants," he muttered. "They look like ants pouring out of an anthill. Sister," he ordered, "better gird your loins for battle."

That got him a weird look from Sister. She was sitting in a window with two AK-47's and banana clips full of ammo. Hellfire started praying "Our father, who art in heaven, hallowed be thy name. Thy kingdom come, thy will be done, shoot these godless cocksuckers!" he yelled. Sister's AK chattered its death song, taking down five fighters.

Hellfire stood up, blasting the fighters with loads of buck shot. One jihadist jumped into the window, knocking the sister on her fat ass. She shoved the AK into his crotch and pulled the trigger. Blood blew back on her face. A bullet hit her in the back, she turned and shot that fighter in the head. They were being overrun. One AK empty, she grabbed the other gun as two slugs bored into her gut. Screaming for Hellfire, she sat against the wall. She blasted the fighters crawling through the window until the gun was empty. She reached for another clip and a fighter cut her hand off. She tried to stand up, but a blade cleaved her head down to her chin. Hellfire was behind a concrete wall blasting away with the shotguns. One of the jihadists tossed a stick of dynamite over the wall. It went over the wall and onto what composed the roof of the church. Hellfire's church came crashing down on him.

28

NIGHT WAS FALLING AND Firefly had heard the shooting and explosions. "Time to feed the beast," he said, finishing off the bottle of vodka. With a twisted grin on his face, he opened the valve on the tanker. "You'll will feast tonight, my friend," he chuckled. He watched the raw gasoline pour down the hillside and form a huge pool at the base of the hill.

Hussan, leading the jihadists, smelled the fuel. One of his men ran back to him. "There must be some kind of fuel leak."

Hussan yelled at him, "Pull the men back! It's a..." A loud whooshing sound killed that thought as Firefly tossed a lit book of matches into the gasoline.

The fire roared down the hill and the pool erupted in a huge ball of flame. Fighters became human torches. Firefly laughed insanely, but that drew him unwanted attention. The fighters that had pulled back peppered the area with bullets. Firefly caught a slug at his beltline. He screamed and doubled over in agony. "No," he screamed, "not this way!"

He staggered to the tanker. "Bastards always wanted the beast." He spit out blood. "Now they can have her." He picked up a hammer and hit the valve, gas gushed though the opening . Firefly had tied the hood of a car over the back of the tanker to camouflage it. Bleeding profusely, he crawled on top of the tanker and cut the ropes. The hood shifted and fell into the flaming river with Firefly still holding the ropes. Flaming droplets of gas hit Firefly, but he was enraged and beyond pain. He surfed the hood though the flames, a human torch, screaming his rage as the flames consumed him.

HUSSAN WAS TRYING TO rally his men when he heard screaming. He turned as Firefly jumped and crashed into him, locking his arms in a death grip on Hussan. Hussan screamed as his nightmare of a fiery demon came to fruition. Firefly turned him into a heap of charred flesh that barely resembled a human being. The tanker erupted into a huge fireball, illuminating the area.

THAT EXPLOSION HAD everyone in the compound up and running. Sal found Angelo and Leo. "I think our roadblocks are all used up," Sal said.

Leo looked at the fires in the distance. "I'd be a fool to think that blast got all of them," said Leo. "We better get ready, odds are they be knocking at our door come daybreak."

SYLVIA STORMED UP TO a shaken Kareem. "Where is Hussan?" she asked.

"Dead," Kareem muttered. "He's dead."

"Why aren't we attacking, why are you holding back?" she snarled.

"Because half of our force was incinerated," he shot back. "This isn't working."

"Allah will help us prevail over these unbelievers," Sylvia said.

"You honestly believe that crap?" spat Kareem.

"Blasphemer!" she yelled in his face.

"Fuck you, Sylvia, all this Allah crap is a means to an end and you know it. We like dominating people, we like rape and torture and we like to kill. Then the ultimate evil—we ate the flesh of who we killed. There are no 77 virgins, no rewards, no paradise, no nothing."

"You will die for those words, Kareem, you turned your back on your faith!" she screamed.

"No," said Kareem softly. "I'll die, but only because I underestimated who I was fighting."

"Order them to attack," Sylvia ordered.

"I will," said Kareem softly. "Now go back to your 'charges' so you're out of the line of fire as usual."

Sylvia fumed. "You can't talk to ..."

"Get out of my sight!" Kareem roared. Sylvia slunk off, muttering dire threats.

Kareem figured he had about a couple of hundred jihadists left. Other than a full-frontal attack, there was no other way to storm the compound. Kareem rallied his troops. "Time to rid the world of these infidels and claim our rightful place with Allah in paradise!" he yelled. "We will have our final victory! We will kill the men, make whores of the women, and leave no trace of their foul existence on this earth," he proclaimed.

A cheer went up and the jihadists poured into the pass and discovered hell, not paradise.

ANGELO HAD GOLDSTEIN muscle an old truck engine into the catapult. Angelo calculated the distance. "Incoming!" he yelled, as the catapult let go with a loud twang.

The engine hit the jihadists at chest level, boring though the mass of fighters. "Sweet," Eddie commented.

"Here they come!" yelled Sal. Bullets filled the air like angry hornets. Small battles were breaking out as the jihadists scattered though the pass.

Ace had snorted a pile of PCP and his eyes were bugging out of his head. "Fuck this," he said to Tamera. "I'm going after the kids."

About a dozen jihadists had held back. Ace walked up to them. "Looking for me, boys?" he yelled. Startled, the fighters froze for a second. That's all it took. Ace's hands were a blur as he drew the two Glocks and went to work. Ace was hit high and low, but kept on shooting until the jihadists were down and dead on the sands.

"You're hit!" Tamera cried.

"Don't matter, I'm done any way you look at it. I've been pissing and coughing up blood for the last two days," he snarled. "I know I won't last too much longer. Let's find those kids," he gasped.

Tamera and Ace ran past the bodies. As they turned a corner a shot rang out and Tamera dropped to the ground, shot in the leg.

Sylvia stood with a little girl as a shield. "Drop those guns or I kill her," Sylvia snarled. She shoved the gun against the girl's head, burning her with the barrel. The girl cried in pain and Ace's hand was a blur. Sylvia's knee exploded in a shower of blood, bone and cartilage. Screaming in agony, she let go of the girl and fell. The girl ran to Ace.

Sylvia tried to pick up her gun and a shot from Ace mangled her hand. "Go back with the others, honey," he said to the girl. "You don't need to see this." Ace waited until the girl was out of sight, then stuck the barrel of one of the Glocks in Sylvia's forehead, burning her.

"You won't last the day," she snarled. "I'll see you in hell!"

"Good!" Ace shouted in her face. "Then we can do this all over again, bitch." Ace blew her head off.

Ace staggered back to Tamera. One of the older boys had tried to bandage her leg. Ace had been shot four times, he was dead on his feet. Shouts came from close by. "Great," he muttered. "More of them."

Ace reloaded the Glocks, he then checked his six-shooters. "I have 48 rounds," he said to Tamera. "You stay here with the kids, anyone comes around the bend you don't know, start shootin."

"Ace, maybe I can..."

"No," he interrupted Tamera. "You can't. One favor I'll ask," Ace said, "give these six shooters to someone who can use them." He gave her a cocky salute, then drew his guns. He stepped out and faced the oncoming jihadists.

Ace blasted his way into Valhalla. The carnage was horrific. Heads exploded with every shot Ace fired. Bullets tore through him, but he just kept on coming. The Glocks empty, he dropped to his knees and pulled the six-shooters, loaded with Sal's dum dums. Bodies were blown apart. Covered in gore, Ace smiled and dropped to the ground dead.

29

THE JIHADISTS SPLIT their forces, attacking the defenders of the compound. Angelo and Goldstein filled the catapult with large rocks and sent them flying into the oncoming horde. "Let's give 'em something to think about!" Angelo yelled to Goldstein.

Goldstein dragged out something he and Angelo built. It was part of a telephone pole studded with spikes. He lifted it into the catapult, but a slug clipped his leg. "I'm ok!" he shouted. "Let 'er go."

The catapult let go with a loud twang. The spiked pole spun though the mass of fighters like a deranged top, impaling some and tearing though others.

More jihadists poured into the compound. "They will overrun us!" Angelo shouted.

"Not before we do this!" Goldstein yelled back. He struggled to put a keg of nails into the catapult. The keg had a stick of dynamite in it. It sailed toward the jihadists, then exploded in midair. The shrapnel decimated about a dozen fighters. Fighters ran to one side of the compound and plunged into the pits of punji stakes. A stray bullet caught Angelo in the side. Goldstein threw him over his shoulder and staggered toward The Last Chance.

Apache and his crew hit the jihadists, flanking them. The TEC-9s chattered, spitting death into the fighters. Deke got too close to one fighter and was decapitated by a machete. Jones blasted that fighter to pieces.

A bullet tore through Jones's knee. "I'm hit bad!" he yelled.

"Go back to the bar!" yelled Apache. A bullet slammed into Apache's back, knocking him off the bike. Denny shot by and picked him up. "All of us get back to the bar," Apache groaned. "This hit and run ain't working, there's too many of them." The remaining bikers took off toward the bar.

"This place is getting crowded," said Leo as the bikers limped in. A shaken Apache was propped up by Denny at the bar. "How bad?" asked Leo.

"Bullet's still in me," Apache groaned. "There's too many of them, Leo. We're fucked."

"Angelo, Goldstein, and you are wounded," said Leo. "Others are still out there."

"If they are even alive," said Denny. "Everything is shot up."

Leo had a detonator. "We keep fighting," Leo told the group. "If it looks like we will be overrun, I'll blow this whole place up when they storm us."

Leo addressed the group that were bad shots, older men and some women. "You people just grab guns, stick them out the windows and try to shoot anyone you see," he ordered. "They are not taking us alive." Everyone realized that death was better than falling into the hands of the jihadists. Faces were grim as people took up defensive positions in The Last Chance.

Sal and Eddie had beaten back the jihadists from their position. But the jihadists just kept on coming. Sal had made a few dum dums of his own. Picking his spots, he blasted one jihadist after another. The exploding bullets tore huge holes though anything they hit. Bullets peppered the building. Sal was hit and thrown back.

"Nooooo!" Eddie yelled. He emptied his gun into the onrushing fighters. Standing over the prone body of the man he was sworn to protect, Eddie grabbed his bat and swung for the fences. Heads exploded like overripe pumpkins. Blood, bone and copious amounts of grey matter decorated the walls as the steel covered bat shattered skulls.

"It's the bottom of the ninth!" screamed Eddie. "The bases are loaded, he swings, he hits! And the crowd goes wild!" Another head caved in. Eddie stood panting, covered with blood. A shot rang out and blood gushed from Eddie's head. He fell over Sal's body and lay still.

Blade, Lee, and The Shotgun Girls poured lead into the oncoming jihadists. "Too fuckin many of them!" Blade shouted.

"We should get back to the bar," Lee said.

"You're right," said Blade. "Let the ladies go first, we'll cover them." Blade and Lee laid down a withering cover fire. The girls took off, but a bullet clipped one in the back. She staggered and fell. The other girls dragged her off.

"C'mon Lee!" Blade yelled. "Let's get outta here!" He was knocked over as the door was kicked open. A huge fighter rammed a knife into Blade's back. Lee turned to catch a fist to the jaw and fell back unconscious.

Blade woke up in a world of pain. The knife had gone through a kidney, nicked his liver and mangled his insides. Through a red haze, he saw one fighter raping Lee. Rage fueled Blade as he staggered to his feet. The one fighter got off of Lee's prone body.

"Her pussy is really tight," he said grinning.

The huge man who had stabbed Blade pulled out his knife and said, "I'll open it up a little."

Blade slammed into them, his life leaking out on the dirty floor. Blade's knife cut into the small of the fighter's back and he sawed upward, cutting through ribs and hitting the heart. The huge fighter got off a shot that hit Blade in the chest.

Lee had come to long enough to grab a broken bottle. When the guy shot Blade, she shoved the bottle into his crotch. Blood poured from the hideous wound. The fighter lay on the ground screaming.

Lee crawled over to Blade, who was gone, eyes staring at nothing. She took the knife out of his hand and went back to the screaming fighter. She cut his cock off and stuck it in his screaming mouth. She stood back impassively and watched him choke to death.

30

THE JIHADISTS HAD THE Last Chance surrounded. Using the boulders for cover, they poured bullets into the bar. "We're fucked!" yelled Leo, as a man shooting out a window caught a bullet in the face.

"Keep fighting" Apache groaned. "Let's not make it easy for them."

BLINDMAN WAS ABOUT a mile away. "Pour it on, Sarge!" he yelled. The jeep entered the pass and Blindman sized up the situation. "Fuckers are behind those boulders, damn it." He thought for a minute. "Nydia, you go to the left, I'll go to the right," he ordered.

"What the hell is that gonna do? They have great cover," she shot back.

"Don't shoot at them, shoot behind them at the rock walls. You'll get it."

Nydia thought about it, then smiled. "I get it," she yelled.

"Doc," ordered Blindman, "once we get though the pass, start tossing those grenades behind us." Frightened out of his wits, Patel nodded in agreement.

Nydia and Blindman roared through the pass. Blindman aimed the machine gun at the walls behind the jihadists. Bullets hit the walls, ricocheted off them and became misshapen hunks of lead that tore through the jihadists.

Patel started tossing grenades behind the jeep as it roared through the compound. Blasts of firefrag shrapnel shredded the jihadists' bodies into piles of raw meat.

Jihadists left their cover and were shot down by the crew in The Last Chance. Nydia took a round in the front tire and went sailing off the bike. A fighter stood in front of the oncoming jeep and shot Sarge in the head. His blood and brains splattered Patel.

Thinking fast, Blindman abandoned the gun, pushed Sarge's body out of the jeep, and ran over the shooter, then backed over him again.

He drove over to Nydia, who was slowly getting to her feet. "You ok?" he asked.

"Yeah, nothing broken," she replied, spitting out some sand.

"Good," he said. "Now get in and drive this thing so I can mop up these assholes."

TAMERA STAYED HIDDEN, guarding the kids, as the battle raged on. A voice yelled out, "Put that gun down, bitch!"

Tamera looked up to see a black-clad figure standing on the rock outcropping above her. "Well looky here," he said. Tamera recognized him as one of her rapists. "Now drop that gun, drop those panties and let's get reacquainted," he snarled, rubbing his crotch. "Then I'll sample some of that young stuff while you..."

A brown blur knocked the man off the ledge. Dog rode the man to the ground with the guy's head in his mouth. Dog twisted the man's head until his neck snapped with a loud crack. Dog picked up the dropped AK-47 in his mouth, walked over to the oldest boy, and dropped the gun at his feet.

Tamera looked at the blood splattered cur and said, "More trouble?" Dog just wagged his tail.

One of the boys said to Tamera. "They have those psycho child soldiers and they weren't in the main attack."

Tamera thought for a minute. "Yes, those filthy little murdering bastards, you're right. Where the hell are they?" Dog started growling. "Someone is coming," she muttered.

A group of small, black-clad figures started moving toward them. Dog crouched, ready to attack. Tamera held her Uzi, but couldn't bring herself to fire on the group. "I can't shoot a child," she said in a hollow voice.

"They are not children, they are monsters!" one girl screamed. She grabbed the Uzi out of Tamera's hands and fired into the group. The boy picked up the AK-47 and did likewise. Guns empty, the kids grabbed rocks and sticks and beat the remaining fighters to death.

Dog started barking and running back and forth. "We should follow him," Tamera said. "I think it's over."

BLINDMAN WAS PLAYING havoc with the machine gun. Driven out of cover, the jihadists were blasted to bloody rags. The so-called Army of Allah was decimated.

Those in The Last Chance that were still able to walk joined the fight outside. Leo shot a running jihadist in the back. Marty had his bike up and running and was gunning down any jihadist left. Lee and the Shotgun Girl walked through the carnage, executing wounded fighters with a bullet to the head. Gun smoke hovered in the air like a thick fog. Within a few minutes not one jihadist was left alive.

Tamera limped into the compound with Dog leading the kids.

Blindman stepped out of the jeep. "Looks like it's over," he said.

"We thought you were dead," Leo said.

"For a while, it was even money," said Blindman. "Doctor Patel here fixed my eyes and got me out."

"You're a real doctor?" Leo asked.

"Yes," said Patel. "I am."

"We have a lot of wounded folks, Doc. Can you help?"

"Most certainly," said Patel. "Take me to them." Leo took Patel to treat the wounded.

Blindman looked around the compound. "We lost a lot, didn't we?" he said softly.

"Ace is dead," said Tamera. "He saved the kids and went out shooting. He said to find a home for these." She handed Blindman Ace's guns. "I think he was meaning give them to you," she finished.

Blindman took the weapons. "Thanks," said a choked up Blindman. "I'll take good care of them.

"Everyone who tried to stop them is gone," Blindman said. "We knew we'd take hits, we knew some of those people out in the front would die. But damn, this was a slaughter."

"Mr. Blade is dead," Lee said. "He save my life."

"How about Sal and Eddie?" Blindman asked.

"Not sure," said Leo. "Everyone out in the front got overrun. Let's go look for the... I don't believe this shit. The *balls* of this cocksucker!"

Everyone looked where Leo was looking. A figure walked toward them, waving a white flag. "Kareem," Blindman spit out the name. "Their fuckin leader."

"I come with peaceful intentions," Kareem yelled. Leo, Nydia, Lee and The Blindman walked toward Kareem, tombstones in their eyes.

"I surrender and expect to be treated properly according to the articles of war," announced Kareem.

"Well, do tell," snarled Blindman.

At that moment Patel ran up to the group. "Some of these men are gravely injured, I'll need... You!!" Patel exclaimed upon seeing Kareem.

"Yes, brother Patel, I'm so glad to see that..."

Patel busted Kareem in the mouth, knocking out a piece of bridgework. "You're an abomination!" Patel screamed in his face, "And never call me your brother!" Patel hit him again.

Blindman pulled him away from Kareem, "Ok, Doc, you got your licks in. We'll take care of this prick."

"Keep that barbarian away from me," Kareem spit blood from his ruined mouth.

"He's gonna be the least of your problems before we send you to Allah, your so-called god," said Blindman.

"If things were reversed," Kareem said, "you would have been doing what we did."

"Killing for the sake of killing, rape, torture, perversion and cannibalism?" yelled Blindman. "Your religion is as big a joke as you are."

"No," said Kareem, "I used it as a means to an end, we all did. You Americans are weak and sentimental, my people aren't. We have hated you for decades. We loved to see dead soldiers, dead tourists, all you infidels dead. Religion, bah, nothing more than a tool to control the ignorant and program them to kill. There is no Allah. If there was, I would have destroyed you," finished Kareem.

"You came close," said Blindman, "but no brass ring. Now get out."

"Pardon me?" said Kareem.

"You heard me," spat Blindman. "Leave."

"And go where?" Kareem asked.

"Out into the fuckin desert," Blindman yelled. "I'd love to kill you slowly, but you're a piece of crap stuck to my boot. Why should I waste my time when the wasteland will do it for me?"

"Out there," muttered a shaken Kareem, "no food, no water?"

"No!" yelled Blindman. "And no weapons either. You'll either die of thirst, starve, get bitten by a snake or run into some extremely unfriendly folk."

Blindman turned to the group. "Let's go, we got things to do."

Kareem stood there, seething with anger. He watched the departing Blindman. *He cost me everything,* Kareem thought. *If nothing else, I'll kill him.* Kareem had a .38 special hidden in his clothes. He pulled out the gun and aimed it at Blindman's back. Before he could shoot, his world erupted in pain. The group heard a loud thud. They turned to see Kareem drop to his knees, his arms useless. Standing behind him was a bloody Home Run Eddie.

Eddie's bat had hit Kareem between the shoulders, breaking his spine. He circled Kareem. "It's the bottom of the ninth!" Eddie screamed in Kareem's face. "The bases are loaded! He swings, he hits! The crowd goes wild!" Eddie's bat turned Kareem's head into a bloody pinata.

"Help me get Sal," Eddie panted.

"You're not in great shape, Eddie," Leo said.

"Fuck me," Eddie gasped. "Sal's worse." Eddie could barely stand but led the group to Sal.

Sal had been shot in the chest and hip. "Nice to see you guys are still among the living," Sal groaned.

Blindman leaned over to check his wounds. "Damn," exclaimed Sal. "You got one eye."

"Yeah, and that one eye sees you're still as ugly as ever," said Blindman. "Glad you made it, too."

Sal said, "How bad am I?"

"Near as I can tell, bullet went though and didn't hit anything vital. But you got a slug in your hip, it's gotta come out." Sal looked at Blindman in horror. "Don't worry, we found a real doctor," Blindman told him.

"Thank God for that, I had a vision of you pouring me full of liquor and cutting it out," Sal said.

"That still might happen," Blindman said. "The fill you full of liquor part. But let's leave this up to the Doc."

Patel had turned The Last Chance into an infirmary. Blindman brought Sal in with help from Eddie. "This is not good," said Patel. "Apache, one of the girls and your friend here needs those bullets taken out. I don't have the resources to do surgery," finished Patel.

"Great," muttered Blindman. "And I brought the mountain down on your clinic." Blindman pondered the situation. "What about where we found Sarge? That was a military installation, so they should have an infirmary."

"That's true," said Patel.

"Then let's go for a ride," said Blindman.

"I'm going, too," said Nydia. "Every time you're out of my sight you get into trouble."

"Ok," muttered Blindman. "Next thing you'll want a ring." Nydia shot him a withering glance.

The group started the jeep and took off, with Dog loping out ahead. Once inside the facility, they spread out, searching for the infirmary. "Here it is!" shouted Nydia. "Locked."

Blindman leveled his shotgun and blew the door open. "Go shopping, Doc," Blindman ordered.

Patel started gathering up bandages, instruments and drugs. "We are in luck," he exclaimed. "These antibiotics are still good."

"After this, when things settle down, we have to come back and grab this stuff," said Blindman.

"Yeah," agreed Nydia. "All of it."

When Patel had everything he needed, they returned to the compound at dusk. Patel went right to work. The next day, Blindman rounded up anyone who was still mobile. "Sucks to say this, but we have to bury our friends," said Blindman. Graves were dug. Ace Scanlon, Blade Benson, Deke, Lobo, Sarge, and 27 others, defenders of The Last Chance, were laid to rest. Markers were made to honor the sacrifices of Juan and Manny, Scarecrow, and Firefly. "I hope we never have to go through shit like this again," Blindman said. "I need a fuckin drink," he finished.

"I think we could all do with a drink. Or two, or three. Fuck, just break out bottles," said Leo. "Let's drink to our fallen friends."

The group toasted the fallen well into the night. Dawn broke and plans had to be made.

Epilogue

ALL HE KNEW WAS AGONIZING pain, thirst and hunger. Plus he wanted revenge on the guy who made this happen to him. The Reverend Hellfire was pinned under his church. A week had gone by and he prayed and prayed. Then one morning he heard a sound, someone walking. He tried to speak, but his mouth was dried out. He rapped his hand against a piece of wood.

The footsteps stopped. "Well, what do we have here?" a harsh voice rasped. Someone started pulling the debris off of him. Sunlight blinded Hellfire, but he saw the man standing over him. The man continued to pull boards off of Hellfire. "Now pull yourself out and I got ya covered," the man ordered. Hellfire got shakily to his feet. His 'benefactor' was a man dressed in a blue work shirt and jeans. He had a mean hawk-like face and was missing his right arm.

"Looks like you lost your flock, reverend," the man said.

"I was deceived by the devil," Hellfire muttered.

"Can your 'devil' see?" the man asked.

"No," shot back Hellfire. "He's a drunken fornicator who has created his own Sodom and ..."

"Shut up and listen," the man interrupted. "I could give a shit about that. The only thing I really give a shit about is that I want him dead. And you, padre, are going to help me."

"Why do you want him dead?" Hellfire asked.

"Because of this," the man pointed to his missing arm. "He did this and I want him dead. Get your ass up, reverend, we got plans to make."

Gunfighters of the Drunken Master
Book III: Last Call?

Prologue

The two men sat by a small fire. Not too closely, though. The Reverend Hellfire stunk, something his new 'friend' kept reminding him.

"No offense, pal, but you need to get more down wind of me."

Hellfire had been trapped under debris that once was his church. He had pissed and shit himself multiple times and had no water to clean himself up. His 'rescuer' was Jack Taggart, a former corrections officer from Riker's Island.

Taggart quizzed Hellfire. "You say you know where The Blindman has holed up?"

"Yes," replied Hellfire. "I have a pretty good idea of where The Drunken Master's compound is."

"Pretty good idea ain't gonna cut it, son, you either do or ya don't. If ya don't, I really have no use for you," stated Taggart.

"Ok, I know where it is. What are you going to do?" asked Hellfire.

"I told ya, I'm going to kill the blind bastard and take the place over," responded Taggart. "After the fight with them sand niggers, they'll be weak and ripe for a takeover."

"You must really hate Blindman," said Hellfire.

"I hated all those fuckin cons after a year on the job," said Taggart. "When I knew things were going to shit, I started killing them in their cells. 'Please Mr Taggart, don't kill me'," he laughed. "I just went from cell to cell, blasting the crap out of them. It was fun. Then that blind fuck tricked me, grabbed my gun and blew my arm off. He's going to pay; I'll destroy him and take his place," Taggart finished, almost foaming at the mouth.

"Where does that leave me?" Hellfire asked.

"You? Just get me to him and you can write your own ticket," said Taggart.

"I never liked him," said Hellfire. "He's a drunk, a fornicator and beyond redemption. A plague on this earth."

"He's all that and more, but in the end, he'll be one thing," said Taggart.

"And what would that be?" inquired Hellfire.

"Stone cold fuckin dead, that's what he'll be," finished Taggart.

1

THE MOANING OF THE wounded echoed though the camp. The Blindman sat at the edge of the bar, stiff with the pain of his injuries. The doctor, Patel, who Blindman had saved (or maybe Patel had saved The Blindman), approached him.

"I have done what I could with what I have," he told Blindman.

"I took bullets out of Sal, one of your Shotgun Girls, Angelo, and the rest. Apache is the worst, the bullet is too close to his spine," finished Patel.

"So is it going to be fatal?" The Blindman asked.

"No," said Patel, "but he will be in pain, and he won't be riding. If the bullet shifts, he may be paralyzed from the waist down."

"I don't think he can live with that," said Blindman. "Take away a biker's ride, you take away all he is. Did you tell him yet?"

"No, I haven't," said Patel.

"Ok," said Blindman. "It might be better if I do."

"That big guy left this morning," said Patel.

"Which big guy?" asked Blindman. "We got a couple of big dudes."

"The one with the bat, the one who was shot six times," Patel replied.

"Oh, Homerun Eddie," said Blindman. "Did he say anything?"

"Something to the effect that he had to walk off the pain, that he was getting stiff, not to try and..."

"Ok, I get it," cut off Blindman. "Once he gets something in his head, he just does it unless Sal stops him."

"Sal is resting," said Patel. "Taking that bullet out of his hip left him in a lot of pain."

"All of us are in a lot of pain," said The Blindman. "The booze helps, but I wish we could find some more real drugs like morphine, Vicodin, any of that shit."

"We are thankful that the scavengers left the antibiotics alone," said Patel.

"Yeah, we lucked out there," agreed Blindman. "Maybe I'll take the jeep and go back to that depot. We might have missed something."

"Good idea," said Patel.

Just then Eddie walked through the door. "How ya holdin up, big guy?" asked Blindman.

"I feel like an old whore," Eddie muttered. "Everything hurts and it feels like parts of me want to fall off."

"Have a drink," offered Blindman, pushing a bottle of Maker's Mark toward Eddie.

"Thanks," the big man said. Eddie killed half the bottle in one gulp.

"Hits the spot, it does," Eddie commented. "By the way," he continued, "I found something that belongs to you." Eddie pulled out a blackened .45 automatic. "I think if you clean it up, it should be just fine."

"Damn," gasped Blindman. "That's Blackjack's .45. That cocksucker, Hussan, took it off me. Where did you find it?"

"I found two bodies burned to a crisp," said Eddie. "The gun was next to them. Weird thing was one body had its hands around the other one's throat."

Blindman was silent for a few seconds. "I'll bet that Firefly took out Hussan," he said. "I'll want to bury the man proper like."

"I took care of that," said Eddie. "But I need you to come with me out there."

"Why?" asked Blindman.

"Because you need to see what I found," Eddie replied.

Blindman realized that Eddie wasn't going to talk about it. "Ok, but I'm too fuckin stiff to walk it. Let's take the jeep, or I'll take the jeep and you can trot along, seeing you're trying to get in shape and all that healthy shit."

"Always got a smart mouth answer," shot back Eddie. "Good thing I'm used to you, you old fuck, or I'd whip your ass."

"Don't go just yet," Leo, the 'owner' of the bar, christened The Last Chance, called out to them. "I got something I need to talk to you about."

"And this can't wait until we get back?" inquired Blindman.

"No," stated Leo. "There's a problem you don't know about."

"Alrighty," said Blindman. "What's up?"

Leo began, "While we were fighting, some of us weren't. There's a bunch of slackers that hid during the battle."

"Do tell," said Blindman, his features hardening.

"When things got heavy," continued Leo, "they ran out the back and hid in the gully. I called them out on this and they told me to go fuck myself."

"How many?" asked Blindman.

"Originally about seven, but they've been running their mouth to others and now there might be over a dozen. I think they are going to try and take this place over," finished Leo.

"Take this place over? My fuckin ass they will," snarled Blindman. "Eddie, go find Nydia and tell her to get Lee."

"Will do," replied Eddie. "You want me here, too?"

"Hold back a bit until I call these fucks out, I want to see what kinda crap I'm dealing with," said Blindman.

Nydia and Lee came running. "Trouble?" said Nydia, smiling in anticipation of another fight.

"Maybe," said Blindman. "Seems we got a bucket of chicken shit vaginas that wouldn't fight the Islamics, but think they can take over what we fought for."

"Not going to happen," said Nydia. "Should I tell..."

"No," Blindman cut her off. "Let's see who's really with us."

Nydia looked him in the eye. "Gotcha," she said.

"Good," said Blindman. "Me, you, Nydia, Lee and the girls took this place. We own it, and we are keeping it."

Leo cut in. "Looks like we won't have to wait, here they are."

A group of maybe fourteen—twelve men, two women—approached, fortified by liquid courage.

"Hey blind dude," said Joe, their leader, "we had a little meeting, we decided it's time for a regime change."

"Oh, ya did did ya?" asked Blindman. "You chicken shit punks hid during the real fight, so you think you can take us out now. Think again, you cum guzzling bastard."

"Two old men and two cunts," Joe shot back. "Can you count, old man?"

"Yeah," replied Blindman. "I count a bunch of dead fuckers that I won't bother to bury."

"Now, was that a nice thing to say?" snarled Joe. "No one has your back, Blindman, the rest of these people are with us."

"Really," a new voice added. "I don't like the odds." Goldstein, the butcher stepped beside Leo. "Now it's five."

"No, make us six and seven!" Jones yelled as he and Denny joined the group. They were the surviving bikers that played hell with the Islamics.

"Don't forget me!" bellowed Eddie as he stepped out of the bar.

"Or me." A female voice belonging to Tamera, a black girl that Blindman saved from the fanatics.

Blindman looked at Joe and spat, "Like these odds now, cupcake?"

Joe turned to his group and a hard fist broke his jaw.

"Let's fuck them up!" yelled Blindman. And the fight was on.

Eddie used his huge fists to pummel the first two idiots who charged at him. Blindman dropped Joe to the ground, grabbed another man and ripped an ear off. Nydia punted one of the women in the pussy. She doubled over only to catch a stiff uppercut from Nydia that spread her nose all over her face. Denny and Jones took on about five men and left them bleeding on the ground. Goldstein took a couple of hard punches before choke slamming his attacker on a concrete slab. Lee had taken out one guy, but the remaining woman charged her only to run into clothesline from Tamera. Leo had a guy against the building hammering hard fists into his chest and belly. In about five minutes, the 'insurrection' was put down.

Panting heavily, Blindman addressed the beaten group. "Now you can get the fuck out of here."

"Leroy!" a voice shouted. Blindman turned to see a shaken Sal pointing a snub nose .38 at him. Sal pulled the trigger and Joe's head exploded as the Glock flew out of his hand.

"Surprised you didn't see that coming," muttered Sal.

"Yeah," said Blindman. "Thank you, Sal, guess you're feeling better."

"Better enough to take a hand in this fight," said Sal. "I think Eddie and myself earned our place, so did the rest of us."

"That you certainly did," said Blindman. "These worthless sacks of shit can hit the road."

"You can't do this to us," said the woman with the busted nose.

"Can and will," Blindman shot back. "But I'm not a worthless piece if shit like ya all are. Guys, round up enough food and water for a couple of days for these pilgrims."

"You're not being fair," the women bitched.

"Fair?" Nydia got right in the woman's face. "Fair, to me, would be to shoot you in the head and dump you in with that pack of fanatics so you could rot along with them. Now take what we hand you and leave before we change our minds."

The sullen group of unlucky thirteen took the supplies.

"Oh," said Blindman, "FYI, you come back here or lead anyone back here, I'll kill you. Got it?" The group looked at him with seething hate in their eyes.

Sal limped over to Blindman. "I think we need to talk," Sal said.

"I'm listening," Blindman replied.

"We have a good group here, but too many loose ends, if you get my drift," started Sal. "You guys," Sal motioned to Blindman, Nydia, Lee and Leo, "took this place. the rest of us joined together because of happenstance. We all worked well together, plus we all lost friends."

"I know that," replied Blindman. "All of yas earned a place here, but I get what you're saying. We got a bunch of pretty straight people here that needed protection. Most joined in the fight, but I don't know what to do next."

"Then let's call a meeting," said Sal. "Lay out some kind of plan."

"I'm not a leader, Sal, you know that," said Blindman. "But you're right, we need to know where these people stand because I'm not spending the rest of my life coddling them."

Blindman and Sal told the group to round up everyone.

"Get all the people outside The Last Chance," Blindman said. It took about an hour to corral everyone. There were about 60 people, not including the kids they saved.

Blindman opened the dance. "Ok, people, we just had situation with some people who weren't happy here. Now they're gone. Question is, do you want to stay here?"

One man started to answer, but Blindman stopped him.

"Let me finish. Most of us," Blindman swept his hand to the core group, "are bad guys." The crowd perked up a bit at that statement. "We weren't 'zactly out to save the world, but we saved this place. Now if you want to stay here, you have to contribute. Help with shit, keep this place safe. Most of yas ain't worth a shit in a fight, but yas held your own.

"We," said Blindman, "can fight. So this is the deal, and it's non-negotiable. You people help put this place together, help scavenge for supplies, and use whatever skills you have to help. You people do that and hold up your end, we will defend this place."

A low mummer went though the crowd.

"And to sorta drive my point home, you don't want to pitch in? Fine, there's the road out." Blindman pointed to the only way in or out.

"You'll get what we gave those people. Now are you in or out?"

For a couple of minutes, the groups had discussions among themselves. One of the men, a tall man named Pruitt, asked, "If we go for this, who will be in charge? You can't just drop a leadership role in our laps, none of us have any experience," Pruitt finished.

"Ok," said Blindman. "I see your point in all this. Sal here, has what I'd think you need. He's been in charge of people before, so he'd be my choice. If he wants to do it, that is."

Sal looked a bit shocked. "So you're appointing me mayor?" he said with a chuckle.

"Only if you want to do it, Sal. Plus you're a little banged up and you need to keep busy," said Blindman.

"I'm touched by your concern," laughed Sal. "But it's up to them. I'm not going to accept it unless they want me to, and that has to be 100 percent."

Pruitt spoke up. "We know what you guys were before all this, and speaking for myself, I have a pretty good idea of what you can do. So I would say that you're perfect for the job."

Sal thought on it, then addressed the crowd. "I'll do the best I can," he said. "But I'll need help. Leo and Angelo could be my right and left hands, if they agree to it."

"I'm ok with it," said Leo.

"I, too, am good with this," said Angelo.

"Good," said Blindman. "Now what you all should do is organize yourselves into groups that can get shit done. Now, I'm going to take a ride with Eddie, we have to check something out."

2

AS BLINDMAN AND EDDIE walked over to the jeep, Nydia came running up, followed by Dog.

"Lemme guess," said Blindman. "Youse two don't trust me outta your sight."

"Yeah, something like that," Nydia said with a smile. "You're a magnet for trouble. Any objection?" Nydia asked Eddie.

"No, but let's get going before Sal decides he needs me to do something."

The jeep started with a belch of smoke. Dog trotted alongside. "Go to where Firefly's camp was," directed Eddie.

"What did you see, big guy?" asked Nydia.

"That tanker full of gas," Eddie replied. "I don't think all of it blew up."

"How could it not have blown up?" asked Blindman. "Everyone said there was a blast, then a huge fireball."

"You'll have to just see what I found," muttered Eddie.

They came to what was left of Firefly's camp, a stretch of blackened sand and rock.

"Better leave the jeep here," said Eddie. "Lots of big potholes, rocks and crap that could bust this ride up."

"Good idea," said Blindman. "Breaking it up might void the warranty," he laughed.

Dog trotted up, then stiffened. A low growl came from his throat and the hair on his back stood up.

"Someone is up there," said Nydia.

"Damn," said Blindman. "I see legs, he's sitting in that shady part of that sand dune. Hey!" he yelled. "You friendly?"

No answer.

"He's either deaf or dead," said Nydia.

"I'll take dead for 30 points," Blindman said. "Let's go see, but be ready."

"Looks like you win, Blindman," Eddie said. "This guy is deader than shit."

The man was emaciated, his dead eyes stared into nothingness. The slight wind blew his long, unkempt hair over his sunken face.

"Look at his arm," Nydia said. "He's got a spike in it."

The man had a shoelace tying off his arm, there was a disposable old syringe stuck in his vein.

"A fuckin junkie," Blindman muttered.

"Let's see what he has on him," Eddie suggested.

They searched the man and came up with 3 bags of white powder and a printed notice.

"Is this heroin?" Blindman asked Nydia and Eddie.

Nydia opened bag, took a little of the powder on her finger and tasted it. "I'm no expert," she said, "but it's some kind of dope."

Eddie chimed in. "I don't know, Sal never allowed that. He was old school, ya know. Book making, loans, protection, that stuff. The NYC police left us alone as long as we stayed away from drugs."

"What's that paper say, Nydia?" Blindman asked.

"Listen to this shit," Nydia said. "Reward: Drugs or Money for stragglers. Bring them to Barter Town and get a big reward."

Blindman and Eddie looked at each other.

"Money?" Blindman exclaimed.

"Well, that makes no fuckin' sense at all," muttered Eddie.

"For a fact it don't," shot back Blindman.

"This is all weird and fucked up," said Nydia. "Someone is paying to bring people to this place, for what?"

"Bitch, you'll never know. Don't fuckin move an inch, any of yas!" a voice yelled.

Taggart and Hellfire had crept up on them, the group talking covered any noise the two men made.

"Keep that mutt in check or he goes first," Taggart snarled.

Nydia grabbed Dog by the scruff of his neck.

"Blindman, you don't know how long I've wanted to put a bullet in your blind head," gloated Taggart.

"Can we..." Nydia started to say.

"No, bitch, you can't save him. But maybe if you lay some pussy on the padre and me, I'll let you live," finished Taggart. "Now turn around with those milky, fucked up eyes because I'm going to shoot you in the face."

Blindman had his hands up. "Whatever you say Officer Taggart."

Blindman started to turn, slowly at first, then he brought his arm down and a double barreled .38 caliber derringer was in his hand. He shot Taggart in the belly. Taggart flew back, a horrified expression on his face. Blood gushed from the wound.

Blindman walked to Taggart and stood over him. He started singing, "I can see clearly now, the rain has gone. I can see all the obstacles in my way. It's a bright, bright sun shiny day."

Nydia and Eddie had WTF expressions on their faces.

Blindman said to Taggart, "If you're gonna shoot, you shoot. You don't talk a man to death."

Blindman shot him in the head. He looked up to see Hellfire take off like the devil was chasing him.

"Figures that fuck just had to survive. I'll go after him," Nydia said.

"No, don't," Blindman ordered. "Fuck him. This piece of shit," Blindman said, pointing to Taggart's cooling body, "was using him to find me. Hellfarter won't last a day out there on his own."

"Where did you get that?" asked Nydia, pointing to the derringer.

"It was Ace's hideout gun." said Blindman. "He had it on him when we buried him, so I took it."

"I think he'd be proud of how you just used it," said Nydia.

"Now on to what we came out here for," said Blindman. "Show me what you found, Eddie."

"Ok," said Eddie. He walked over to where the tanker blew up. "See this?" He pointed to a large, blackened area. "That's what blew up, there's another compartment behind it."

Blindman ran his hand over the black wall. "It's metal, alright." He thumped the butt of his shotgun against it, "No echo. I'd have to say you're right, big man, it's still full of gasoline."

"If we could get it out, we could keep these vehicles running for a bit," chimed in Nydia.

"There has to be a valve somewhere," Eddie said.

"Trouble is this thing is half buried. I think any valve is under this sand."
Blindman pondered that. "I think we go back, get some people and shovels,
and..." Just then a bullet pinged off the tanker.

"Get down!" Blindman yelled.

The three hit the sand. "What the hell is wrong with this day?" Eddie
bitched. "First a dead junkie, then our old pal Taggart, now someone
shooting at us. I'm getting slightly pissed here."

"Just stay down," Blindman said, "and listen."

They heard two voices arguing.

"You weren't supposed to shoot anyone, dummy," a deep voice rasped.
"That notice said 'alive'."

Another voice chimed in. "Well, Em, I thought it was wanted dead or
alive."

"You shoulda learned to read, Rufus, they want them alive, not dead."

"Well, maybe I winged one," Rufus whined.

Blindman looked at Eddie and Nydia. "Let's not kill these assholes," he
said. "Let's find out what they know about this reward crap."

"How do you want to play it?" Eddie asked.

"Simple. I'm shot and badly wounded," Blindman said.

"Oh Christ," said Nydia. "You did this when we met. Eddie, get ready for
an Oscar winning performance."

"Nydia," said Blindman, "keep holding Dog, we need answers before he
chews on someone.

"Oh," moaned Blindman, "I'm hurting real bad, where did my friends
go? Come back you bastards, you can't leave me! My leg, oh lord it hurts
something awful."

"See, Em," Rufus whined. "I got one, let's go get him."

The two men ran to where Blindman was 'dying'. Nydia and Eddie were
waiting.

"Freeze, you morons, and drop those guns!" Eddie bellowed.

The two stopped dead in their tracks.

"Drop the fuckin guns, now," Eddie repeated.

The two men dropped the guns like they were on fire. Blindman looked
at them. One was squat and heavy set, with beady eyes. The other was a
skinny runt with a pinched face.

"Ok," said Blindman. "Who the hell are you two?"

"We're the Clement brothers. I'm Emmett, he's Rufus."

"We did have another brother, Frank," whined Rufus.

"Well, get his ass out here," ordered Eddie.

"We can't," said Emmett.

"That's right, we can't," Rufus added. "Poor Frank is dead. Damn, I still see his face."

"You mean what was left of his face after you shot him in it," growled Emmett.

"That's not my fault, I told ya I was just trying to clean my gun," complained Rufus.

"Ever think ya should have unloaded it before you tried to clean it, you idiot?" yelled Emmett.

The two started arguing back and forth. Now they were nose to nose, pushing each other.

"Enough of this crap!" yelled Blindman. "I should shoot the two of yas on general principles, but it's bad luck to kill morons."

The two looked at Blindman.

"What did you call us?" growled Emmett.

"Morons," said Blindman. "You're morons."

"No we ain't," shot back Rufus. "Morons live in Utah, we live in..."

"Oh, just shut the fuck up for a minute!" Nydia yelled at them.

The two got quiet and looked like scolded schoolboys.

"Now tell us what the hell this reward crap is all about," ordered Blindman.

"Well," started Emmett, "we needed a place to hole up and we found this place, Barter Town, but they won't let you in unless you bring someone in with you. So they told us that if we brought some folks in, we could stay."

"Any idea what they wanted these people for?" asked Blindman.

"No," answered Emmett. "But they said something about blood types needed."

"And they had a bar," chimed in Rufus.

"Blood and a bar?" questioned Blindman. "What are they, vampires?"

"He meant 'bear'," said Emmett. "They have a bear."

"Oh, this just keeps getting better and fuckin better," said Nydia. "Bounty hunters, blood suckers, junkies and a bear."

"Should I say 'oh, my'?" chuckled Blindman. "Maybe we should take these two back with us and try to sort this out."

"Ya can't," whined Rufus. "That would leave Ma all alone out here."

"You two have a mother?" asked Eddie.

"Well, don't everyone have a Mom somewhere?" answered Rufus.

"Alright," muttered Blindman, "enough of this, let's go find your Ma."

The two brothers led them to a partially buried RV.

"Better let Ma know we're back," said Emmett.

"Go ahead, but this better be legit or you're dead," said Blindman.

"Ma!" Emmett yelled. "Better come out here."

The RV door opened and a gray haired, slim older woman stepped out with a shotgun.

"Ma'am," said Blindman, "we'd appreciate if you would put the gun down until we parlay."

Ma looked at the group, then turned her attention to her sons. "I see you two dummies decided to do something stupid."

"Ma," started Rufus, "it weren't like that, we just..."

"You wanted to collect some fake bounty and you got caught," Ma finished. She turned to Blindman. "Guess you was the ones they tried to take," she said. "Not very smart of them."

"Beggin your pardon, Ma'am, but we've been with these two for the last couple of hours and I can't say that they've done anything smart in that time," said Blindman.

"I told them that this bounty is just bullshit," said Ma. "Offering money and drugs. If it was food or water, maybe, but something else is going on here."

"What do you think it is, Ma'am?" inquired Blindman.

"Somethin rotten," she shot back. "You can't go into this Barter Town place without a prisoner. Then," she continued, "something about blood. And what the fuck can you do with money? Wipe your ass with it? No, mister, somethin else is happening in that place and it ain't no good," she finished.

"Well," said Blindman. "We do have a place. We have supplies, but if we take you back, what can you throw into the pot?"

"I'm a good cook," stated Ma. "When I actually have something I can work with. As for Emmett and Rufus, they'll do what I tell 'em to."

"Now, wait a minute, Ma," Emmett bellowed. "Why would we just up and go with people that..."

"Shaddup," Ma shot back. "It's better than you two idiots getting yourself killed for nothing."

"Yeah," said Blindman. "You will get your ticket punched by someone. Let's go back, then you two are going to tell us everything you know about this Barter Town."

3

THE GROUP RETURNED to the compound. Blindman got Leo, Sal and Angelo in the bar to hear what the Clement boys knew about Barter Town.

"Well," started Emmett, "we never actually got to the town itself. We wuz headed there, but we found a place called The Outpost."

"What kind of place is that?" asked Blindman.

"It's a bar," replied Emmett. "There's some bosses there. They told us we had to bring people though there first, then we get let into Barter Town."

"Who runs the place?" asked Blindman.

"Two mean bastards," Rufus chimed in. "Captain Coonsley and Shotgun Harker. Piss Harker off, and he decorates a wall in the bar with your brains."

"Sounds like a charming individual," said Sal.

"I get the impression Harker likes to kill," said Leo.

"Ok," said Blindman. "I don't like two things. One, they are too close to us. Two, this bringing people back, the blood and the drugs I want to check out this Outpost place. You two," Blindman pointed to Emmett and Rufus, "are going to bring us there like you rounded us up."

"Then what?" asked Emmett.

"I'll either get some answers or punch their tickets," answered Blindman.

"They'll do it," cut in Ma, "or I'll whip their asses."

"Ma," whined Rufus, "I don't..."

"Shaddup!" bellowed Ma. "You'll do like I tell yas."

"Leo," Blindman started, "Ma says she can cook, think you can put her to work?"

"You mean you're tired of my gourmet treats?" laughed Leo.

"Cans of pork & beans are wearing a little thin, plus they don't go well with bourbon," said Blindman.

Angelo, the midget scientist, cut in. "I have to show you people something." Angelo dumped the contents of a sack on the bar. It was the dead rattlesnake Blindman brought back after luring the terrorists into their den.

"I was curious as to how these snakes were still living," said Angelo. "I dissected this guy and found a rat in its stomach. Rats must have survived by eating the food left in that Costco we found. The snakes are eating the rats. My point here is, these snakes are fresh meat, and we can use fresh meat."

"And dangerous meat," said Blindman.

Rufus walked up to the bar and examined the snake. "You said you know where there's a den of these?" he asked.

"Yeah," said Blindman. "Hundreds of the ugly fuckers, why?"

"Because I can catch them," Rufus said with a goofy smile on his face.

"Bullshit," muttered Eddie.

"No," cut in Emmett. "The dummy has a way with snakes."

"Em," snarled Rufus, "stop callin me a dummy or I'll beat your ass." The two started screaming threats at each other.

"Enough of that shit!" shouted Ma. "Both of you back off." The two sulked like scolded children.

"You really can catch these snakes?" Blindman asked.

"Yeah," said Rufus. "I hypnotize them, or use duct tape."

"Duct tape?" Leo asked. "How do you catch snakes with duct tape?"

"Well," started Rufus, "snakes ain't too smart. You lay some duct tape in their path, they crawl over it, it sticks to them, they start biting it and get wrapped up in it. Then you can grab them after they wear themselves out."

"This could work," mused Blindman. "It's risky, but it could work."

"Gentlemen," cut in Angelo. "It's too bad we don't have a freezer, we could stock up on snake meat."

"Maybe we will have a freezer," said Blindman. "Eddie found out that Firefly's tanker still has gas in it. I'll bet there are generators and freezers in that Costco or that army depot. So why don't we get a couple of groups together, one to find the valve on the tanker, the other to scrounge up some stuff we need."

"Can I go after the snakes?" asked Rufus.

"You seriously want to do that?" Blindman asked.

"Well," whined Rufus, "you said we should pitch in, so I'm pitchin in."

"Ok," said Blindman "somebody go find Denny, he would remember where the den is."

"I'll go find him," volunteered Goldstein. "he's been sitting with Apache."

"Leo," said Blindman. "Go find Pruitt and tell him to round up some guys. I'll have Arnold take one group and scavenge the Costco and the depot. Eddie can take the other group and dig for the valve on the tanker."

Goldstein returned with Denny. "What's up, boss?" he asked.

"I need you to take Rufus to that rattlesnake den."

"Are you fuckin serious?" Denny asked.

"He says he can catch snakes. We can eat them, fresh meat," replied Blindman.

Denny looked at Rufus and shook his head. "Not so sure about this," he said.

"I can do this," Rufus snarled. "I ain't never been bit."

"Denny," said Blindman. "It's worth a shot, unless you're really fond of eating pork & beans for the rest of your life."

Denny thought a bit. "Alright, but we are taking shotguns. Those things get rowdy, we blast 'em and jet. That ok with you, mister?" he said, looking at Rufus.

"Yeah, that's fair," replied Rufus. "I ain't lookin to get bit either."

"Ok, pal, get what you need and I'll get my bike. Oh, Blindman, Apache wants to see you."

"How's he doing?" asked Blindman.

"Not good," answered Denny. "You two need to talk."

Blindman went to the makeshift hospital where Apache was recovering.

"Hey brother, how are ya feeling?" Blindman asked.

"When I'm loaded on pills, I'm ok. Without them, not very ok," replied Apache. "I talked to Dr. Patel, the bullet is stuck against my spine. He can't get it out without it paralyzing me."

"Well," started Blindman, "maybe we..."

"No," interrupted Apache. "I'm not stupid, there is no maybes. I won't be riding again, but I'm not going to just lay here and die either."

Blindman felt like he had been gut punched.

"I understand," Blindman said. "What can I do for you?"

"I hear that something may be brewing, something that could be trouble," Apache stated.

"We ain't exactly sure what's going on, but there's some fucked up shit happening and it's too close to us to be ignored," answered Blindman.

"Then promise me this," asked Apache. "If something does go down, let me go out like a man."

Blindman stepped back, deep in thought. "You want to go out in a blaze of glory?" he asked.

"Better that than dying here on my back," Apache countered.

"As I would want the same for me," muttered Blindman. "Yeah, you have my promise. If and when the shit starts, take the cocksuckers to Valhalla." The two men shook hands on it.

Blindman went back to The Last Chance. Nydia was at the bar, smoking a joint. "In the mood for a little trip?" he asked Nydia.

"Sure, where to?" she asked.

"I want to shake the tree and see what falls out. I want the Clements boys to make like they are taking us in. Then we go to this Outpost place and see if these clowns are really a threat," answered Blindman.

"I'm in," she said. "Who else are we taking?"

"Eddie and the two brothers. They know where the place is. We gotta wait until Denny brings Rufus back from his snake hunt, though," Blindman finished.

4

DENNY HAD A SIDECAR attached to his bike, Rufus was in the sidecar. Rufus took a couple of burlap sacks and a couple of rolls of duct tape that hadn't dried out. There was a horrible stench in the air.

"We're getting close to the den," Denny told Rufus. "Lotta dead scumbags rotting out there."

"Smells nasty," whined Rufus.

As they got closer, they saw bloated bodies burst open by the heat. Several snakes were basking on rocks.

"They don't act like they are pissed off anymore," whispered Denny. Rufus began unrolling the duct tape.

"Coulda been they might have been mating," said Rufus. "They get real mean around mating season." Rufus made a couple of big mats of duct tape. He laid them out in the sand. "I'm going to catch one, you can stay here if you want."

"No shit," said Denny. "I'm not fucking with them, but I'll cover you."

Rufus approached a snake that was about four or five feet long. The snake's head rose and it started rattling. Rufus motioned his left hand in front of the snake. The snake attempted to strike, but Rufus caught it with his right hand. The snake thrashed around; Rufus brought it back to Denny.

"Smack its head in!" yelled Rufus.

Denny brought the butt of his shotgun down on the hissing reptile's head. Rufus shoved it into a sack.

"You're fast," remarked Denny.

"Not fast enough," answered Rufus. "Look."

Several snakes were slithering toward them.

"Back up and let them hit my little traps," Rufus ordered.

Denny and Rufus retreated to where the snakes would have to go over the tape to get at them. Three hit one trap, four hit the other. A couple slithered past the trap and Denny's shotgun boomed. The snakes exploded in a welter of blood and flesh.

The snakes caught in the tape thrashed around, biting the air. "They'll wear themselves out, then we can get 'em," said Rufus.

"I have an idea," said Denny. He went to his bike and pulled a machete out of his pack. "Be easier this way." He started chopping the snakes' heads off.

Rufus peeled the dead snakes from the tape and stuffed them into the sacks. "Ma will cook these up tonight," Rufus said proudly "We'll have us a regular feast."

5

HELLFIRE WAS EXHAUSTED. He had run for hours, it seemed. Then he spotted a group of people, the people Blindman had kicked out of the camp.

"Hold up a bit," Hellfire yelled.

"Who the fuck are you?" one of the men asked.

"I'm a man of God," Hellfire explained. "Some barbarian tried to kill me."

"Would that 'barbarian' be blind?" someone asked.

"How did you know?" asked a shocked Hellfire.

"Because the son of a bitch ran us out, that's how. The fucker thinks he's lord and master," spat the man. "He had all his buddies beat us up and run us out."

"There is supposed to be another camp," said Hellfire. "Let's try to find it, maybe they would be interested in cleaning out that bunch of filth."

The group kept moving for a couple of hours. Night fell, but they saw a light about a mile or so in the distance.

"That might be the place," one of the two women in the group said.

"Well, let's just hope it is," replied Hellfire.

After some walking, the group came to a sun blasted building. Someone had carved 'Outpost' on the door.

Hellfire opened the door. Lit by candles and lanterns, the place was dim, smoky, and smelly. A squat, bald man with a scarred face was behind the bar. A hulking man with a huge gut was standing by the bar.

"Oh, now what do we have here?" he asked.

Before anyone could speak, Hellfire blurted out. "I have brought these sinners to salvation."

"So now you want into Barter Town," the barman said. "And you brought us pussy to get there."

"Wait a fuckin minute," one of the men said. "They are with us."

The big man at the bar walked over and punched him in the face. The guy went down, but tried to get back up. He was kicked in the head. The group moved forward until the barman brought a sawed-off shotgun from under the bar.

"Move and you're dead!" he shouted.

Everyone froze.

"You got guns, drop them now or I'll blast you," he told the group.

One of the men tried to beat the odds. The shotgun boomed and pieces of his head decorated the wall. "Anyone else want to get stupid?" he said.

"No more," chimed in Hellfire. "Am I in? I delivered the goods, didn't I?"

"Why, you treacherous son of a bitch, I'm going to break your fuckin..." The man didn't finish as the big man broke his nose.

"Nice work, Coonsley," the barman said. "Now tie these boys up, take the cunts in the back, and we'll spend the night breaking them in."

AFTER A NIGHT OF SEEING the women raped and beaten, Hellfire and the rest were escorted by Coonsley to Barter Town. Entering the town, and it was an actual main street of sorts, the stench of death was in the air.

"What is that horrible smell?" Hellfire asked.

"Nothin to be concerned about," mumbled Coonsley.

"Where are you taking us?" asked Hellfire.

"To the blood station," replied Coonsley.

"What is a blood station?" asked Hellfire.

"Y'all got to many fuckin questions," shot back Coonsley. "King Crump wants everybody who comes here to get their blood tested."

"King Crump," said Hellfire. "You mean our President?"

"Yeah, well now he's our king," said Coonsley. "He's gonna bring us back to power."

"That's good to know, that he's still with us and leading us," said Hellfire. "He's a moral, God-fearing man, just who we need to bring us salvation and smite these sinners."

"Yeah," chuckled Coonsley. "Now just get in line and roll up your sleeve, padre."

6

WITH THE FRESH SNAKE meat, Ma cooked up a huge feast.

"Never thought I'd say this," said The Blindman, "but this is some tasty stuff."

"Sure is," said Nydia, wiping some grease off her chin. "I could get used to this."

"Well, now that we have a freezer and a couple of generators, we can store the meat," Goldstein said.

"That was a real score," replied Blindman. "Youse guys did good digging that stuff up."

"Oh, it wasn't that tough," said Goldstein. "No one touched this stuff. They tore the place apart looking for drugs and weapons, but pretty much left everything else alone."

"Tomorrow," said Blindman, "we are going to check out that outpost place."

Rufus said, "Back in the day, a guy named Barney used to own it."

"I'm betting whoever is there now killed Barney," said Blindman. "But that's a good thing to know. You and Emmett can take us there, then maybe we can figure out what's going on in Barter Town. Eddie and Nydia are coming too, lets shake the tree and see what falls out of it."

7

"LEAVE DOG WITH LEE," Blindman said as they piled into the jeep. Dog whined. "Don't worry, boy, I'll have someone you can chew on shortly."

If a dog could grin, Dog did. After about a 20-minute ride they were close to The Outpost.

"Let's leave the jeep here and walk the rest of the way," Blindman said.

After a short walk, they were within sight of the building. "You said this Harker guy likes to use a shotgun?" Blindman asked Emmett.

"Yeah, he does," said Emmett. "He's real proud of the wall with all the blown apart heads splattered on it."

Blindman reached into a bag he brought with him. He took out a really cut-down double-barreled 12-gauge shotgun with a pistol grip.

"What are you doing with that?" asked Nydia as Blindman stuffed the gun inside his shirt.

"A little surprise for Mr. Harker if he fucks with us," replied Blindman. "Ok, Emmett," he said, "You two act like you're bringing us in."

Rufus walked into The Outpost ahead of the group with Emmett bring up the rear.

"Mr. Harker," Rufus blurted out. "We brought you some people so we can get into Barter Town."

Harker glared at the group. "An old man, a big dummy, and some pussy," Harker muttered. "Well, the pussy will work. As for these two, let the King decide."

"You have a King?" Blindman asked.

Harker glared at him. "Did I ask you to talk, you dried up old fuck?" Harker snarled. "This is called 'I talk, you obey', if you don't then you can be part of my wall," he snarled. Harker motioned to the wall behind Blindman. It was splattered with bits of skull, brain matter, and a couple of eyeballs and ears. It stunk of stale blood and rotting flesh.

"Well," said Blindman, "ain't you just the artist. What happened to the guy who used to run this place?" he asked.

"What guy?" Harker growled.

"Barney," said Blindman. "His name was Barney."

"He's buried out there somewhere," said Harker, smiling.

"Is that a fact," said Blindman. "I didn't know he was feeling sickly."

"You got a smart mouth on you, old man," Harker spat. "Coonsley, take the cunt into the back room so you and the boys can break her in. I'll keep our guests here busy."

"Not going to happen, big mouth," snarled Blindman.

Coonsley grabbed Nydia's tit in a hard squeeze. The two other guys got up to join him.

"Now, you people don't seem very hospitable," said Blindman. "Nydia, take the fucker out!" he yelled.

Then shit got nasty.

Nydia shook a switchblade out of her jacket and drove it up to the hilt in Coonsley's huge gut. She turned it upward and pulled. A huge pile of grey intestines hit the floor with a big splat. Harker reached for his shotgun only to have Blindman's new toy shoved under his chin.

"Please don't shoot," Harker pleaded, frozen on the spot.

"And how many of these other poor bastards asked you the same thing?" Blindman snarled. "Have a nice fuckin day."

Blindman pulled the trigger and Harker's face disintegrated into raw meat. One of the other jerks rushed Eddie. Eddie threw him into the wall and his spine snapped in three places.

Coonsely was trying to stuff his guts back inside him. Nydia kneeled down beside him and said. "Hurts a bit, don't it?" She cut his throat.

The group turned and looked at the last guy, who had just pissed himself in fear. "Well," said Blindman, "unless you want to join your friends, you're taking us to Barter Town."

8

HELLFIRE WAS TAKEN into a room with two other people after the bloodwork was done. A pinched-faced man in a dirty white coat, doctor Cruz, walked in with a clipboard.

"Well, you people have the right blood type, but not the type needed to cure our King."

"It saddens me to hear the great man is ill," said Hellfire. "If there is anything I can do, maybe send thoughts and prayers..."

"Actually," interrupted Cruz, "you will be making the ultimate sacrifice to keep King Crump healthy."

"What do you mean 'ultimate sacrifice'?" asked one of the women, who had obviously been beaten.

"Simple," said Cruz. "Our King has a blood destroying disease and needs fresh blood, so you three will have the honor of supplying that blood."

"Now wait one minute," said Hellfire, "I'm a man of God, not some guinea pig for..."

Hellfire was slapped by Cruz.

"Take them to his chambers," ordered Cruz. Hellfire and the women were dragged kicking and screaming down a passageway.

They entered a chamber that stunk like an open sewer. What looked like a bloated mass of orange colored flesh was in the center of the room. Two barely alive, emaciated men were strapped down on tables. They had tubes in their arms draining their blood into the bloated mass. When Cruz entered, the thing's head turned around. It had strands of orange cotton candy like hair on it, and its beady eyes peered out from thick folds of flesh.

"Did you find the right one yet?" it croaked at Cruz.

"No, your highness, not yet, but these three will tide you over for a while."

"President Crump," yelled Hellfire. "I protest my treatment, I voted for you, you promised to bring about the rapture, I..."

"Shut him up," croaked Crump.

Two guards beat Hellfire to the ground, breaking his arms and legs. The two almost dead men were taken off the tables and thrown on a gurney.

"Our friend will feast tonight," said Cruz. Then, leaning over to a barely conscious Hellfire, "You should have shut up. This might have gone easier." Cruz tapped a needle into Hellfire's arm. "Don't worry, you're serving the greater glory, and you'll be dead in a few days."

9

"I KNOW YOU AREN'T GOING to like this," Blindman said to Nydia, "but I need you to go back and tell Sal and Leo about this crap."

"I hate to miss out on a good fight," she said, "but yeah, our people need to know what's going on here."

"What's your name, boy?" Blindman asked their prisoner.

"Rudy is my name," he muttered sullenly.

"Ok, Rudy, here's how it gonna go. You're taking us to Barter Town," ordered Blindman.

"You'll all die there," blurted Rudy. "The King will kill you all."

"Now, we'll just see how that plays out," said Blindman. "Rufus, stand behind our new friend and if he gets stupid, you get stupid."

"So I blast his ass if he gets stupid?" asked Rufus.

"You got it. Emmett, make like you're sorta bringing us in, can you do that?"

"Sure, boss, not a problem," Emmett replied.

"I'm going to head back," announced Nydia. "I'll see you boys on the flipside."

"Just be careful," said Blindman. "There might be more of these scumbags roaming around out here."

"Will do," said Nydia as she started back.

"How do we play this?" asked Eddie.

"We waltz right in like we are stupid pilgrims looking for swag," said Blindman. "Consider the fact that right now we don't really know what's going on," added Blindman. "Don't eat or drink anything they offer us."

"This whole deal stinks," muttered Eddie.

"I know it does, but let's keep 'the stink' away from our camp," replied Blindman.

"I agree," said Eddie. "Best to get a handle on this right now.

10

BACK AT BARTER TOWN, there was a meeting of the minds. Dr. Cruz called in former Congressman Fratboy Ryan, and what passed for 'the law' in Barter town.

"Doc" Pritchard was a former dentist turned skip tracer before the world went crazy. He was a lean old man with a face full of stubble.

Steele was a former drill instructor and an ex-Marine. He didn't talk, he bellowed.

David Sanchez was the King's personal muscle. 6'4" and bald with a vaquero mustache, he liked beating people to death with his fists.

Cruz opened the meeting. "Our King is not getting any better, the blood from these people we catch is just barely keeping him alive."

"So we catch more assholes," bellowed Steele. "What's the big deal?"

"The big deal," interjected Ryan, "is that we aren't finding that many stragglers out there."

"And that," said Cruz, "will be a huge problem sooner than later."

"How so?" asked Doc.

"We will have to use some of our troops," replied Cruz.

"This shit is out of hand," said Doc.

"Watch your mouth, old man," spat Sanchez. "We keep the King alive no matter what the cost."

"Then why don't you hook your big ass up to a blood line and contribute?" Doc shot back. "You fuckin ass kisser."

"Could be we'll use you, you useless old fuck," said Sanchez.

Doc backed up. "You can try, greaser, you can try..."

"Enough fighting!" shouted Cruz. "We will keep him alive and bring back this country."

"Bring it back to what?" shouted Doc. "He pretty much fucked it all up before the flares did."

"I don't like your attitude," bellowed Steele. "You're either in, or you're in the way."

"I'm in," muttered Doc, "but I don't have to like it."

"We have some entertainment for the men tonight," said Ryan.

"You mean we have another execution to watch," said Doc.

"It keeps people in line," said Ryan.

There was a huge cage in an area between the bigger buildings. that cage was home to a sixteen-foot-tall grizzly bear that was kept starving. A crowd of scary looking men surrounded the cage. Bloodlust was written on their faces. Two men were dragged through the crowd.

Steele screamed to the crowd, "Listen up, these two fucked up big time. They didn't do their jobs, they used our dope to get high with and did nothing to earn it," he continued. "Now they are gonna earn it."

The bear was agitated by the crowd. It roared and swiped at the men who were standing a respectable distance from the cage, where bones and crushed skulls littered the floor. The stench of rotten meat and bear shit permeated the air.

Steele went to the opposite side of the cage and distracted the beast. The two men where quickly shoved into the cage.

As soon as the bear heard the door open, he charged. The terrified men ran in opposite directions. One guy tried to climb the cage. The bear swiped his back, exposing his spine. His hands locked around the bars, the bear sunk its teeth into the man's back, then dragged him down. His arms tore out of their sockets and were left hanging from the cage. The bear tore off chunks of flesh and ate them.

The other man was running circles around the cage. The bear pushed aside its meal and charged him. He was luckier than the other guy. The bear swatted him and he hit the cage head first, crushing his head. The bear ripped him apart.

"That's what happens when you fuck with our rules," Steele bellowed.

11

NYDIA WAS ABOUT A THIRD of the way back when she realized she was being tracked.

"Fuck," she muttered. "I have to shake off these assholes, I can't lead them back to our camp." She drew out her Glock and checked the clip. "Good," she said to herself. She approached a sand dune and a scarecrow-looking figure popped up.

"Flinch, bitch, and you're a gone goose!" he yelled.

Nydia shot him in the throat. Arterial blood shot out in a four-foot arc as he toppled over.

"She just killed Phil!" a voice shouted.

"We need her alive, try to wing her!" another voice yelled.

Damn, thought Nydia. *How many of these fucktards are out there?*

Nydia threw herself in a gully as bullets whipped all around her. "This is real bad," she said to herself.

She pulled out her back up gun, a Phoenix Arms .22 automatic. "I won't go down easy," she promised herself.

She heard a thud. A bigger man with a bullet-shaped shaved head was running toward her position. She turned and put a round from the Glock in his belly. He sat down with an astonished look on his face. A round from the .22 crashed into his forehead.

A voice asked, "Did you nail her, Joe?"

"Fuck this guy," she spat. "Oh," she moaned, "I'm hit."

A weasel-faced guy ran right into a round from her Glock and did a 360 in the air before hitting the ground. "That's three," she told herself. "Can't be too many left."

Then she made a mistake. She belly-crawled along the gully and a weight came crashing down on her back.

"Got her!" the attacker yelled.

Nydia's finger was on the trigger of the Glock when he dropped on her. Now that finger was broken. Roaring in pain, she flipped over, pinning the guy under her. With her left hand she pulled out her switchblade and sliced the guy across his thigh. Blood spurted from a ripped open artery. Nydia tried to get up, but caught a boot to her face.

Dazed, the knife was ripped from her hand. Her attacker pulled her off the guy who was now bleeding out. Nydia threw a punch that broke someone's nose. Hard fists and boots beat and kicked her into semi-consciousness.

"Hold the bitch down while I sample that pussy," a voice roared.

Hard hands pinned her to the ground, but she still fought. Someone used a box cutter to cut her jeans off, doing some damage in the process. Bleeding and beaten, she tried to bite the guy raping her. She tore part of his cheek off and spat it back in his face. Screaming with rage, he knocked her out. Then his three companions took turns. The ordeal was just beginning.

12

THE FIRST THING BLINDMAN and the others noticed was the smell of rotting meat. Barter Town was a sun scorched collection of decrepit buildings, bleached gray.

"What a shithole," Eddie said.

Human debris staggered around, looking more dead than alive. "Junkies," said Blindman. "Now we know why they get these guys to bring others in. They must have a shitload of dope on hand." Blindman looked at their prisoner. "Ok, Rudy, take us to your leader."

"First you have to get your blood checked," said Rudy. "Those are the rules."

"Then lead on, and no tricks," Blindman told him.

They saw a huge cage-like structure. "What's that thing?" asked Blindman.

"That's where they keep the critter," Rudy replied.

"What kind of 'critter'?" Blindman persisted.

"It's a big bear, ok? They feed people to it for sport or if they fuck up," Rudy told them.

"I hate this place already," Eddie said. "Junkies, assholes, and a bear, oh my."

"Forget the bear for now," Blindman said. "Let's see who running this circus."

CRUZ DID NOT LIKE THE look of the four men Rudy brought in. *These guys can handle themselves,* Cruz thought. *I should talk to Steele about taking them down quickly.* Cruz put on his happy doctor face and drew the samples.

"Rudy," said Cruz. "Why don't you take these gentlemen for some refreshments while I check these samples."

"Sure Doctor, no problem," Rudy said.

Blindman saw the look exchanged between the two. *Ok,* he thought, *this dance will open sooner than later.*

Rudy took them to a big, barn like structure. "Set these fellows up with a round of our best," Rudy yelled to the bartender.

Blindman took in the scene. Men were openly snorting white powder. Crack pipes were passed around. A couple of guys huddled in dark corners, shooting God knows what into their arms.

"Nice homey joint this is," Eddie muttered.

"Clean, too," Blindman chuckled as a junkie puked on the floor after snorting too much dope.

Steele and Sanchez were seated at a table in the back. They watched the group through bloodshot eyes. The bartender filled five shot glasses.

"Drink up, boys," Rudy said.

"You first," ordered Blindman as he switched drinks with Rudy.

"What the fuck is this?" said Rudy.

"Drink this drink or you die," growled Blindman.

"Fuck you," snarled Rudy. Then he dumped the drink on the floor.

Blindman grabbed Rudy by the face and poured Eddie's drink down his throat. Rudy's face went pale. He started convulsing and fell to the floor.

"I figured as much!" yelled Blindman. He pulled out the sawed-off and held it to the bartender's head.

"Eddie, see if that fucker still has a pulse."

Eddie knelt down and checked. "Yeah, he's still breathing."

"Explain yourself before I count to ten," Blindman ordered the bartender.

"He don't have to explain nothin," a voice bellowed.

Steele and Sanchez were up and moving. Eddie got right in Sanchez's face. Blindman swung the shotgun in Steele's direction. "Don't talk," Blindman ordered.

"Fuck you," Steele bellowed.

Blindman fired at Steele's feet. "Now back up until I tell you to stop."

Steele went to say something.

"Shut your big yap and back up. Your goddamn big mouth is giving me a headache."

Glowering, Steele backed across the room. "Happy, asshole?" Steele asked.

"Thrilled to death, now just stay put," ordered Blindman. "Every time you open your big mouth your fuckin head disappears." Steele glared at him.

Rufus and Emmett had their guns out, covering the rest of the patrons.

They'll stand, thought Blindman.

"Well, Leroy," a voice said. "We meet again."

Blindman looked for the source of the voice. "Oh fuck," Blindman said. "My old pal Pritchard, figures you'd be with this pack of assholes."

"You know this guy?" asked Eddie.

"Old Doc here is a bounty hunter," explained Blindman. "He's the one who turned me in. Right, asshole?"

"It was a job, Leroy, nothing personal," Doc said.

"Yeah, nothing personal except money," spat back Blindman.

"Remember a guy named Jack Taggart, Doc?" asked Blindman.

"That mean guard at Riker's?" asked Doc. "Yeah, he was a friend. Why?"

"Well, I hate to be the one to inform you of his untimely passing," said Blindman solemnly.

"I didn't know he was feeling poorly," said Doc.

"Oh, he wasn't feeling poorly until I shot him twice," said Blindman. Doc's face clouded with rage.

"So are we going to rock and roll or what, boys?" Blindman challenged.

"Don't kill him," a worried voice shouted.

It was Doctor Cruz. Cruz ran to Ryan and whispered something to him. "No one is to harm this man!" Ryan shouted, pointing to The Blindman.

"And why the hell is that, sonny?" Blindman asked.

"It's your blood," Cruz said. "Your blood can cure King Crump."

"Well, why would I want to cure the bastard who destroyed the country before all this other shit went down?"

"It's your civic duty as an American," Ryan told him.

"Civic duty," Blindman laughed. "Excuse the fuck outta me, but there is no America. The world got destroyed, in case you failed to notice."

"We will bring it back to what it was," said Ryan.

"Oh, in other words, a shithole of hate, racism, and guys like Doc over there making a living hauling corpses. No thanks, fuck Crump, I'll pass."

"You don't have a choice," Ryan told him.

Blindman strode over to Ryan and said "How's this for a choice, I tear one of those baby blue eyes out, make a keychain out of it, then skull fuck you. Sound good?"

Terrified, Ryan backed away. A loud rumbling started and a big door started to open. A foul stench permeated the room. Blindman, Eddie, and the Clements looked at the abomination that was once the leader of the country.

"Is this him?" it croaked.

Blindman took in the scene. "You want to give my blood to this thing? This is what all those posters and reward crap was about?"

"We have to keep him alive, he will restore our..."

Blindman cut him off. "There's nothing left, get it? Nothing. It's all gone."

"Blindman," a voice moaned. "Kill me."

Blindman looked for the voice and saw what was left of Hellfire. "Aw shit, even your sorry ass don't deserve this."

Blindman flipped his wrist and shot Hellfire in the head with the derringer. All guns were pointed at Blindman, but Eddie and the others were covering him.

"You cocksuckers want a fight, try us!" Blindman bellowed.

"Everyone stand down!" Ryan yelled.

Sanchez started toward The Blindman. "I'm going to stick that gun up your ass, old man," he threatened.

Eddie blocked him. "Just try it, Pancho, just try it." The two men started to square off.

"How about a contest?" croaked Crump.

"What kind of contest?" asked Blindman.

"Your tough guy against my tough guy," Crump slurred.

"So let me get this straight," said Blindman. "These two fight for what?"

"Simple," said Ryan with a smug look on his face. "Your guy loses, you give us your blood."

"And if he wins?" asked Blindman.

"We won't feed you guys to our friend," Steele bellowed.

"Didn't I tell you to shut up?" said Blindman. "After Eddie takes care of the Frito Bandito here, we walk. You don't follow. Get it?"

13

"HE WON'T WIN, SO YOU have a deal." said Ryan.

"Ok, but no help. Just knuckle and skull, no toys," Blindman ordered.

"I won't need any toys to beat this faggot," Sanchez spat.

"Hold this," Eddie said, handing Blindman his bat.

The steel collar that Blindman gave Eddie was hanging loosely around the bat. Sanchez tried to sucker punch Eddie, but Eddie saw it coming and ducked. Eddie clipped Sanchez's knee and nailed him in the jaw with a right cross. Sanchez shook it off and bored in swinging. Eddie blocked most of the punches, but some got through. Eddie backed up a bit, bleeding from some cuts on his face. Then he uncorked a vicious backhand that sent Sanchez crashing over a table.

Eddie punted him in the ribs. Sanchez rolled and staggered to his feet. Roaring his rage, he caught Eddie in a bear hug and drove him against the bar, knocking the wind out of him. Sanchez hit Eddie with punch in the jaw. Eddie spit a mouthful of blood into Sanchez's face. When Sanchez went to wipe the blood out of his eyes, Eddie head butted him, breaking his nose, then staggered him with an uppercut. Sanchez spit out a couple of teeth.

Sanchez put a head lock on Eddie and started pounding a fist into the top of his head. Eddie picked up Sanchez and threw him across the room, crashing into some furniture. Sanchez pulled himself to his feet. Sanchez was panting, one eye was swollen shut, and he was bleeding from cuts on his face. Sanchez now had fear in his eyes. Eddie wasn't even breathing hard. Sanchez threw a chair at Eddie. Eddie, showing real agility for a guy his size, grabbed the chair and smashed it over Sanchez's back. Sanchez hit the floor. Eddie went to finish him, pummeling him with hard fists. Then Sanchez pulled out a knife and slashed Eddie's arm.

"I knew you couldn't take me, you fuckin puke!" Eddie yelled at him.

"I'll gut you like a fish!" Sanchez yelled, moving in with the knife.

Blindman yelled, "Catch, Eddie!" He tossed Eddie the steel collar. Eddie caught it, slipped it over his hand, then smashed Sanchez in the side of the head.

Sanchez screamed in agony. His right eye was hanging out of the smashed socket. He swung out with the knife, but Eddie dodged it. Eddie swung a vicious blow as Sanchez staggered past him. That blow nailed the back of Sanchez's head and he hit the floor, brain matter leaking out of a crushed skull.

"Looks like we have a winner," Blindman announced.

14

THERE WAS A DEAD SILENCE. Panting and bleeding, Eddie stood over his dead opponent, glaring at Ryan. "Anyone else want a shot at the title?" he challenged.

Ryan looked at Steele who looked real uncomfortable.

"Give that loser to the bear," croaked Crump.

"Well, now we'll be takin' our leave," said Blindman. "I would advise you people not to follow us."

Just then four men came into the bar dragging someone.

"Hey," announced one, "guess we missed the show, but we caught us some pussy. Me and the boys broke her in."

Blindman turned and said to the man, "You broke her in?"

"That's right, I tore her a new one," the smiling thug told him.

Blindman slowly pulled out his .45. "Was it fun?" he growled.

"Sure was," the man gloated. "'Specially when we turned her over and corn..."

Blindman shot the man in the crotch, blowing his balls off. He fell back screaming, trying to stanch the blood gushing from where his junk was.

"That's my woman, you rotten motherfuckers!" Blindman yelled. He fired three shots into the rest, all low. The men lay on the ground screaming and bleeding out. Eddie and the Clements brothers had guns out.

Blindman checked Nydia, she was barely conscious.

"Eddie," growled Blindman, his teeth clenched in rage. "Help Nydia out of here. Boys, any of these people move, kill 'em." Eddie gently picked up Nydia.

"Get her to Patel, take the jeep," Blindman said. "I'll be along shortly. Emmett, you and Rufus stay with me, these fucks need to know the error of their ways. You guys wanted a war, now you got one," he told them. "You just pissed me off to the highest power and now I'm throwing a jihad on your asses. I intend to kill every last one of you worthless fucks. And I'll start with you."

Blindman pointed the sawed-off at Ryan and pulled the trigger. The blast picked Ryan up and bounced him off a wall. Blindman stood over him. "I said I'd use your eyeball for a keychain." He stuck his finger in the eye socket and pulled the eyeball out. Then he threw it at Crump.

"Fuck you, fuck all of you!" Blindman screamed. "Anyone else want it now? How about you, big mouth?" Blindman motioned to Steele. "How about it, Doc? You want to try and bring me in again?"

"Blindman," said Emmett, "let's get out while we can."

"You!" Blindman yelled, pointing at Cruz. "You're coming with us."

Cruz backed up "No, I won't, I'm..."

"I'll blow a hole in this orange bastard then and leave it at that," Blindman yelled at him. "Move, motherfucker, or I'll do it."

"Better listen to him," said Doc. "He's not fooling."

Blindman put a gun to Cruz's head and they backed out the door. A horde of ragged men were waiting outside.

"Don't shoot!" yelled Cruz.

One man raised his gun, Rufus blew him out of his boots with a blast from his shotgun.

"Nailed that one," he announced with a goofy smile.

"Anyone else want to die?" Blindman yelled.

The men backed away.

"Didn't think so. Now we are leaving. Follow us, you die."

Blindman saw that the jeep was gone. "Good," he said. "Eddie got her out of here."

Blindman turned to Cruz. "I should just waste your ass, but you can go back to that nest of snakes and tell them they wrote a check their ass can't cash. I know you'll have your army of junkies come after us. Just get this though your head, Cruz. I'm killing you all."

Cruz still looked defiant.

"Oh, yeah, you have tombstones in your eyes looking at me, but it won't help. I'll see that orange turd you worship gets fed to that fuckin bear. Now git before I change my mind!" Blindman yelled.

15

CRUZ SCURRIED OFF LIKE an ugly little insect. Blindman and the Clements returned to the camp. "Find Patel and tell him I need to see him," Blindman told Emmet.

Eddie and Sal came out of The Last Chance. "How is she?" Blindman asked Eddie.

"Patel is working on her," Eddie told him. "She was out until I got back here. I'm not going to lie to you, they really fucked her up."

Blindman's face was a storm cloud. "I need to see her."

Blindman went to the makeshift hospital. Patel was waiting for him.

"She's sleeping," Patel told him. "Luckily I had something to relieve the pain for her. She has a concussion, some really deep cuts on her legs, a broken nose and index finger, and cracked ribs. What happened to her?" Patel asked.

"I sent her back because I wanted her out of danger and she got ambushed," Blindman said. "Can I see her?"

"Yes," said Patel, "but she's unconscious right now."

Blindman went inside the hospital. Apache was sitting near Nydia's bed. He looked at Blindman. "Do I have to ask?" he said.

"No, but the score ain't close to even. Give me a minute with her."

Apache left. Blindman knelt down and took Nydia's hand.

"I should have never left you alone," he said softly. Nydia's eyes were swollen, her hand and legs swathed in bandages. "I won't leave you alone again, but right now I have to get the boys organized. Rest, Kid. This won't stand." Nydia squeezed his hand, then drifted off to sleep.

BLINDMAN GATHERED HIS crew in The Last Chance. "I'll get right to the point here," said Blindman. "Soon there will be an army of nut jobs coming for us. Those posters about a reward, well, it's all a trap. Seems that the former president is being kept alive with the blood of others." Shock registered on the faces in the bar. "He has a bunch of followers that think he can bring back the country." Blindman explained. "So they've been capturing people, draining their blood and feeding the dead to a bear."

"A bear?" asked Leo.

"Yeah, a fucking real big one they have in a cage. They keep a bunch of crazies hooked on heroin and they'll be coming our way."

"Wait a second," said Pruitt. "Our President is alive?"

"Your so called 'president' is being kept alive with people's blood. In other words, he's a bigger parasite now than he was in office," said Blindman.

"Maybe you have it all wrong," said Pruitt. "He was the best thing that happened to this country in a long time, we should..."

"Kill his ass and everyone with him," finished Blindman. "Not for nothing, pal, but did you see what they did to Nydia? Remember our old pal Hellfire? They were draining his blood in a way that was so horrible that I put him down."

"Ever think you might be wrong about him?" asked Pruitt with a smug look on his face.

"The only thing I might be 'wrong' about is letting you stay here. That fuck divided and destroyed this country. Now there's a bunch of morons that think he's the second coming. I'm going to nail that orange fuck to a cross."

"That remains to be seen," said Pruitt. Then he walked out, his back stiff with anger.

"Sal," Blindman said, "keep a watch on him. I forgot Crump's people are like a cult. If he starts getting others riled up, he's gone. Now I know they are going to hit us, so let's get a reception party ready. I want some pits dug way out before they get close to the path in here. Make them about five or six feet deep. Rufus, can you get some of those snakes alive?"

"Yeah," said Rufus. "How many do you want?"

"As many as you can catch without getting yourself killed."

"You're going to fill those pits with snakes?" asked Sal.

"Among other things. Yeah, I am."

Blindman turned to Goldstein. "In the midst of all this other stuff, did you uncover the valve on that tanker full of gas?"

"We did," replied Goldstein. "Eddie showed me where it is, a couple of days ago we cleared it."

"Good work," said Blindman. "Now here's your job, get any container that will hold gas and fill them up. Leo, I'm sure you have a pile of empty bottles, so we are going to make super bombs."

"Just fill 'em with gas?" Leo asked.

"No, not just gas, find bits of Styrofoam and powdered laundry soap and mix it in. That way it will stick to whatever it hits. How are we fixed in the way of explosives?" Blindman asked.

Leo said, "We have a couple of cases of grenades, a lot of dynamite, and a bunch of artillery shells that don't work in anything we have."

"Ok, here's what I need done," said Blindman. "Angelo, you have a gentle touch, so I need you to take those shells apart. We'll make bombs out of the powder and primers."

"I'll get on that right now," replied Angelo. "I'll need Arnold to help me lift the shells, though."

Blindman looked at the big ex-butcher. "You ok with this, Arnold?" he asked.

"I'm fine," replied Goldstein. "Let's end this before it starts."

16

RUFUS HAS GATHERED up sacks, pillowcases, and the like. He found Denny at the bar. "Blindman wants me to gather up some snakes," he told Denny.

"Yeah," said Denny, "he told me that was our job. How are we going to do this without getting bit?"

"I'll grab the snakes, you hold the sacks open," Rufus replied.

"No, fuck that," said Denny, "Those fuckers are big and hardly cooperative."

"Let me ponder on this a bit," said Rufus. "I see your point, but we need those snakes."

The two wandered around the compound trying to figure out how to capture the deadly reptiles. Then Denny saw a bunch of old, plastic fifty-gallon drums.

"Follow this idea," he said to Rufus. "Those things chased us last time. What if we took these drums, lay one down with the lid off, make them chase us and trap them in the drum?"

"Might work," muttered Rufus, "but we have to hide them so they run right into them."

"Best way to do that is to have one hidden around a bend by those dunes," suggested Denny. "One of us stays on top of a dune, then the other has them chase him toward the barrel. We tie a rope around the barrel and when they get into it, we pull it up, slap a lid on it, and we got them."

"Worth a try," said Rufus.

The two men got three of the drums secured in the jeep, then went hunting.

PRUITT WAS ANGRY, VERY angry. "How can this blind fool plot the murder of the President of the United States?"

What people didn't know about Pruitt was that he embraced the whole bullshit MAGA. Pruitt was a closet racist and a coward. He only stayed in the compound because he feared for his life. Yeah, he fought the Islamics, but he hated Muslims anyway. He would have been content to stew in his own juices, but now he was emboldened by the fact that Crump was alive.

There has to be others here that love our President, he thought.

I'll just have to find them.

LEO FOUND BLINDMAN sitting in front of The Last Chance, whittling.

"Having fun?" Leo asked.

"Tons," replied Blindman.

"Well, the pits are dug, about a dozen of them," Leo informed him.

There was a couple of dozen stakes piled up next to Blindman.

"Are those what I think they are?" asked Leo.

"Punji stakes," said Blindman. "The gloves are off with this bunch."

He picked up the stakes and walked to the latrine. Curious, Leo followed. Blindman started dipping the sharp ends of the stakes into the foul mixture of human waste.

"That's some seriously fucked up shit," said Leo.

"I told you I ain't fucking around with this bunch," snarled Blindman. "A scratch from this will turn septic and that's a miserable way to die."

"How do you think they'll come at us?" asked Leo.

"Straight on, because they don't know any better," said Blindman. "They have a loudmouth ex-military guy who could know tactics, but I doubt any of those druggies can be whipped into any kind of shape. They'll try to steam roller over us with sheer numbers," he continued. "Remember, I'm the only one they need to take alive, so we blow the shit out of them here, then go right after them and wipe out every last one of them."

"Sounds real personal," said Leo.

"They made it that way when they fucked up Nydia," Blindman spat. "Then thinking I'd give my blood to keep that bastard piece of shit breathing? Fuck no, that prick had us on the verge of World War Three before the flares took everything out. Let's save our little piece of the world," he finished.

17

BACK IN BARTER TOWN, the scene was chaotic at best. Steele was now in charge of 'rallying the troops', so to speak. Crump had Steele, Pritchard, Cruz and a man named Benton, who was 'promoted' from the ranks, in his foul chambers. Benton was a lean man with black hair and a pock-marked face. He was also a meth addict. "Blindman," Crump croaked, "has to be taken alive."

"Yes," agreed Cruz. "Nothing else matters but getting that man's blood into the veins of our leader."

Doc had been laying back, then he spoke. "You think this will be easy? Think again. I know this man, he's tougher than a $3 steak. The people with him are organized and know how to fight."

"We outnumber them," bellowed Steele. "At least three to one."

"Oh, so you know the layout of Blindman's camp?" asked Doc.

"Doesn't matter," muttered Steele.

"What do you mean it doesn't matter?" shouted Doc, getting angry. "You're an arrogant fuck, Steele. Yeah, we outnumber him three to one with a pack of junkies. Think they won't cut and run when half of them wind up dead? Think again, mouth almighty," Doc finished.

"I'm getting tired of your mouth, old man. I'm starting to doubt your loyalty here," bellowed Steele.

"Glad you brought that up, because right about now, you won't be getting behind me," snarled Doc. "You can lead the charge, I'll be watching my back from here on in."

"Not much of a team player, are you, old man?" Benton asked. "Go smoke some more of that shit that rots your teeth out, you junkie fuck."

"No, I'll stay here and babysit the King."

"You're a fuckin coward, Doc," Steele spat. Doc's hand started to reach for his gun.

"Stop this now," Cruz said. "We need to get along to make this work. I can use Doc here to guard the King, you two get this rabble ready to take out Blindman's people and get him back here alive."

Steele looked happy that he was completely in charge. He looked at Doc. "After this is over, old man, you and me will settle this."

"You mean you'll try," said Doc. "And I'll knock your dick in the dirt." Doc walked away.

18

RUFUS AND DENNY HAD one barrel ready. It laid on its side in between two dunes. Rufus screwed an eye hook under the lip of the barrel. That way Denny could yank it up with a rope, then put a lid on it. Rufus found the den and noticed that there were a lot more snakes around than the last time they were here. To get their attention, Rufus tossed a rock at the sunbathing serpents. Loud rattling filled the air as the agitated snakes seemed to be warning Rufus. Rufus threw another rock and they slithered toward him.

Rufus ran toward the trap when he realized he miscalculated something. To escape the rattlers, he had to run up the dune. Now he knew they would follow him. So he ran right at the barrel and dove over it. The snakes crashed into the barrel so hard that Denny didn't have to use the rope. The impact of the snakes hitting the barrel up righted it. But two snakes went around it. Rufus got his gun up in time to blast them. Denny had slammed the lid on the barrel.

Rufus was shaken.

"I gotta rethink this thing," he whined nasally.

Denny hammered the lid tighter with the butt of his shotgun. "I don't know how many we got," he said, "but this sucker is full."

It took both men to lift the drum into the jeep.

"I say let's take these back and see if they are enough," said Denny. "If not, we can come back. Leave those other drums here just in case."

19

BLINDMAN WAS IN THE Last Chance alone. He had a bunch of 12-gauge shells that he was 'modifying'. He was also very angry. *I can't remember ever being this pissed off,* he thought. *I've been stomping around here for the last two days screaming at people. Now I'm wondering why these crap heads got under my skin so bad.*

Then another voice in his head gave him the answer. It was because of Nydia.

No, he thought. *Well, yes.*

Then he flashed back to when they met, that first fight, when she actually had the upper hand on him until Dog stuck his snout into it.

That's when we became a team, he thought. *Then the thing with the terrorists, me getting captured, her not giving up finding me. Then her finding me with tears in her eyes.*

Blindman broke open a shell and dumped out the shot. He filled the shell with jacks. Remember that old kid's game? Nasty little pieces of metal.

"Ok," he thought, "am I in love with her?"

In Blindman's world, that was an alien concept. He always worked alone, except when he found Dog. Then she showed up, full of piss and vinegar, and a real bitch on wheels in a fight.

"How old am I?" he asked himself. "Late 60s, early 70s? Shit, the last time my dick got hard is when I broke Cal's neck." Then he smiled. "Nydia showed up right after that." Then his features hardened.

"I fucked up," he told himself. "I shoulda sent one of the guys back with her." But she would have taken that as a sign that he thought she was weak. He stopped working.

Blindman decided to take a walk. He wound up at the makeshift hospital. Nydia was sitting on the edge of her cot. Her face looked like she stuck it in a hornet's nest. Her index finger was in a splint. She looked at him though swollen eyes.

"How's things going out there?" she asked.

"We're getting ready," Blindman told her. "You feeling any better?"

"Compared to yesterday, yeah. I'm really pissed about my finger though. Had to be my fuckin trigger finger," she answered.

Then she stared right at him. "Can I ask you something?"

"Yeah," answered Blindman. "What's on your mind?"

"After I was knocked out, I don't remember much. But I do remember something I heard," she said. "I heard you say I'm your woman."

Blindman had no answer.

"I know what I heard, Leroy," she continued, "and you know you said it. I'm not trying to paint you in a corner, either. You're a hardcase, I'm a hardcase," she continued. "For the record, I care about you. When those people had you, I thought that was it. I thought..."

"Ok," interrupted Blindman, "I was never good at this. I just sat around thinking about what happened. In my own alcoholic way, I care about you."

Blindman continued, "I went crazy when I saw it was you they dragged in. Oh, and I killed them all. I shot their balls off."

Nydia snickered at that.

"Then I killed one of the big shots out of sheer meanness."

"Look, you don't have to explain yourself," said Nydia. "I get it, we forged a bond when we took out The Drunken Master. We could have just went our separate ways then, but we didn't. I'm not pushing you for anything, Leroy. We respect each other and we fought side by side. We are just two misfits that found each other in a fucked-up world."

"I wish I was 30 years younger," Blindman groused.

"It's not about age, it's about us. We're a team and I'll have your back again when Crump's people attack."

"Fair enough," Blindman answered.

Then he did something completely out of character. He stooped down and kissed her cheek.

"Thanks" he told her. "Now get better. I have to go look at something Goldstein found scrounging that old depot."

20

BLINDMAN FOUND GOLDSTEIN helping Angelo take apart some shells. "Arnold," Blindman asked, "Leo said you found something interesting?"

"That I did," answered Goldstein. "Let me get it." Arnold dragged a long case out from under their work bench. "When I was looking for a generator in that Army depot, I found this in the officer's quarters. I was going to leave it, but then I found a few cases of shells for it."

Arnold opened the case and this was the biggest gun any of them had ever seen.

"What is it?" asked Blindman.

Goldstein had a book that was in the case with the gun.

"It's a Barrett M82," Goldstein told him. "According to what I read on it so far, it's the Rolls Royce of sniper rifles. It fires a 50-caliber shell."

"Just like Scarecrow's old Sharps," Blindman added. "And I'm out of shells for that gun."

"Not a problem for this gun," Arnold told him. "I found plenty of ammo for it."

"Wonder what this sucker was worth?" Blindman thought out loud.

"Thousands," Arnold told him. "This isn't military issue, someone bought this. There was a receipt in the case for $8,000, discounted from $10,000. The shells alone are five bucks each."

"Holy shit," Blindman exclaimed.

Angelo chimed in. "To quote an old movie, Dawn of the Dead: 'The only one who could miss with this gun would be the sucker that could actually afford to buy it.'"

"Why don't we see what this baby can do?" asked Blindman. He lifted the gun out of the case. "This thing isn't exactly light," he announced.

"This scope came with it," said Goldstein, handing Blindman the item.

"Damn, Arnold," said Blindman. "Even with just one eye, I can see for about a mile."

Angelo handed Blindman an empty old spackle bucket. "Fill it with sand," he said.

"Good idea," replied Blindman. "I'll set it out a ways, then we'll see what it can do."

Dog trotted up, curiously. Blindman looked at him. "You ain't gonna like this, pup," he told Dog.

Blindman sighted the bucket and squeezed the trigger. It sounded like a cannon going off. The bucket exploded and Dog took off yelping. The recoil almost dislocated Blindman's shoulder.

"This has a worse kick than the old Sharps," said Blindman. "This will be good when we take the fight to them."

Nydia, helped by Dog, walked over to the group.

"I need to move around, I'm getting all stiff here," she said. "What's with the baby cannon?"

"Super sniper rifle," Blindman told her. "You just missed the demonstration."

"I heard the fuckin thing and Dog almost ran me over," she said. "Just what you needed, a new toy."

"I'll save this for when we go on the offensive. If I can take out the heads of state with this, it will be over," said Blindman.

21

JUST THEN, RUFUS AND Denny returned. Denny yelled to Blindman "We might have a problem here!"

Blindman, Nydia, and Goldstein walked over to the jeep. A loud buzzing filled the air.

"We got the snakes," Rufus explained. "A lot of them, but I don't know how we are going to get them out of the barrel and into the pits."

Emmett strolled over. "Rufus, why did you fill the barrel right up to the brim, dummy?" he got in Emmett's face.

"I told you to stop with the dummy shit, now I'm going to kick your ass."

Rufus dropped his shotgun and tackled his larger brother. The two rolled around in the dirt kicking and punching each other. Denny dragged Emmett off of Rufus.

"Knock it off!" he yelled at Emmett. "We had no choice and you weren't there."

Blindman cut in, "Save your fight for the one coming at us, or I'm going to tell your Ma." The two brothers glared at each other.

"Somebody better figure out how to get these snakes into the pits because they are getting pissed off," said Nydia.

The buzzing got louder.

"We need to stun them," Denny said.

"Yeah," replied Blindman, "but with what?"

"I have an idea," said Nydia.

"I'm all ears," said Blindman.

"Wrong answer," Nydia chuckled. "But you'll want to cover your ears."

"What are you thinking?" Blindman asked.

"Put your new toy next to the barrel and pull the trigger. It's a long shot, but the noise might stun them."

Blindman thought on it. "This will be real tricky," he said. "So let's be ready. Back the jeep real close to the pits."

He turned to Rufus and Emmett. "If you two can take time out from beating on each other, go get some long poles, shovels, whatever, so we can push these little bastards into the pits."

"You think this will work?" asked Denny.

"If they stop rattling after I fire the shot, yeah."

"And if it doesn't?" pressed Denny.

"Remember that catapult Angelo built?" answered Blindman.

Denny just smiled. "Ya know, it would be worth getting another drum full just to toss it in the middle of those fucks."

"Hold that thought, let's deal with the matter at hand."

Rufus had a smile on his face. "I like that idea, Denny."

"Let's just do this," urged Blindman.

Denny backed the jeep as close to the pits as he could. Blindman loaded the Barrett. Nydia backed up.

"Here goes nothing," he said and pulled the trigger.

"I can't hear nothing!" Blindman yelled. "Am I deaf?"

"No," Denny yelled back, "but the rattling stopped. You guys get those shovels ready."

Blindman kicked the barrel off the back of the jeep. The lid popped open and the snakes poured out. They flopped on the ground like fish out of water.

"Push the fuckers in the pits before their brains unscramble!" Blindman yelled.

The group moved quickly and the snakes fell into the pits.

"Ok, it worked, now let's cover these up and tell everyone to stay out of here," said Blindman.

22

"ARE YOU TWO REALLY up to getting more snakes?" Blindman asked.

"What do you think would happen if we dropped a barrel full on these guys when they are trying to get in here?" asked Denny.

"It would demoralize the piss outta them." Blindman thought on it. "If you're up to it, why not? We left two drums there, waddya say buddy?" he asked Rufus.

"Well it worked once, no reason why it wouldn't work again," said Rufus.

"Ok," said Denny. "Let's do it."

The two drove back to the den.

"Is it just me, or are there more of them?" Denny asked Rufus.

"Well, they have no more natural predators thinning them out," pointed out Rufus. "So they're getting overpopulated."

"Ya know, you're pretty smart with this stuff. I don't know why your brother thinks you're a dummy," Denny said.

"Because he cain't do it, that's why. But he's family, so I put up with it until I get real pissed off like what happened today."

"I get it," said Denny. "Let's switch places. I'll have them chase me, you work the barrel."

Denny cautiously approached the den. *If I live though this,* he thought, *I'm never going near this place again.* He tossed a rock into the basking serpents. The buzzing started and the snakes crawled after him. Denny dived over the barrel. Rufus pulled the rope, righting the barrel. Then he butt stroked Denny's foot with his shotgun.

"Are you fuckin crazy?" Denny yelled.

Rufus pointed to his foot. A snake had its fangs sunk into Denny's boot heel. The snake now had a crushed head.

"Didn't think you wanted a pet," Rufus smirked.

"Thanks, man," Denny said. "Let's put a lid on this and get them back to camp."

BACK AT THE COMPOUND, Angelo and Goldstein were working on their catapult.

"We used up all the heavy junk we had lying around on the terrorists," Angelo said.

"What if we made some kind of bomb that we could rig to explode over them?" asked Goldstein.

"Possible," mulled Angelo, "but I'd have to play with fuses to get the timing right."

"Why don't we try it with dynamite?" suggested Goldstein. "We have a lot of that to experiment with."

"Explosives are tricky, especially when they are old," explained Angelo. "But it's in our best interests to have the edge over what's coming at us."

23

BACK AT BARTER TOWN, Steele was trying to whip his 'army' into shape. Problem was that a lot of them were brain damaged from all the dope they had ingested. Steele fumed over this. He didn't do drugs, but he drank, and liquor made him mean. He screamed, yelled, punched, and kicked men that didn't move fast enough to suit him. Steele had been convinced that he could over run Blindman's people by sheer numbers.

He didn't care about casualties. These people would die, one way or another. He just wanted to win the fight, bring back Blindman. Then his 'position' would be secure. He decided his best chance was to stay behind his troops until they secured Blindman's camp.

"Why take chances?" he told himself. "Someone has to survive and get that blind fuck back here."

Doc was watching Steele harass his 'troops'.

"This fuck must have watched a lot of Lee Marvin films," he snickered.

"What's so funny?" asked Cruz.

"I'm getting a kick out of watching Sergeant Sphincter out there."

"Steele is the best man for the job," Cruz told him.

"Steele is the only one here dumb enough to take the job," Doc shot back. "I'm willing to bet that he will fuck up big time, and the rest of us will be paying the price."

"No price is too high to pay to keep our King alive," said Cruz.

"Back on that, are we?" asked Doc. "The whole blood type thing, it must run in his family, right?"

"I guess so," muttered Cruz.

"Well," said Doc, "didn't he have a couple of sons?"

"He did," said Cruz.

"Well, logic would dictate that they should have the same blood type, so why not use them?" asked Doc.

"Because we never got a chance to test their blood, that's why," answered Cruz.

"Oh," said Doc, "how convenient that the privileged don't have to kick in like the rest of us."

"That wasn't the case," Cruz shot back.

"Well then, why, pray tell?" Doc pressed.

"Because they pissed off their father and he fed them to the bear," Cruz blurted out.

Doc stared at him, truly shocked. "He killed his own kids? Does that register in that sick mind of yours that this man is fuckin insane?"

"N-no," stuttered Cruz. "He's a genius, he put this country together, he will do..."

"Shut the fuck up!" Doc screamed in his face. "I should have kept on moving, but no! I had to stop here and get tangled up in this shit. I'm a dead man walking, you get that? And you are, too. Blindman threw Taggart in my face as a message. He's going to even the score between us."

"We need his blood. Steele will capture him, you just wait," said Cruz.

"I have no choice but to wait," said Doc. "Wait until death comes a callin. By the way, Cruz, I never asked, but where did you find the bear?" asked Doc.

"Some fellow has a circus, the bear survived. He didn't," explained Cruz.

"In other words, you killed him and took his bear," Doc interrupted.

"Something like that," said Cruz. "We had some welding equipment, so we built this cage. Anyone who gave us trouble got tossed in. That kept people in line, plus it was entertainment."

"You're a sick fuck, you know that, Cruz?"

"And you're not?" smirked Cruz.

"I may be a lot of things," admitted Doc, "but I'm not in your league. Not even close."

"We all have to do things we may not like to set things right," said Cruz.

"You're a fanatic," said Doc. "So was your buddy, Ryan. Now he's been done in. You don't seem to get it, Cruz, you fucked with the wrong guy. Worse, you hurt someone he actually gives a shit about. You saw how he took out those four guys, then Ryan. He's not going to stop until we are worm food," summed up Doc.

"We are the righteous, and the righteous will never fail," preached Cruz.

"Cruz," said Doc. "Go fuck yourself. Do it today and tell a friend."

Cruz had a shocked look on his face as Doc walked away.

24

PRUITT HAD BEEN MAINTAINING a low profile. He was watching the compound get ready for the impending attack. *If I could get the upper hand here, I could take this place over, then give it to the President's forces,* he thought. *I'm sure that would put me in a position of authority.*

Pruitt had found about two dozen 'kindred' spirits who shared his devotion to Crump. Pruitt had a meeting and outlined his plan.

"If we act like we are on board with Blindman's plan, we get close in, then take them."

"How do you propose to do that?" a man asked.

"Simple," answered Pruitt. "All those killers take to the front lines like bees to honey, they enjoy it. So we'll be behind them as the second wave. When the President's army gets close, we throw down on them, kill a couple to show we mean business. Then we hold the rest until they get here," Pruitt finished.

"You make it sound easy," the man said.

"It will be if we take out the big guys first. You know, the guys that are loyal to Blindman," said Pruitt.

"Why not just kill him and be done with it?" the man said. "He's the glue holding the rest together."

"No," answered Pruitt. "They want The Blindman. We make it happen, we write our own ticket. When this thing starts, just follow my lead," Pruitt finished.

BLINDMAN WAS TRYING to get things organized. He had Denny and Jones alternately being lookouts as they could get back quick on their bikes. Blindman went to see how Apache was doing.

"I'm hanging in," Apache told Blindman. "Is it true that Crump is alive?"

"Alive and uglier than ever." Blindman told Apache everything he knew. "That bastard targeted Hispanics and Native Americans for extinction," Apache spat. "How come only scumbags seemed to have survived?"

Blindman laughed at that. "We aren't exactly members of the clergy ourselves," he chuckled.

Apache laughed until the pain cut in. "You're right," he said. "But at least we ain't politicians."

"Yeah," agreed Blindman. "Politicians are one notch below pedophiles in my book."

"Promise me a shot at them," Apache asked.

"What do you have in mind?" Blindman asked.

"Something you won't want me to do, so I ain't telling you. Just let it happen."

"Fair enough," said Blindman. "I won't ask."

"Can you tell Angelo I'd like to see him?" Apache asked.

"Sure, him and Goldstein are blowing shit up today and I was just going to see what they came up with. I'll tell him to drop by."

ANGELO AND GOLDSTEIN were testing distance with their bombs. Tamera, the black girl that Blindman saved, was watching them.

"Boys and their toys," Blindman said as he joined her.

"How's Nydia?" Tamera asked.

"Getting better," Blindman answered. "She was walking around a bit today."

"These people are beasts," said Tamera. "How come the worst seemed to survive?"

"I just had this same conversation with Apache," Blindman said. "We both agreed that heaven isn't where we are headed."

Tamera laughed. "After all this, don't be so sure." Then she got serious. "You know, under Crump we were a police state, and they went after people of color."

Blindman just had a thought and vocalized it. "In all the bullshit that happened when we were there, I didn't see one woman, one kid, or any person of color," he said. "In fact, all the junkies were white trash."

"What do you think is going on?" she asked.

"I'm thinking that any non-white or anyone who disagreed with them was killed. "They were feeding people to a bear," he finished.

Tamera looked at him in horror. "You can't be serious," she said.

"I wish I wasn't, but we didn't linger too long there. I think it's like Circus Maximus, like the Romans did. Brutal death for entertainment. After Eddie killed their big gun, then getting Nydia out of there, I never thought to ask for a brochure about the entertainment. I will tell you this, I intend to kill every last one of them, including the fuckin bear. But if for some reason I fuck up, don't let them take you alive. In fact, spread the word on that.

"Angelo," called Blindman, "when you get a chance, Apache wants a word."

25

ANGELO TOLD GOLDSTEIN to take a break while he went to see what was on Apache's mind. Angelo entered the tent and saw the pain etched on the biker's face.

He saw Angelo. "Thanks for coming over, brother. I need a small favor."

"Anything you need, just ask," said Angelo.

"You might not be down with this, but I can't just lie here with all this shit coming down. In other words, I'm not going out like this," said Apache.

"What do you need from me?" asked Angelo.

"I need you to rig up my bike with explosives and a hand detonator," said Apache.

"You're going to suicide bomb them?" Angelo asked, astonished.

"No, I'm gonna homicide bomb them. Big difference. Understand something, amigo, in my world the ride is everything," Apache continued. "Now I can't ride, but I want one last ride and that ride will take some of Crump's people with me."

"I will respect your wishes," said Angelo solemnly.

"Just don't tell Blindman," laughed Apache. "He might try and talk me out of it."

BLINDMAN WAS ORGANIZING people as to what to do when the attack came. "Realize something," he told them. "No mercy whatsoever. The men coming at us will be loaded on dope, that will give them false courage and they'll keep on coming. Shoot the fuckers to rags if you have to. This is a big bloody party to these guys. They win, we all die, some of us worse than others."

One man spoke up. "Speaking for myself, I'm scared shitless," he said. "How many are we facing?"

"I figured a couple of hundred," answered Blindman. "I know you're scared. Use that fear to make yourselves mad, get angry, get fuckin mean. In this case we have to be harder than they are."

"And that means...?" asked the man.

"No fuckin mercy, no matter what. Those snakes we caught are more trustworthy than Crump and his men," answered Blindman. "But remember, we have quite a few surprises that may make them cut and run."

BLINDMAN WENT TO SEE what Angelo had come up with. Eddie was helping load something on the catapult.

"Wait until you see this shit," Eddie chuckled.

Blindman saw six five-gallon water cooler jugs. Angelo explained, "Eddie found these empty jugs. At first we were going to fill them with sand and drop them on their heads. Then Eddie came up with a better idea."

Eddie took over. "This ain't a confession," he laughed. "We used to torch cars for insurance money. I'd mix gas with those packing peanuts. They'd turn the gas into gunk that would stick to stuff and keep burning. So I tore up some crates and took out the Styrofoam packing, so here you have my homemade napalm bombs," Eddie said proudly.

"You're just in time for the test," said Angelo. "I set the fuses for fifteen seconds."

Angelo lit the fuse and the device let go with a loud twang. The jug flew over the pass and as it started to drop, it exploded. The pass was showered with jellied fire that stuck to the rocks and kept on burning.

"I love it" said Blindman.

Sal had agreed to man the 50-caliber machine gun. They had taken it off the jeep and set it up covering the pass.

"Sal," said Blindman. "You're the second line of defense here. Any of them get past our surprises, mow them down, then get out of here. There's only a couple of hundred rounds left for this thing."

"I'll strafe the pass until I run out," said Sal.

"Just don't get overrun," said Blindman. "Blast 'em, then get out of here."

26

STEELE WAS RALLYING his 'army'. "Tomorrow is the day!" he yelled. "We're going to have a huge victory and reap the spoils of war."

"What spoils?" a meth addled junkie asked.

"Anything they have, food, liquor, even pussy." replied Steele.

"Ya mean we get our pick of the wimmen?" a slovenly ex biker asked.

"Sure," said Steele. "The ones we don't kill you guys can fuck all you want. Now rest up, we march tomorrow at dawn."

STEELE'S 'TROOPS' WERE woken up by his bellowing orders before dawn. Either still drunk, hung over, or jonesing, they milled about.

Doc rubbed sleep from his eyes as the yelling woke him up. "Guess those are Steele's 'shock' troops," he chuckled. "I'm shocked that they are even standing."

Benton had smoked some crystal and was ready to go. Cruz and Steele were talking things over. "I'll have transportation back," Steele told Cruz. "I'll drag that blind bastard back here behind one of his own jeeps."

"As long as he's alive, I don't care what condition he's in," said Cruz. "Good luck, this will be our defining moment."

Steele slapped off a salute and moved his men out.

Cruz walked over to Doc. "We will await Steele's triumphant return," he said.

"Oh, he'll return alright," replied Doc. "Running like the Devil is biting his ass, which he will be."

"Your constant negativity is pissing me off," Cruz snarled. "You can't seem to grasp..."

"Shut up, you fuckin lap dog," Doc snarled. "You and that loudmouth never went against anyone with teeth. Anyone that was brought here, you had the upper hand. Those people will chew that bunch of junkies up and spit them out. Then they'll come for us."

"That remains to be seen," said Cruz smugly.

Doc spit on the ground and walked away.

DENNY WAS KEEPING LOOKOUT when he saw a cloud of dust in the distance. "Fuckers are on the move, guess it's show time," he muttered to himself.

Denny rode back into camp. "Company's coming!" he yelled.

Blindman yelled, "You all know what to do, so let's kill some assholes!"

People scurried to get in position. Angelo and Goldstein were putting the barrel of snakes in the catapult. Goldstein's head exploded and Angelo was splashed with gore.

"None of you move!" someone yelled. Everyone turned. Pruitt stood there with smoke drifting out of the AR-15 he was holding. "Don't anyone try anything or you can join the Jew."

Angelo went for his gun and someone shot him.

"Anyone else?" spat Pruitt. "Blindman," he snarled. "Tell your people to drop their guns or we start taking out the niggers and spics first. Where's the other big guy?" he yelled.

"You're looking for me?" Eddie bellowed. He shouldered his way through the group toward Pruitt, bat in hand.

"Swear alliance to our President and you can join us," Pruitt told him.

"And if I don't?" he yelled.

"We'll plant you next to the Jew," Pruitt told him.

"You mean you'll try," said Eddie.

Pruitt drew a bead on his barrel chest. "Your choice. Now die," Pruitt answered.

A blast picked Pruitt off his feet and slammed him into the side of a building. Pruitt looked at the huge hole in his chest. The last thing he heard was a woman screaming.

"Try takin this spic out you bastard!" Nydia had shot him with the Barretts.

Tamera blasted six of the men to hell with her Uzi. Eddie waded into the group, crushing skulls with his bat. Blindman fired the shotgun into the group, shredding two men. Denny, Jones and the Clements poured bullets into the retreating scumbags. Within seconds Pruitt's group was finished.

"Someone check Angelo!" Blindman yelled. "If any of these fucks are still breathing, finish them," he ordered.

Sal turned Angelo over, his sightless eyes glazed over. Sal closed them.

"He's gone," Sal told Blindman. "Both of them, gone."

Blindman's back was stiff with anger. "Sal, can you and Eddie work this contraption?" he asked.

"Yeah," cut in Eddie. "Can and will."

"Good," said Blindman. He looked at the bodies of his friends. "You will be avenged," he snarled.

Blindman found Nydia clutching her hand to her chest. "I re-broke my trigger finger," she moaned, tears in her eyes. "They killed two of the most decent people here."

Blindman stared at the bodies of his friends, his face mottled with rage. "Take them out of there," he asked the Clements. "Leo, I need you to handle the machine gun."

"I'm on it," said Leo, shaken to his core. "These poor bastards, after all the shit we went through, to go out like this."

27

"WERE THOSE GUNSHOTS?" Benton asked Steele.

"Sure in shit sounds like it," Steele answered.

More shots were heard in the distance.

"I'll bet it's a coup," Steele chuckled.

"Some of those fools saw the light and turned on Blindman. Hope they didn't kill his ass. Let's move faster here!" he yelled.

Steele's 'army' surged forward. Then hit the pits. Men fell in the pits and jumped out screaming as the enraged rattlers struck furiously. Snakes were wrapped around arms, legs and heads striking flesh. Faces turned purple, then black from the venom. Men were shooting each other as they missed the snakes.

Steele was appalled by the carnage. "Go around them!" he yelled.

They did and fell into the pits of stakes. One man crawled out with his legs perforated. "There's poop on these things," he moaned.

Steele picked up a stake. "Bastards rubbed shit on them!!" he yelled.

Then Sal and Eddie launched the barrel. It overshot the milling men and landed right behind them. The barrel hit the ground and broke open. Dozens of angry reptiles slithered toward the men. "Run!" someone yelled. They did, and Leo opened up on them. The 50-caliber bullets ripped through a few dozen men. Blindman, Tamera, Rufus, Emmett and others kept a withering fire on the pass. Half of Steele's army lay dead or dying.

Benton looked at Steele. "We're trapped!" he yelled in a panic.

Steele yelled, "Hold your ground, dammit!"

Snakes behind him and guns in front of him, Steele didn't know what to do.

Sal and Eddie loaded one of the firebombs into the catapult. "Remember, Angelo set these for fifteen seconds, so let's be quick," said Sal.

Eddie lit the fuse "Let 'er rip!" he yelled.

The catapult let go with a load twang. The barrel seemed to almost hover in the air. Then it exploded, showering jellied gasoline on the men below. Screams of the burning men filled the air. Facing snakes and firebombs caused the men to make an insane charge into the compound.

"Sal!" Eddie yelled. "Get the fuck out of here!"

The men surged forward, some of them on fire. Sal shot three before Eddie grabbed him and sent him toward safety.

"Fuck these junkie cocksuckers!" Eddie yelled, swinging the bat.

One clown hit the ground, his head shattered. "It's the bottom of the ninth!" Eddie screamed. "The bases are loaded! He swings, he hits! And the crowd goes wild!"

People were running past Eddie and not shooting at him. The bat was slick with blood and Eddie was covered in gore. One guy ran at him, trying to pull something out of a gunny sack. Eddie clipped him under the chin and heard his neck snap. A vintage Thompson machine gun fell out of the sack.

"Holy shit!!!" Eddie exclaimed. He picked up the weapon and found it loaded. Eight guys rushed him as he pulled the bolt back and let it rip. The .45 caliber slugs picked the men up and threw them back. There was an extra drum in the sack. Eddie grabbed it and backed up, firing into the confused raiders.

Leo ran out of ammo for the 50-caliber. He abandoned it and ran back to The Last Chance with four men hot after him.

"Leo, duck!" someone yelled.

Leo hit the ground as bullets cut through the air above him. Ma cut loose with an AK-47, blowing the men out of their boots and leaving them bleeding out in the dirt.

"Get inside!" she yelled at Leo.

Leo scrambled though the door. "Thanks, Ma," he told her.

"You're welcome, now grab a gun and let's kill these bastards."

Dog had been staying out of sight behind a pile of junk. Three men were sneaking around, trying to get behind The Last Chance. As they rounded the pile, Dog launched himself into them. He tore off a kneecap on one guy. That guy shot at Dog with a 357 Magnum but hit one of his own in the gut by mistake. Dog's teeth clamped on his arm and ripped off his gun hand. Dog heard a click and moved in time to dodge a bullet that hit his victim in the side of the head. Dog launched himself at the guy before he could get off another shot. He ripped the guy's throat out and was doused with a jet of arterial blood. Dog turned to see the gut-shot guy fall over dead. Dog went back behind the pile to wait for more kills.

A group of Steele's men turned to get behind The Last Chance and ran into Lee and her Shotgun Girls. They opened up on the men, dropping two of them. One of the girls was spun around as she caught a bullet in the shoulder. Another girl went to help her and took a round through the head. A huge, bald man with meth rotted teeth was the last standing. Lee stood up and pumped five slugs though his chest. The man fell back, then got up, daylight streaming though the holes in him. Lee muttered something in Chinese that, translated, meant 'junkie fuck', then blew his head off.

STEELE AND BENTON WATCHED what was left of their army come running, crawling and limping back.

"They killed us all!" a man yelled. "You said it would be easy."

Steele had nothing to say. He had about two dozen men that could still walk.

"We gotta jet," Benton said.

Steele had to agree at this point. "Fall back!" he yelled.

"To where?" someone yelled. "There's fuckin snakes back there!"

Angry rattlers were blocking the way out. Steele grabbed an AR-15 from one of the men. "Follow me!" he yelled.

Steele blasted a path though reptiles. Utterly demoralized, the men ran.

28

BLINDMAN SURVEYED THE carnage. Dead junkies littered the compound and the pass. The smell of charred flesh and ruptured bowels filled the air.

"We have to move quick and finish this," he said.

Sal came over. "Did anyone see Eddie?" he asked.

"I thought he was with you," Blindman replied.

"He was, but we got overrun, he pushed me out. After that..."

"I'm ok, boss." Eddie limped up to the group. "Here, Sal. Al Capone sends his regards." Eddie handed Sal the Thompson.

Sal looked at the gun, then looked at Eddie, then broke out laughing. "Where the hell did you get this?" he asked.

"One of them gifted it to me after I broke his neck," said Eddie.

For some reason that comment caused everyone to bust out laughing.

"Let's get back to the matter at hand," said Blindman. "We need to finish this. "We have to go after them," he told them. "I told you I'm killing them all and I meant it."

"Every last one of them dead will never equal the people we lost," Nydia said.

"Who can still fight?" he asked.

"I'm in," said Eddie.

"No," said Blindman. "You ain't in. In case you haven't noticed, you're shot."

Eddie had been nicked a couple of times, but one bullet went through his left side and blood was oozing out of the wound. "Don't argue with me on this, big guy. You'll bleed out," Blindman told him.

"He's right," Sal cut in. "Go see Patel and get patched up. You're staying too, Sal, you and Leo. Someone has to hold what's left together.

"We're going," said Emmett. "Right, Rufus?"

"I'm in," said Rufus. "I'll go get some extra help." Rufus picked up the gunny sack that previously held the Thompson.

"Are you going to get those snakes?" asked Blindman.

"We might need 'em," Rufus said. He marched off with a purpose.

"I'd better go with him just in case there's any stragglers hiding out," said Denny.

"Good idea," Blindman said.

"I'm going, too," Nydia announced.

"Like hell you are, you broke your trigger finger and you're still limping," said Blindman.

"I fixed my finger," she said.

Nydia held up her hand. Her index finger bent into a curl with a crude brace around it.

"Doesn't that hurt?" he asked.

"Terribly," she said. "But it's worth all my pain to get that orange motherfucker in my sights and blow his shit away." She held up the Barretts. "See, I did a little modification."

Nydia had put padding around the trigger guard. "All I have to do is get my finger in there and give it a little squeeze."

Blindman knew arguing with her was useless. "Ok, you use that cannon to cover us, and don't argue. I'll set you up where you can see their hideout and you tag anyone you see, got it?"

Nydia threw him a sloppy salute. "Aye, aye sir," she wised off.

29

STEELE, BENTON AND about two dozen walking wounded crawled into Barter Town. Cruz looked shocked. "What happened?" he asked Steele.

"They were just about ready to give up," bellowed Steele, "then..."

"Why you lyin fuck," Benton cut in. "We were beat from the get-go, they were more than ready, we got annihilated."

"Why you lousy..." Steele started to say.

"Hey, go fuck yourself, Steele. I'm going to smoke some shit." Benton shot back. "Hey Cruz, better tell the King that the executioner is on the way." Benton stormed off, looking for dope to smoke.

Cruz looked at Steele. "Is he right, they are coming here?"

"Yeah, they are. And I'll end this shit then."

"You were supposed to end it at their camp," Cruz spat. "No excuses, now I have to tell the King.

"You go do that," muttered Steele. "I'm not done with this yet."

Doc walked up. "Well, Sergeant York, you fucked up like I said you would," he baited Steele.

"If I didn't need your gun, I'd blow you away!" Steele shouted.

"You don't have my gun," Doc told him. "I'm going in that bar and have my last drink, then wait for my reckoning. If you're around when this is over, you and me will have our own 'reckoning'. You're a dead man walking, Steele, and so am I. Deal with it." Doc walked away as Steele sputtered with rage.

CRUZ WENT INTO CRUMP'S chambers. The place smelled like an outhouse. Crump's beady eyes looked out from his bloated, mottled face.

"You brought me The Blindman's blood?" he asked Cruz.

"No, Your Highness, we failed," Cruz answered.

"You failed me," Crump bleated. "How could you let this happen? How are we going to make this country great again without my leadership?"

"I'd worry more about The Blindman coming here, and he *is* coming here," Cruz replied.

"Nooo," wailed Crump. "He can't come here, he'll hurt me, you have to stop him."

"I have no way to stop him," Cruz spat back.

"Find a way," Crump bleated, his bloated body trembling in fear. "I don't want him to hurt me. I'm your King, you have to protect me."

"I'll do what I can," Cruz told him.

30

BLINDMAN HAD THE CLEMENTS, Denny, Jones, Nydia and Dog ready to go. He called Sal and Leo off to the side.

"If we don't get back, don't come looking for us."

"Now wait a minute..." Leo started.

"No," interrupted Blindman. "I don't know how many they have left. You have enough food and water here to last a bit. Give us two days. If none of us get back, blow up the pass."

"You're serious about this?" asked Sal.

"Very much so," said Blindman.

"Then all any of us can say is good luck, and come back," said Sal.

"We will try," promised Blindman.

Jones and Denny started their bikes. The Clements, Nydia and Blindman got in the jeep. Dog trotted alongside. After about an hour, they were close to Barter Town.

"Find some place that overlooks the town," Nydia said.

They pulled the jeep up on a ridge that gave a good view of the town. Nydia picked up the Barretts and looked though the scope.

"I see a couple of people, looks like they are guarding a building," she said.

Blindman adjusted the derringer rig on his arm. He had his sawed-off in one hand and his .45 automatic in the other hand. "Pop one of them," Blindman said. "Let's send them a message."

Nydia drew a bead on a big man holding a TEC-9. She squeezed the trigger. The man was thrown against the building and left a red smear as he slid to the ground. Barter Town erupted in gunfire.

"Now we got their attention," Blindman said.

Denny and Jones had Uzis strapped to the handlebars of their bikes. "You guys swoop in on them, one on the left, the other on the right,"

Blindman ordered. "Me and the boys will go straight in. Nydia, keep picking off anyone who gets close to us. Let's go!!"

Cruz looked out a window and saw a fighter's head explode. He heard the chatter of Uzis as the bikers roared in. Steele was screaming orders that no one was listening to.

We need something to stop them, Cruz thought. Then he had an idea. Cruz went to the bear cage. The huge beast hadn't been fed for days. Cruz was unlocking the cage.

"They won't be able to handle this," Cruz said aloud. The bear watched him though pain filled eyes.

As soon as the lock clicked, the bear rushed the door, slamming into it. Cruz was pinned behind the door, dangling a foot off the ground. The beast ripped him open and stuck its snout into his guts, eating him alive. Cruz was shredded from his neck to his feet as the bear ripped off chunks of bloody flesh and devoured them.

Steele ran into one of the buildings for cover. Blindman and the Clements blasted their way into town. Four men charged them; Blindman blasted two of them with the shell full of kid's jacks, shredding them. Rufus blew one guy away with a shotgun blast. The last gun was taken out by Emmett's thrown Bowie knife. They took cover behind a wall. They traded shots with some men hiding behind a junked car.

There was a terrible roar as the bear burst out of a building and charged the men behind the car. They scattered, but the bear caught up to one and swatted him with a huge claw. The man went down spewing crimson from a huge gash in his back. The bear started eating him alive.

"As if we didn't have enough shit to deal with," Blindman said.

The bear looked up and, with a roar, charged them.

31

"WHAT IS THAT SINGING?" Sal asked.

"It's Apache," Eddie answered. "I remember something I read about Injuns," he said. "When they know they are going to die, they make peace by singing their death song."

"I'll go see if I can..."

"No, Sal," said Eddie. "Leave him be, it's what he wants. Blindman said leave him be."

Apache painfully staggered to his feet. His legs were barely working. Patel tried to stop him. "Amigo, I appreciate everything you done for me. One last favor, help me get on my bike," Apache said.

Patel put his arm around Apache and got him on his bike. With a pain-filled kick, Apache started his bike.

"Tell the others I wish them well," Apache said. Then he took off toward Barter Town.

THE BEAR STARTED CHARGING toward Blindman and The Clements. "I heard that if a bear charges you, you shouldn't run," said Rufus.

"I don't think this particular bear heard the same thing," spat Emmett.

"Don't argue," Blindman shouted, "run for cover!"

The three ran in different directions, but the bear went after Rufus. Rufus ran like a marathon runner, but the bear was closing in.

"Throw the sack at him!" Emmett yelled.

Rufus threw the sack over his head right into the bear's gaping maw. Rufus ducked into a building as the bear ripped the sack apart. The rattlers were all over the bear, sinking fangs into its flesh. The bear tore one off and bit it in half. Screaming in rage, the bear rolled on the ground, trying to dislodge the rattlers. The snakes slithered off, but not before the bear ate a couple of them.

Blindman ran into the bar, then into Doc Pritchard. "Sit down, Leroy," Doc ordered. "Have a drink and we'll finish this." Doc was sitting at a table with a half empty bottle in front of him.

Blindman sat across from him. "In case you haven't noticed, Doc, this place is finished," Blindman said.

"Yeah," chuckled Doc. "Big mistake getting involved with this bunch."

"Well," said Blindman, "you never were too smart about picking your friends. I'll take a shot of that Makers you're hording there."

Doc poured him a big glass. "I agree I picked a bunch of winners this time," Doc answered. "Crump couldn't wipe his own ass unless he had either help or a map. But this is about you and me, Leroy," Doc continued. "I have a gun pointed right at you, under the table here. Second time in my life I got the upper hand on the notorious Blindman."

"It's gonna be the last time in your life you do anything, Doc. You and Taggart fucked me over big time," said Blindman. "He shoulda quit when I cost him his arm."

"But he didn't," Doc spat back, "and you killed him. I see you got some sight back in one eye," he said. "Now you're going to see the man who is going to kill you."

Blindman downed his drink in one gulp, the residue dripped though the stubble on his face as he grinned. "Tell you what, Doc, neither one of us is leaving this room alive."

The two gunshots sounded like one.

32

NYDIA HAD BEEN PICKING off anyone she could. She heard the sound of a bike behind her. Apache drove up, looking like death. "Jesus fuckin Christ, are you..."

"Just point me in Crump's direction, muchacha," Apache moaned. "I'm his pale rider."

"The big building in the middle," Nydia said. "He's hiding in there."

"Gracias and vaya con Dios," Apache said, then gunned his bike into Barter Town.

THERE WAS SPORADIC fire between The Clements and what was left of Crump's men. Jones heard Apache's bike and made the fatal mistake of stopping to look. Steele blasted him off his bike.

"Got one!" Steele bellowed.

Apache roared by and Steele shot him in the back. "Make that two!" Steele yelled.

A ribbon of blood streamed out of the wound, but Apache kept on going. Apache crashed through the doors and plowed through the equipment keeping Crump alive.

The two men were almost face to face.

"Don't hurt me," Crump bleated. "Who are you?"

"Who am I?" Apache said. "I'm the one motherfucker you're gonna wish you deported. Die, bitch."

Apache pushed the detonator and the building blew up, raining debris everywhere. The concussion knocked everyone standing off their feet.

Emmett was looking for Rufus when he ran into Benton. Emmett pulled out his Bowie knife and drove it into Benton's guts. Benton fell back, his intestines spilling out on the ground. But he was so doped up, he didn't feel it. He shot Emmett twice in the chest. He was standing over him for a coup de gras when Rufus ran in and blew him in half with both barrels of his shotgun.

"Em, I'll get you back!" Rufus yelled.

"I'm done," muttered Emmett, blood running out of his mouth. "Say goodbye to Ma for me. And Ruf, I'm sorry about the dummy shit." Emmett's eyes closed.

Enraged, Rufus went looking for revenge. He walked out of the building and blasted a guy who had just knocked Denny off his bike.

"How bad?" he asked Denny.

"They killed my fuckin ride," Denny spat. "Where's Emmett and Blindman?"

"Emmett's dead," Rufus answered. "I haven't seen Blindman since that bear got out."

"Jones bought it, too," Denny said sadly, "but Crump got blown up."

"We should try and find Blindman," Rufus said.

"There are still assholes trying to kill us," said Denny, "and that bear is still around somewhere, so let's be careful."

The two men went looking for Blindman.

DOC HAD AN ASTONISHED look on his face and a hole where his throat used to be. He tried to say something, then hit the table face first. Blindman had a smoking derringer in his hand. He also had a bullet in his chest.

"Life is full of little surprises," he said to Doc. "You're surprised you're dead and I'm surprised I'm sitting here with a bullet in my chest." Blindman took a deep breath. "Well, it didn't hit a lung, that's a plus," he muttered.

Blindman staggered to his feet. Pain went through him as he walked. "Bullet is still in me, dammit," he muttered. *I best see if anyone else is left,* he thought.

He went outside and was near the big cage where the bear was kept. "Shit," he muttered. "Forgot about that big bastard." Then he heard a snort. He saw a flash of brown fur between two buildings.

It's stalking me, Blindman thought.

Blindman weighed his options; he was too injured to run, and the closest thing near him was the cage. "If I can climb on top of that thing, he might not see me."

Blindman hobbled toward the cage. He had just reached it when a voice bellowed. "Now I got you, you blind bastard!"

Steele was between two buildings and marching toward Blindman with a triumphant grin on his face. The bear heard Steele bellow and changed direction.

"Steele," Blindman yelled, "if you've never listened to anyone in your life, listen to me now. Shut your big mouth and run!"

"You're a coward, old man," he bellowed, raising his gun. "Time for you to die."

A blur of brown fur crashed into Steele. Blindman lost sight of him as he started climbing the cage. Steele staggered out in the open, screaming, both his arms ripped off. Blood spurted from the stumps. The bear followed him, knocking him down, then tearing his screaming head off. Then it turned its attention to Blindman, who was halfway up the cage.

Nydia was watching the scene unfold though the scope of the Barrett. Her hand throbbed with pain from pulling the trigger.

"I have to nail that big bastard," she said to herself. She fired, tearing a chunk of meat from the bear's side.

Nydia, Blindman thought.

The wound seemed to spur the beast on as he climbed further up the cage. Blindman aimed the sawed-off at the bear, hoping to hit it in the face and blind it.

When he pulled the trigger, a bullet from the Barrett missed the bear and hit the cage. The buckshot raked the bear's back, knocking it off the cage. Dog charged in, he sunk his teeth into the open wound and ripped off a piece of meat.

"Dog, no, get back!" Blindman yelled.

But Dog was in his element. He dodged the huge claws and was biting chunks from the bear's hind legs. Blindman had no more shotgun shells, so he took out the .45.

He aimed it at the back of the bear's head. As he pulled the trigger, Dog charged the beast again. The bear dodged Dog's attack, but smashed back into the cage, causing Blindman to miss his shot and drop the gun.

"Motherfucker!!" Blindman yelled. "Can anything go right today?"

Dog sunk his teeth into the bear's front paw and tore. The bear threw Dog about twenty feet away. Dog crashed to the ground and didn't get up.

"You cocksucker!" Blindman yelled. "I'm gonna skin you for that!"

The bear turned and looked at Blindman with hate filled eyes and started climbing the cage toward him. Blindman had nowhere to go and no weapons except a pair of brass knuckles. He slipped the knucks over his hand.

"I ain't got a prayer," he muttered.

Then he smashed the bear in the snout as hard as he could. The metal knuckles cut the bear's tender nose. Blindman hit it again.

The bear roared in pain. Nydia squeezed off a shot that hit the bear, knocking it away from Blindman. Rufus and Denny were watching the battle.

"We gotta help him," Rufus whined.

"Yeah," Denny agreed. "But how?"

"Maybe with this." Rufus had a stick of dynamite with a long fuse. "I'll get its attention, then blow it up."

"It's a long shot. I'll cover you as best I can," said Denny.

Nydia kept trying to hit the bear, but the pain in her hand was throwing her aim off. The huge slugs were hitting the cage instead. Blindman felt the cage shift.

This thing isn't going to hold much longer, he thought.

Rufus then made the incredibly dumb move of lighting the fuse and shooting the bear in the ass with his shotgun. The bear swiped and broke Rufus's arm. Rufus flew back and the dynamite flew out of his hand. The enraged bear was after Blindman again.

Nydia fired one last shot before her hand was just a throbbing mass of pain. The shot hit the cage and it started to topple over. Blindman dove off and hit the ground hard. The bear was now pinned under the weight of the cage but was roaring and struggling to get out.

Blindman staggered over to Rufus and tried to get him up, but Rufus was out cold and dead weight. Dog limped past Blindman with something in his mouth.

Dog had picked up the lit stick of dynamite and limped over to the struggling bear. Blindman watched in horror as Dog dropped the stick next to the bear and limped away. Blindman covered Rufus as the blast threw Dog into the air. Bloody chunks of meat rained down on them.

"Jesus Christ!" Denny exclaimed as he helped Blindman up.

I might be seeing him sooner than later," Blindman muttered. "You hurt?" he asked Denny.

"No, but you and Rufus are. Everyone else is dead."

"Take me to Dog," Blindman asked.

Dog was lying on his side, panting.

"I don't think he can walk," Denny said.

"Then I'll carry him," Blindman said.

"You can barely walk, yourself," said Denny. "Let me rig up a travois to help him."

Rufus got up, favoring his broken arm. "He killed the fuckin bear," Rufus muttered, pointing to Dog.

"Let's get him and us out of here," said Blindman. Some movement caught his eye. "What the hell are they doing?"

Several men were taking something out of a shed. Denny looked over. "I think they just found the drug stash," he said.

The men paid no attention to anything except the packages they were carrying out. One guy cut one open and snorted the powder on his blade.

"Fuck 'em," said Blindman. "That pile of dope will finish them. Let's get out of here."

Denny rigged up a travois and they put Dog on it. They went back to where they left Nydia with the jeep. Nydia's face was white with pain.

"You're all that's left?" she asked. Blindman just nodded. "The Jeep is fucked," she told them. "Somehow when I was picking them off, one of them shot back and hit the radiator."

Blindman slumped down next to her. "I won't make it back," he said, looking at her, "and neither will you or Dog."

"We can get you back," said Denny.

"No, you can't and you'll only die trying," Blindman said.

"We can go get help," Denny almost pleaded.

"You can try, that's about all you can do. And don't think I don't appreciate it, but we're done in. It's gonna take you a day or more to get back," Blindman continued. "Take all the water you can carry, we won't need it."

"Nydia..." Denny started.

"Save it," said Nydia. "I stay with them."

"Rufus," said Denny. "Let's go. We'll be back for you, count on it."

"Guys, it was an honor fighting beside you. Get back safe," Blindman said.

Epilogue

They watched the two men head back for help.

"How you holding up, Kid?" Blindman asked.

"Everything hurts, but I'm getting a little numb right now," she said. How bad are you shot?"

"I don't know," he said. "Bullet is in me, I'm pretty spent. So is Dog."

"Strange," she said. "The three of us started out together and now we go out together."

"Better than going out alone, in some crappy place," Blindman said.

"Yeah," she said. "All my life I wanted to belong to something that matters. Then I ran into you and found something that mattered, something I became a part of, something worth defending."

"I was just trying to survive," Blindman said. "I never considered myself a 'good guy' or a leader. Then I met people who put me in that position. People that made me care about them."

"What do we do now?" she asked.

"Why don't we just enjoy this sunset?" he said.

Nydia pulled herself next to him and put her head on his shoulder. Dog dropped his big head on Blindman's leg. They watched the sun go down.

The End

Author's note: Myself being a fan of series fiction, I sort of hate to see a series end. You grow to like certain characters, you follow their adventures, then the writer ends that series and goes on to another. Sometimes they bring characters back by either reviving the series or having them show up in a different series. When I wrote the original book, I was going to leave it as a stand-alone. Then fans dug The Blindman and wanted more.

So I wrote a second book, which I felt topped the first one. As for this one, I toyed with the idea of just not having anyone survive. Then I thought on it, and came up with the ending I did. Will The Blindman be back? That I'll leave up to the fans.

Pete Chiarella aka 42nd Street Pete
5/25/18

About the Author

Pete Chiarella has written for Screw Magazine, Chiller Theater Magazine, Shock Cinema, Something Weird Video Blue Book Vol. 1 & 2, Ultraviolent Magazine, Uncut, Dangerous Encounters, Spaghetti Western Digest and Sleaze Fiend Magazine. He also helmed twenty issues of his own magazine, Grindhouse Purgatory. He has a new magazine out now called Grindhouse Resurrection!

OTHER WORKS INCLUDE
42nd Street Pete's Big Book of Grindhouse Trivia
Two Fisted Tales of Times Square
A Whole Bag of Crazy

Milton Keynes UK
Ingram Content Group UK Ltd.
UKHW011956281223
435113UK00001B/75